UNWRAPPED:
Erotic Holiday Tales

Edited By
Eric Summers

Herndon, VA

Copyright © 2009 by STARbooks Press

ISBN-10: 1-934187-59-3
ISBN-13: 978-1-934187-59-3

This book is a work of fiction. Names, characters, places, situations and incidents are the product of the authors' imaginations or are used fictitiously. Any resemblance to actual events, locales, or persons, living or dead, is purely coincidental. All rights reserved, including the right of reproduction in whole or in part in any form.

Published in the United States by
STARbooks Press, PO Box, 711612 Herndon VA 20171.

Printed in the United States

Herndon, VA

STARbooks Press Titles by Eric Summers

Muscle Worshipers

Love in a Lock-Up

Unmasked – Erotic Tales of Gay Superheroes

Don't Ask, Don't Tie Me Up

Ride Me Cowboy

Service with a Smile

Never Enough – The Lost Writings of John Patrick

Unmasked II: More Erotic Tales of Gay Superheroes

Can't Get Enough – More Erotica Written by John Patrick

Unwrapped: Erotic Holiday Tales

Teammates

CONTENTS

INTRODUCTION

About a year ago, I was approached by STARbooks Press to put together a holiday-themed anthology as part of our twentieth anniversary celebration. I agreed as long as the stories wouldn't all be about Christmas.

So, as I solicited stories, I made it clear that I wanted a mix of tales to include Christmas, Hanukah, Kwanzaa, or any other holiday or celebration that happens during the winter months. I also made another request: These tales were not to be cookie-cutter stories about two people meeting over the holidays and having sex. As a result, I rejected more submissions than I ever have while putting together an anthology. However, what I ended up accepting were among the most creative stories I have ever included. Our authors, many of whom are STARbooks Press veterans, were forced to think outside the box, and that provided some fun and downright sexy stories that incorporate the themes of the season along with characters whom you would never imagine going at it during this season.

I am very proud of what we present for you on the following pages, and I hope you enjoy these stories as much as I enjoyed editing them. In addition, I am thankful to the many authors who utilized their talents to create what I consider a great collection of well-written erotica.

Eric Summers

Senior Editor, STARbooks Press

ELF SEX

By Stephen Osborne

Big Red, as some us refer to old Claus, was in one of his moods. Normally, he stays in his office, going over his lists, but today he was stomping around the work room with a frown on his face. He would stop and grumble at each table, using the tip of his damn pipe to point out imagined flaws he saw in the toys. "The paint is too thick on that Choo-choo!" he told Oliver. Glowering at Percy, he growled, "You're over-stuffing the Teddy Bears! That one looks pregnant, for goodness sake!"

I narrowed my eyes at Clyde, the elf who shared my table. "Someone woke up on the wrong side of the bed this morning."

Clyde nodded.

Clyde and I were in charge of dolls. I was in the process of attaching long black tresses to one while Clyde was putting a dress on another. He leaned toward me conspiratorially. "I hear that Mrs. Claus is withholding S-E-X. That's what has got him acting like one of the reindeer rammed him in the ass with his antlers."

That made me snicker. Big Red spun around to locate the sound, and I concentrated on my work until he moved on. When I was sure he was out of earshot, I asked Clyde, "What is it, anyway?"

"What is what, Gary?"

"S-E-X. I mean, I sort of know what it is. It happens in a bedroom once it gets dark and you smoke cigarettes after. I know that much. But what exactly does it entail?"

Clyde frowned. “How should I know? I just know that if Big Red doesn’t get it he gets cranky.”

We hadn’t been paying attention, and somehow Claus was standing behind us. I don’t know if he heard any of our conversation, but he certainly was ticked. “Clyde and Gary,” he bellowed, “apparently you have time for chit-chat, despite the fact that you’re behind in doll production!”

I bit my lip. Behind in doll production? Well, if the fat bastard wouldn’t set impossible goals, we wouldn’t be. I mean, elves are magical beings, but even so, there is only so much we can accomplish. I’d like to see him put hair on a Poopy Suzie doll. His big old sausage-like fingers can barely hold on to his stupid pipe.

“We’re working as fast as we can, sir,” Clyde said, ever the dutiful elf.

“Well,” the big man said, puffing on his pipe, “you’ll get plenty of opportunity to catch up. The two of you can come back here tonight for an extra shift!” With that, the fat man thundered out of the room, leaving a lot of shaking elves in his wake.

After my shift, I went out to the reindeer pen to visit with my pal, Dasher. I found him in his usual stall, munching on some oats. I picked up his brush and began to work on his coat, even though he really didn’t need it. Like us, the reindeer are magical creatures and don’t need grooming. That’s not to say they don’t enjoy it, though.

“Bad day?” Dasher asked. To anyone else it would have sounded like a grunt followed by a small whinny, but I understood it fine.

I groaned. “Santa was in one of his moods.”

“Oh, tell me about it,” Dasher said with a snort. “He was out here this morning, telling us we’d better shape up or he’d replace us with flying dachshunds. I mean, can you picture the sleigh being pulled by dachshunds? That'd make for a stupid looking Christmas card!"

"He was just grousing," I told the reindeer. "He doesn't really mean it. He gets this way whenever Mrs. Claus withholds sex ... whatever that is."

Dasher turned and cocked an eye at me. "You don't know what sex is?"

I felt my face flush, even though Dasher's tone held no derision. "I know what sex is," I said. "Sort of."

"You either do or you don't," Dasher said. "You should check out the stuff that Roland keeps in the bottom drawer of his desk. That stuff should answer any questions you have."

I frowned. Roland was one of the Elf foremen, who oversaw the production of rocking horses, toy ponies, and cowboy outfits. As a foreman, he had his own office located just off the main workroom. Being in dolls, I didn't have much contact with Roland, but he seemed a friendly enough guy. Whenever you walked by him, he always patted you on the butt and told you how pretty you looked that day. "What exactly does Roland keep in his desk, and how do you know about it?"

Dasher snorted. "I can fly around the world and hit every house in a single night. Finding out what an elf keeps in his desk is considerably easy in comparison."

I nodded. He had something there. "Well, Clyde and I have to work a shift tonight. No one will be in the workshop. Maybe we can take a few minutes to check out Roland's desk while we're there."

"I'd recommend it," Dasher said. Under his breath he added, "Anything to annoy Big Red."

I put Dasher's brush aside and patted his neck. "Thanks, Dash. You're a good friend."

"You are, too, Gary. Hey, have you ever noticed how full and firm Clyde's butt is?"

I thought a moment. "I have noticed that. Why do you ask?"

It almost looked as if the reindeer smiled. "Just wondered," he said.

The workshop seemed eerily quiet without elves busy at every table. I looked around, thinking that the room looked a lot larger. Clyde and I clocked in and made our way over to our doll station.

"Let's get this over with," Clyde said. "I don't want to be here all night."

I eyed our table, which had only a few dolls on it. "We really don't have much to do. Despite what Big Red said, we're actually ahead of schedule on doll production. We're really just being punished because he was in a grumpy mood."

Clyde shrugged. "So how are we supposed to spend our time? We really should stay for at least a while, just in case the fat bastard checks our time-cards."

I thought about what Dasher had said. "We could check out Roland's desk."

Clyde's frown was so deep that it brought his elf cap forward, nearly covering his dark eyebrows. "Why? What's in Roland's desk?"

"I'm not sure. Dasher claimed he hides some interesting things in the bottom drawer, though."

Clyde laughed. "Dasher knows everything. I've always said it pays to be on the right side of that reindeer."

"Want to check it out?" I asked.

With a shrug, Clyde answered, "Can't hurt."

Even though the workroom was empty, Clyde and I moved quietly to the door to Roland's office. With only a few of the lights on, weird, phantasmagoric shadows were thrown up onto the walls as we walked. I suppressed a shudder.

Clyde tried the door. It was locked.

He looked at me, amazed. No one locked anything up at the North Pole. "What's he got in there that he's so keen to keep secret?"

There being no locking mechanism on the door, it was obvious that Roland had a spell to keep people out of his office. That made Clyde and me all the more interested in getting inside. "He must use a voice command to override the spell. Maybe open sesame?"

The door remained locked.

Clyde smiled. "I know what it is." He faced the door and shouted, "Dog farts!"

The door squeaked open.

"How did you ..."

"It's his favorite expression," Clyde explained. "He says it every time he hits his thumb with a hammer, which is often. The clumsy idiot."

We crept into the small office, afraid to make even the slightest sound. There was little chance of anyone coming into the workshop at this time of night, but one hates to take chances. We didn't want to turn on a light, so Clyde produced a magic candle, and we used the light from it to guide us over to Roland's rickety old desk.

We crouched down, and I reached out a hand and pulled. The bottom drawer was locked. I looked at Clyde. "What's his second favorite expression?"

We both thought for a second and then said, simultaneously, "Poopy butt!" The drawer slid open.

Inside was a treasure trove of books and magazines the likes of which I'd never seen. They were intended for humans, not elves, for the covers were adorned with pictures of male humans in various stages of undress. I picked up one of the books. Clyde reached for a magazine and flipped through it.

His eyes popped open. "I don't understand. What are these guys doing to each other? Are they wrestling?"

I showed him the title of the book I held, *The Manual for Gay Love.* "They aren't wrestling. They're having sex. This book explains it all."

Clyde put the magazine aside and got another book out of the drawer. This one appeared to be a storybook of men having sex. The title was *Ride Me Cowboy.* He flipped it open. "Whatever they're doing, they seem to be having a lot of fun. Listen to this."

As Clyde read a passage aloud, I began to feel very strange. My penis seemed to grow in size, making my pants very uncomfortable. My face felt flush, and I became aware of my skin in a way I never had before. A look at Clyde's crotch showed that the effect was the same for him. His mouth must have gone dry because he had to keep clearing his throat to continue reading.

He got to the end of the passage and tossed the book back into the drawer. "I don't know about you, but this sex sounds like a blast. What does the manual say?"

I leafed through several pages. "It seems there's quite a lot of sex things to do. One thing is called fellatio."

"Fellatio? What's that?"

I licked my lips. "Stand up. It will be easier to show you."

Clyde stood and I scooted over to him and yanked down his pants. His penis sprang out, looking large and full. It almost looked angry. Taking my instruction from the book, I took Clyde's elfhood into my mouth. It tasted of musk with a hint of salt. I moved my head, sliding his dick further into my mouth. It felt nice, but the effect it had on Clyde was amazing.

"Oh, my sainted Aunt!" he gasped. "That's fantastic!"

For two elves who didn't want to be caught, we were being way too noisy, but I don't think either of us cared at this point. Sex must have some instinctive elements because Clyde began to move his hips, thrusting his penis between my lips, and I hadn't even told him about that part of the book. It seemed to me that Clyde's dick grew even larger as I sucked away. It affected Clyde's breathing as well because he began to pant.

Then something happened that I didn't expect. Apparently, I should have read further. In any case, Clyde penis suddenly shot out a thick goo, which nearly made me gag. I pulled my head away, and he even shot some of it onto my cheeks. I wouldn't have thought his dick was big enough to hold all that goo, but he seemed to have a lot of it.

When the eruption finally ended, Clyde stood there, shaking. He was sweating and a huge smile crossed his face. "That," he said, "was the most amazing thing ever! What else does that book say to do?"

I looked at another section and immediately saw why Dasher had asked me about Clyde's rump.

"Let's try this. Bend over the desk."

Clyde arched a questioning eyebrow at me but did as I said. I got behind him and pulled my pants down, releasing my aching penis. I had to check with the book again to make sure I was proceeding correctly. Having nothing called "lube," I simply spit onto the end of my dick. Another load of spit, I rubbed into Clyde's crack.

"What are you doing?" he asked.

"I'm not entirely sure," I replied honestly, "but apparently it's called fucking." I shifted my position and shoved the head of my cock into his ass.

The howl Clyde let out surely woke a few elves from their slumbers. I stopped, afraid I was killing him.

"Don't stop," he said, sounding out of breath. "I was surprised, that's all. I mean, it hurts but it kind of feels good, too. I can't explain it. Just put more of it in me!"

I obliged. It felt good, sliding my dick into Clyde's ass. All warm and cozy. I began slipping it in and out. Amazingly, the warmth spread to my entire body. I felt as if I was electric. I shoved harder and faster, slamming Clyde against the wooden desk. He seemed to be enjoying the sensations as well because he kept telling me to give him more. I felt a sudden tightening from deep within me and then ... Oh my goodness. Fireworks. Goo came out of my penis, shooting into Clyde's warm, firm butt. Every synapse in my brain fired at once. This was true magic.

Clyde and I couldn't speak for several minutes. We just panted. Eventually we pulled our pants back up and looked at each other.

"We've got to get a copy of that book!" Clyde said.

"And, share it with the other elves!"

Clyde's eyes were wide. "We can have sex parties!"

"And Big Red definitely won't be invited!"

The next day I brought Dasher some extra reindeer treats. It was the least I could do.

MASTER BELSNICKEL

By Pepper Espinoza

Nothing gets your imagination, and your heart, racing faster than a sharp knock on the door in the middle of the night. A dozen different scenarios raced through my mind. Was it the police? Did I have my television up too loud? Were they coming to tell me about a horrible accident? Did I know anybody who worked in a mine or a dangerous factory? Or maybe it was a neighbor who wanted to complain about my loud television? Most people didn't take the time to deliver their complaints personally anymore. Everybody relies too heavily on the police, as if they don't have enough on their plates. Could it be my parents? Or could it be a stranger with hard eyes? I remember seeing a story on the news once about a crazy guy who dressed as a clown, knocked on doors, and shot the unsuspecting homeowners in the face. I saw that story when I was a kid, but I have to admit, it still lingers with me. And, it comes to mind every time there's a sharp knock on the door at two in the morning.

I swallowed, trying to will my pulse into slowing. I didn't have my television on, so chances were good it wasn't the police or a neighbor. And, most people will live long and happy lives without ever crossing paths with a psychopath. I pressed my eye to the peephole, but it was too dark. I couldn't even see an outline. My heart still thudded hard against my ribs, but my fingers didn't shake as I unlatched the door.

Whoever was on the outside yanked it open as soon as the lock clicked. My mouth dropped as I stared at the tall figure in the doorway. I recognized it, but my mind wouldn't let me form the words. The world stopped moving, and sweat drenched the back of my shirt. Why couldn't it have been the police? Or my neighbors? I would have even accepted a clown with a shotgun.

"Hello, Henry," the figure rasped. "Have you been a good boy?"

"You're ... you're not real ..." I managed through numb lips. The figure chuckled as I spoke, and I could almost understand his amusement. Of course he was real. He was standing there, wasn't he? Standing there in his furs and his mask, chains hanging over one arm, a whip hanging loosely from his fingers, and a brown, muslin sack slung over his shoulder. Belsnickel. Saint Nicholas's companion. Nothing more than a myth, and even if Belsnickel was real, he tested children on the night of Saint Nicholas's feast. Not adults. I've been called many things, but I haven't been called a child in twenty years.

"Do you deserve a treat this year?" The question vibrated through my body. "Or do you deserve a birching?"

"I'll ... I'll call the police."

I couldn't see Belsnickel's face, but I could imagine his grotesque smile of amusement easily enough. The police couldn't touch him, and we both knew it.

"Let me in, Henry, so I can see your trick."

I don't know if he pushed me out of the way, or if I stepped back and let him waltz in. But the door clicked close behind me, and I was left standing in front of the imposing figure wearing nothing but my boxer shorts – what else would I have on at two in the morning?

"I don't remember any tricks," I whispered.

"Not one? Not a single Bible verse? Not one song?"

I shook my head, my palms and neck tingling. I probably knew many Biblical verses, and even more songs, but not a single one entered my mind.

"Are you sure?" Belsnickel hit his palm with the whip, echoing the steady thump of my heart. Despite the distance between us, I felt each tap of the leather against my skin. I couldn't look away. "You do know what happens to naughty boys who don't know their scriptures?"

Each word burrowed under my skin, digging deeper into my flesh. I knew, and my stomach rolled with that knowledge. Sweat dotted my brow, and my tongue was dry and thick, resting against my bottom lip.

"I ... I don't remember."

"What about the Lord's Prayer?"

I shook my head mutely. I wish I could see Belsnickel's face – but then again, maybe not. Maybe he wore a mask to hide an even more hideous visage than the long tongue and demonic eyes painted over the wood.

"The Beatitudes?"

"I ... I haven't been to church in a long time."

Belsnickel shook his head. "That's very bad." The whip continued to slap against his hand. "Take off your shorts."

The command wasn't one I could ignore. It resonated with authority, and it put me back in high school when the assistant principal – James Hollinsworth – would bellow at me with a deep voice, his blue eyes flashing with annoyance and maybe something a little bit more, his thick neck bulging against his collar, his jet black hair standing on edge. One word from that man was enough to make me stand a little straighter and make my pants a little tighter. Something about Belsnickel had the same effect on me. The boxers pooled at my feet, wrapping around my ankles like a hobble.

"Bend over," Belsnickel rasped. "Hold your ankles."

I did as he instructed, surprised by how icy my fingers felt. I always kept the heater turned up high in the winter, but now a chill had settled over me, and goose bumps covered my legs and my back. I knew as soon as that leather strap touched my freezing skin, I would scream. Would my neighbors hear me? Would they call the cops then? Somehow, the thought didn't comfort me. I didn't want the police to come.

"Not a single scripture?" He laid the whip across my ass. Even though he chose the fleshiest part, I still yelped from shock – and from pain. A low ache began in my groin. The ache grew stronger and spread as Belsnickel whipped my ass again. "Not a single song? What do you have to say for yourself?"

I groaned. I didn't have an answer. I just hoped he didn't ask why my cock was stiff, jutting between my legs, vulnerable to the tip of the ancient leather. I had a feeling that boys who got off on the stinging whip would top Belsnickel's naughty list.

The third blow was a little lower than the first two, across the tender flesh of my thighs. Ragged breath filled my ears – and there was a strange doubling effect. As though I wasn't the only one who was gasping for air. My cock twitched, fresh pre-cum coating the tip. I thoughtlessly reached up to wipe it away, but Belsnickel hit my wrist with a sharp tap. The unexpected sting startled me back into position, and he chuckled.

"I never said you could move." He dragged the tip of the whip up and down my length. "Don't do it again."

"Yes, sir."

Belsnickel didn't take the leather from my cock. The tip felt cold against my heated flesh, and I throbbed at every point he touched me, as though suffering from a fresh bruise. My balls hung heavy and aching, and occasionally, the tip skittered across the loose skin. Somehow, the anticipation of the blow hurt more than the actual blow ever did. I imagined the pain radiating through my body, imagined my flesh screaming in protest, imagined the sharp sting behind my eyes as the pain finally became too much without an outlet.

The expected blow against my balls, when it finally came, was both better and worse than anything I imagined. The pain was sharp and exact, and my eyes watered instantly. But my cock also throbbed with fresh excitement, and I rocked backwards, unconsciously straining for another blow. I knew that soon the pain would bend itself around the pleasure until all distinctions were lost, and my body was nothing more except desperate, hungry sensation.

Belsnickel cackled with glee. Or maybe it was with satisfaction over my response. The whip whistled through the air, connecting with my sac in one, two, three, four rapid blows. By the time he paused, I was sobbing for breath, and words fell freely from my mouth. But I wasn't begging him to stop. I would never beg him to stop.

I was working myself up into a frenzy. There was no question of that. I couldn't help it. Whenever I felt the cold, indifferent, yet oddly personal, texture of leather against my skin, my brain shut down and my body came to life. When the tip of the whip finally slapped against my wet cock, I almost blacked out from the pleasure. My knees went weak, and my stomach clenched into a tiny, hot ball. All the blood rushing to my head was hot, and I felt it close to the surface of the skin, turning my cheeks and neck a high red.

And Belsnickel was breathing harder. I knew it wasn't just my imagination. He was panting for breath beneath his mask, and I tried to watch him from between my legs, but all I could see were his fur pants and his thick, waterproof boots. I wanted to see his eyes glow like cinders, and I wanted to see the bulge in his pants – a man who sounded like that must have been wound tight. Right to the breaking point.

He lashed my hard cock again and again, and I felt the red welts rise on my skin. In my position, I couldn't quite see my own erection, but I thought it probably resembled a thick candy cane – white with red strips all the way down.

"You know what I think?" Belsnickel said, his voice oddly casual.

I couldn't respond with words, but I made a choking sound that might have sounded like a what?

"I think you're bad all year long precisely because you want me to punish you."

I shook my head, realized he couldn't see me, and whispered my denial.

"No, don't try to tell me that. You think about me all year. All those stories your parents used to tell you. You wonder if they're true ..." I heard the rustle of Belsnickel's pants as he moved, and then he was standing right in front of me. I tried to look up without lifting my head, but even the mask was obscured at my angle. "You hope the stories are true. You used to watch for me when you were a kid, didn't you?"

"No ..."

"Would you ask me to stop, if I gave you the chance?"

I didn't need to think about my answer. "No."

“Straighten up.”

I did, my back popping with protest after being locked in position for so long. Belsnickel towered over me, and that close, the smell of leather intoxicated me. I wanted to rub my cheek against his coat, just to see if the fur was as soft as it looked. I shifted my weight from one foot to the next, but I kept the litany of questions from spilling out.

“Put your hands in front of you. Cross the wrists.”

As soon as I did, I realized what he planned to do. The chains that had been on his arm were suddenly wrapped around my wrists, heavy and cold, the links pinching my skin. Once my hands were secure, he squatted in front of me and wrapped the long chain around my ankles. I couldn’t move. I couldn’t even shuffle my feet. Locked in place, I could do nothing but shiver as my erection bobbed in front of me. Even my new fear couldn’t dampen my arousal.

As he straightened, he took a deep breath, as if he was savoring the smell of my sweat and excitement. Now that I had a clearer view of him, I tried to check out his crotch, but his coat blocked my view. Still, it wasn’t too difficult to believe that he was hard for me. Why else would he continue with my punishment? Traditionally, Belsnickel only punished children with one or two hits from the whip and then forced them to promise they would be good in the future. I had never heard a single story of Belsnickel using chains – though it was becoming increasingly clear that the adults kept all the good Belsnickel stories to themselves.

“How many years has it been since you read your Bible?”

I blinked. Who kept track of that sort of thing? It’s not as if I marked the day on the calendar and spent the next decade or so chuckling about all the fools who still read their scriptures.

"I don't know ... maybe fifteen years."

"Fifteen?" He nodded. "Fine. Count it off."

"Count ...?" My question was cut off by the sound of the whip slapping against my chest. I cried out, my skin immediately turning a bright red. "One."

"Good."

He slapped my chest again, the long leather strap laying across my body. He always paused long enough for me to shout the number. At first, my tone was as crisp as the leather snapping against my flesh. But my voice faltered as soon as he found the more sensitive areas. My cock again. My inner thighs. The flat of my stomach. At one point, the tip stung my throat like a wasp, and I almost dropped to my knees. But even when I struggled for breath, I didn't forget to count. Two. Three. Four. I also didn't close my eyes. I wanted to see Belsnickel, wanted to try to catch a glimpse of the features beneath the mask, or the shape of his body beneath his coat, or a hint of his arousal. But everything was completely hidden from me. The only thing he couldn't disguise was the way his breath came in rapid pants.

Five. Six. Seven. Eight.

Halfway through, I wanted to beg him to stop. I also wondered if it was possible to come this way. I had never had an orgasm beaten out of me before, but I had also never been this close to the edge. My thigh was covered in clear fluid, and I felt it crawling down my cock, nestling in the hair at my balls. Sweat streaked down my sore back and sensitive thighs, gathered beneath my arms, and painted my brow. The earlier chills were forgotten. Now I just felt heat. Heat from the whip. Heat roaring under my skin. Heat like long waves from Belsnickel's body.

Nine. Ten.

“We’re almost done.”

The promise startled me – and alarmed me a little. He wasn’t going to get me all worked up and then leave, was he? My left hand often did a fantastic job, but I was going to need something more. Still, I couldn’t imagine Belsnickel kneeling in front of me to give me head – or even deign to jerk me off.

Eleven.

“Do you promise to be a good boy from now on?”

“Twelve. Yes ... yes, sir.”

Two more hits in rapid succession. Belsnickel stood behind me, and I looked up, trying to catch a glimpse of him, but he caught my chin and forced me to look forward. “Just one more to go. And then you shall have your treat.”

My spine stiffened at the promise, and I barely felt the final lash across my shoulders. My fingers trembled, and as soon as I uttered the magic word – fifteen – that tremor raced through my body. My hands shook. My knees knocked together. My heart, already racing, went even faster, until I was certain it would explode out of my chest. I felt like an over-eager puppy, my entire body moving with uncontained excitement. I just hoped my tongue wasn’t hanging out.

One strong arm went around my waist, holding me tight against his body. His coat was softer than I thought it would be, and I didn’t mind the texture against my raw back. In fact, I wanted to squirm against him, but between the strength of his arm, and the tension in the chains, I didn’t have a lot of room to move. His other hand slid over my thigh, aggravating the welts there, his long, gloved fingers seeking out my cock.

I would have preferred to feel his skin against my mine, but any thought of complaint fled my head as the hard fingers closed around my aching cock. His suede gloves were cool and smooth against my heated skin, and I couldn't remember the last time I had felt anything so soft. My knees buckled, and I pushed against his hand, desperate to feel the smooth texture soothing the red stripes on my shaft. He stripped my cock, moving from the tip to the shaft in an easy, slow motion. I didn't stop shaking. And I was grateful he held me.

"You want the rest of your treat?"

"Yes. Please. Please."

"At least you have good manners," Belsnickel murmured.

I almost smiled at that, but another hard stroke pulled a moan from me instead. The chains rattled as I rocked my hips, moving as much as I could despite his hold. He moved so slowly at first, I was certain that the torture would continue all night. I tried to encourage him to quicken the pace, but he ignored the silent hints, as well as the vocal pleas. He followed his own rhythm, forcing me to accept it. I couldn't do anything except relax against Belsnickel's chest. As soon as the tension went from my body, he finally jerked his wrist faster, as though he had just been waiting for my silent submission.

I didn't want to come too soon. I didn't want him to leave me. But there wasn't anything I could do about it. I cried out each time his palm rounded the crown of my cock, smearing the clear fluid there, and applying too much pressure to the sensitive skin. I tilted my head back, resting it against Belsnickel's shoulder. I caught a glance of a bare patch of skin beneath his mask – just below his jaw. I wanted to lick it. I wanted to taste the cold winter night on his skin. I wanted to taste snow and bitter north winds. And then I wanted to find his mouth and see if the winter clung to his lips.

Somehow, that was the thought that sent me over the edge. My cock throbbed, and cum erupted from me, staining Belsnickel's gloves, smearing over my skin. The trembling finally stopped, leaving the muscles in my legs completely weak. Wave after wave of pleasure rushed through me, until I could do nothing but sag against Belsnickel's arm.

"I think I want my own treat," Belsnickel rasped.

I whimpered, partly out of surprise, partly out of consent. I didn't know what would count as a treat for the devil, but I didn't care, either.

"Get on your knees."

He pushed me to the ground without further warning. I hit my knees hard, and then felt his hand between my shoulder blades, pushing me forward, until my brow touched the floor. The chain pressed against my stomach, and my shoulders cried at the pressure from the awkward angle.

"Don't look," Belsnickel warned. "You'll be punished if you do."

"Yes, sir."

"I know you're going to be tempted ..." He ran his bare hand down my spine. "But you'll be sorry." He slapped the flat of his hand across my sore ass. "You understand me?"

"Yes, sir. I absolutely understand."

"Good. Starting now."

I kept my gaze locked on the floor between my arms, my ears straining to catch every rustle, every hint at what he might be doing. I heard the heavy coat fall from his shoulders and hit the floor. I heard the snap of his buttons. I heard his moan as he dragged the tip of his thick cock down the crack of his ass. He felt massive. I instinctively tried to pull away, even as all my muscles tightened in anticipation.

Slick fingers probed my hole, forcing me open, stretching me in preparation for his prick. I wanted to bite my arm to keep from shouting, but I couldn't even bring my arm up to my mouth. The floor muffled each moan, but I knew Belsnickel appreciated every shout – whether it was from pleasure or pain.

His cock quickly replaced his fingers. I didn't feel ready. I wasn't prepared. I tried to force myself to relax. I knew it would be better for me if I did. Of course, that thought completely disappeared from my mind when his crown pushed past my pucker. I tensed and tried to pull away, resisting the initial stab of pain. He grasped my shoulder and forced me to remain still, holding me in place as an inch, then another inch, then another inch, filled my passage. I stopped breathing. I stopped thinking. Everything went dark. Nothing existed, nothing moved, except Belsnickel's dick, sinking deeper and deeper into me.

"Yes. Please. Yes."

Seconds later, he was fully seated, his cock twitching and straining inside of me. I felt his pulse. It changed my own heart beat, echoed inside of me. I screwed my eyes closed, doing everything I could to stop myself from looking over my shoulder. It was so hard to listen to his instructions, but I didn't want another punishment. I only wanted his glorious cock, stretching me, splitting me, marking me.

The thick arm looping under my torso surprised me – but not as much as when he pulled me into a kneeling position. I could tell that his mask was gone. A thrill of fear raced through me. All I had to do was crack open an eyelid, and I would finally know. I kept my eyes closed, wishing he had blindfolded me. He set a rhythm of shallow, earth-shattering, mind-numbing strokes. Putting his mouth close to my ear, he whispered, "You're a sweet little treat. I think I'm going to visit you again and again. Would you like that?"

"Yes."

"Yes, what?"

"Yes, sir."

My flaccid cock stirred. He licked and nibbled at my lips, catching each moan, swallowing each plea. A new sheen of sweat slicked my back, amplifying the sound of flesh slapping against flesh.

"Say it again."

"Yes, sir."

He forced me to bend again, the chains dragging across the floor. His hands went to my hips, his fingers digging into the flesh.

He forced me to remain still and plowed into my ass as if it belonged to him. My brow scraped across the floor, and the chain hit my stomach and cock, and his balls slapped against mine with each punishing drive forward.

"Don't stop," I begged. "Don't stop. Don't stop. Please ... please ..." The pleas blurred, but they didn't cease. I shouted them with each breath, pleasure bursting through my body like small electrical charges. My cock dangled between my legs, thick and throbbing. Even though it had just been minutes since I orgasmed, I was ready for another one. More than that, I needed another one.

"Close ..." The devil warned.

"No, no ... please ... don't stop ... just a little bit more ... please ..." I sounded desperate. I sounded like the cock slut I am. But somehow, it worked. Despite the warning, the hard thrusts continued, and I clamped down around his shaft each time he filled me. I wanted to hold him as long as I could, until neither one of us could tolerate another second.

"Now."

I tensed, waiting for his hot liquid to fill my ass. Each powerful jerk of his cock sent me closer and closer to the edge. I pushed back, wiggling my hips, trying to get more of him. A stinging slap on my ass reminded me to hold still, until his prick stopped twitching, and the cum leaked from my stretched hole to roll down my sac. He gradually eased away from me. I missed him immediately.

"Don't look."

He dressed quickly, then grabbed me by my hair and forced me to my feet. He carefully unwound the chains, slinging them over his shoulder thoughtlessly, as if they didn't weigh more than a feather. He briefly touched my cheek with gloved fingers, and his eyes glowed a bright yellow through the mask. I stopped believing in Santa Claus when I was seven, but I never really stopped believing the legend of the Belsnickel.

"One more treat for you," he rasped, catching my chin and forcing me to look away, to the floor. My shoes were full of candy. "Try not to be too good next year."

"I'll do my best, sir."

He released me and stomped away. The pictures rattled on the wall from his heft. As soon as he slammed the door shut behind him, I raced to the front window, desperate to catch a glimpse of him. But his dark shadow was already gone, swallowed up by the night.

There wasn't even a footprint in the fresh snow.

The next morning, I catalogued the bruises left on my body. Ten long bruises, the perfect size and shape of massive fingers, as well as two yellow circles around my wrists. Welts colored my cock and my inner thighs. Bite marks and hickeys were bright purple spots on my neck and shoulders. Not to mention the rug burns on my knees and elbows. It felt as if every inch of my body had been marked by my punishment – and my reward.

FESTIVAL OF LIGHTS

By Jay Starre

Joch watched the lighting of the menorah with mixed feelings that third night of Hanukah. His father placed the glowing candelabra in the window of their living room with loving hands as snow fell softly outside to frame it. The burning oil lamp in the window was actually a common sight in that bustling Jewish section of Montreal.

Surrounded by his family, the familiarity of the ceremony he'd grown up with brought a definite glow to his heart. The tradition of Hanukah, The Festival of Lights, stretched back for more than two millennia, and was familiar and comforting. He'd always enjoyed this time as a happy Jewish holiday with light and gifts, especially since his own family tradition tended toward less emphasis on ghastly events of the ancient Jewish past.

Then his eyes strayed to their guest and his cock rose up as more lustful thoughts intruded on his somewhat pious feelings.

With glowing golden eyes under silken brown brows, Ariel was an actual Israeli. Visiting Montreal, he was without immediate family of his own. Earlier that afternoon, Joch had bumped into him at a downtown gay bar.

They had literally bumped into each other, colliding in the hallway outside the busy upstairs bathrooms. Their eyes met, and an instant mutual attraction edged them both into an impromptu grope, quickly followed by a deep, tongue-stabbing kiss.

As others crowded past and either ignored the smooching couple, or checked them out with a grin, they exchanged drool in a total lip-lock that lasted and lasted. Their hands roamed up and down, noting firm pecs, solid butts, slim waists and rearing cocks all hidden under Montreal designer clothes.

Joch had been amazed. Not the slightest bit drunk himself, he tasted the handsome stranger's lips and tongue and knew he couldn't be either. What had come over them?

Their kiss broke with a wet smack. It was Ariel who spoke first. "You, my hot friend, just have to be my Hanukah gift!"

Stunned that this remarkable golden-eyed stud was a fellow Jew, he blurted out the first thing that came to mind. "It's a fucking miracle!"

Breathless, they both howled with laughter. Spontaneously, Joch invited Ariel to his family's Hanukah celebration.

After the traditional blessings and a few intoned songs, Ariel was asked as a guest to speak to the family.

"Judah Maccabee, The Hammer, liberated the Temple in Jerusalem from Antiochus IV to find only a single consecrated bottle of olive oil to light the menorah. Yet even by this third night, the oil still burned, and beyond until the eighth night when newly consecrated oil was finally prepared. This is the miracle we celebrate."

Ariel offered the family a crooked grin as he spoke, an admission that the story was all too familiar. White teeth between full pink lips glowed much like those golden eyes.

He was a strange mix. A modern Israeli yet with his skullcap and trimmed beard and speaking of events steeped in antiquity, evoking the orthodox. And perhaps even something more unusual and distant.

Gazing at that full mouth and those glowing eyes, Joch found his own undeniable sexual urges tumbling into other flights of fancy. Did Ariel's distinctive looks remind him of a Seleucid? Those inheritors of Alexander the Great's splintered empire, Kings of Syria and ruling over the Jews in Israel, those vile foreigners Judah and his brothers had defeated?

There was that grin again and a look directly into Joch's eyes. He smiled back. The menorah glowed in the window, letting all who passed know the miracle was reaffirmed.

What more awaited him that night?

# # # # #

Jochanan placed the torch in an iron wall sconce and stepped forward to inspect the loitering figure before him. Gowned in Greek garb, he was either a very brave or a fool. Of course, men who met other men down in these narrow tunnels beneath Jerusalem were that, either very brave or fools.

Golden orbs gazed directly into his. He exuded a quiet confidence, no doubt born of his superior station in the hierarchy of the Holy City under the rule of the Hellenic Seleucids.

But that was no more, now that his brother Judah had been victorious in liberating Jerusalem.

A sudden fierceness gripped him. They'd won back their city, and most importantly their Temple, from those who'd defiled it with the sacrifice of pigs and the worship of Zeus in the holy precincts. Who was this arrogant cretin to so brazenly parade his Hellenic loyalties? He reached out, grasping the offending gown with both hands and roughly spinning the fool around to shove him face-first against the stone wall.

"This is what all you Zeus-lovers can expect from now on ... a big prick up the ass!"

He hissed the words, a sibilant echo reverberating in the narrow tunnel. His hands yanked up the man's gown and found bare flesh, warm globes more solid than expected, and a deep and inviting crack he wasted no time in spreading.

He thrust against those naked buttocks, his prick stiff and jerking under his own more simple robe of striped wool. One hand probed into that heated butt valley while the other clutched at his own gown to yank it up and reveal his twitching tool.

"Prepare for the Hammer of God," he hissed again, leaning in close to breathe in the offender's ear.

His prick found hole. His instincts were to shove and be done with it, but something even more crude came to mind. He hawked down onto the bared ass-crack, a great gob of spittle landing there to drool down over his probing prick crown. He spit again, and again, rubbing the goo in over the flared head, teasing the snug entrance with a pair of spit-wet fingers. The hole twitched nervously between those firm mounds, to his angry delight.

Surprisingly, the silent Greek thrust backwards to meet that pumping pole. His hips writhed in little circles, then humped up and down. He was grinding that warm ass-valley against the spit-lubed prick buried in it!

In his surprise at the man's lack of shame and outright eagerness, Jochanan experienced a moment of hesitant uncertainty, but the sensation of gooey crack and waiting hole banished any last minute doubts. He aimed and shoved. Piercing the tight rim, his fat knob drove deep into the heated bowels beyond. Half his thick shank was inside, clinging ass-lips surrounding it.

The deep grunt exploding from the Seleucid's open mouth was supremely satisfying, but his own heated moan betrayed him. The warm hole felt so good! The man's mouth was so close he could feel and smell his breath. As much to fend off another of his own moans of pleasure, he clamped his lips over the Greek's.

Another surprise! The lush lips parted and sucked in his tongue! The slim but solid body in his arms pushed back against his; the mouth opened wide and sucked him in much like the tight but willing hole between the Greek's firm butt-mounds.

He tongue-fucked that wet mouth, slobbering and drooling. He stabbed deeper into the warm asshole, humping upwards with his knees and hips to impale the offender with more and more of his lengthy cock.

The man took it, hole gulping up as much cock as it was fed. It remained tight, amazingly so, but the convulsing sphincter seemed only to want more and more of the thick meat invading it. Although he'd yet to speak, the Greek's body broadcast an undeniable message. He writhed and humped, fucking his own asshole over the big cock ramming into it from behind.

Jochanan's tension, mostly due to the demands made of him as brother to the famed leader of the revolt, boiled over as he found the tight hole he'd intended on brutalizing instead welcoming him, and more. The Greek slammed back against the Jew, devouring all the prick he was offered. He wriggled his firm buttocks in tantalizing circles, rising up on his toes, dropping down to swallow prick to the balls.

He actually struggled to keep up, tonguing mouth furiously, one hand gripping the back of the man's silken brown hair, the other clamped over one heaving butt-cheek slick with sweat and hot as a molten metal. The bearded face was mashed against the slick stone wall, turned sideways, mouth agape as tongue swabbed it inside out, the hips rearing back and pounded full of angry Jewish prick. Yet the harder Jochanan fucked, the harder the Greek fucked back.

And then, another surprise, stunning in its implications, wracked Jochanan to the core. In the heat of the brutal fuck, one of his hands slid around the Greek's writhing torso, at first meeting a smooth chest, then a flat stomach, and then below that a rearing, drooling prick.

That stiff pole testified to the Greek's excitement. He was loving the rough ass-fuck, yes. But there was something else, something totally shocking. The man was circumcised! It was unmistakable! The foreskin wasn't merely pulled back, it was not there!

He was a Jew!

Caught up in the intense pleasure of hot mouth and hot hole and squirming male flesh, Jochanan didn't miss a beat. He gripped that stiff prick and squeezed, then pumped. The man, now a Jew not a Greek, only grew more frenzied in his arms. He wriggled his solid ass in circles, eating up the prick piercing it. He sucked at Jochanan's tongue like it was life-giving manna.

Regardless, this final shocking turn of events set loose a train of thoughts and emotions that Jochanan felt as intensely as the physical pleasure of that amazing fuck.

It was the third night since they'd taken back the Temple. The holy oil they'd used to light the sacred lamp still burned. Three nights when it should have been only enough for one. It was a miracle.

And, Jochanan's part in this miracle was ongoing. He'd been designated by his brother, Judah, to ensure the new olive oil was properly and speedily pressed, prepared and consecrated. It would take eight days for this preparation; that was certain and impossible to alter.

The city was alive with the talk of it. The expectations were enormous. Eight days was a sacred number to the Jews. God would answer their prayers, and the oil would last. The Holy City was awash in hope and faith.

Yet Jochanan was faithless. He had always been so. His father, Mattathias had been the High Priest who launched the Maccabbean Revolt. His brother Judah was leading it to completion. Those two had always been rock-solid in their beliefs.

As he pummeled the willing hole of this Greek-revealed-as-Jew, Jochanan's entire perceptions of faith and hope were upended. He'd witnessed the miracle himself, the flame in the Temple still alight when it should never have burned this long.

And this man in his arms, not an enemy, but a brother, taking his cock so willingly, offering up himself totally. Another miracle.

He groaned, pulling away as he thrust deep inside heated guts and spewed. The moment was sublime. Emotional revelation matched physical orgasm. His balls roiled, his cock erupted. The writhing Greek-Jew continued humping the prick up his ass.

He felt light-headed, flushed and sweat-soaked by his exertions, emptying of seed and grinning with an ecstasy he'd rarely experienced.

The miracle did not end there. It was only the beginning. The man turned, cock slithering from his creamed asshole. The sputtering torch lit his golden eyes and full lips. He smiled!

"Now it is my turn to provide prick up the ass, to a fellow Jew victorious over the oppressors!"

The voice was rich and soft at the same time. The crooked grin entirely disingenuous. The man had to know he'd revealed himself when Jochanan had seized his prick and found it circumcised. Jews alone practiced that custom.

Still reeling from his orgasmic revelation, he stumbled slightly as he turned and bent over, the cold water that ran down the center of the tunnel a welcome relief as it washed over his sandaled feet.

"Take me," he muttered, his body shaking as firm hands gripped his robe and yanked it up over his waist.

His naked ass, heavy with muscle, furred with a down of silky dark hair, opened up as he spread his own feet and offered himself. Prick, not as long but much thicker than his, slid up into his parted crack.

He moaned. The feel of that hot weapon sliding up and down, so thick and threatening, grazing his tight, fearful asshole, sent another spurt of cum out of the slit in the end of his prick to dribble into the water below.

Spit landed in his crack. He flushed and moaned again. He was about to suffer the same fate as the Greek-Jew! Goo coated his ass-crack and hole. A prick-head smeared in spittle pressed against his trembling sphincter.

He bit his lip and grunted. Rather than await the inevitable, he reared back and impaled himself. Searing pleasure, to his total surprise, engulfed his sphincter and the tunnel beyond.

He'd done exactly the right thing, pushing outwards rather than fighting the invasion. His hole expanded and swallowed. He was taking prick!

"So wondrous! Yes! It is a miracle," the voice behind him proclaimed.

Pride, bolstered by a secret guilt at his lack of faith, had prevented him from an experience like this before.

Now, he gripped his knees and surrendered to it. He pushed back against the hands on his hips and the prick goring him. His asshole cooperated, gaping wide to the invader, eased by slippery spit, and on fire with an overwhelming sense of the miraculous.

He fucked himself over that thick tool. His beefy ass rammed against the slim but sturdy hips behind, settling down into the half-bent knees and lap, naked as his own. The feel of bare flesh against bare flesh was almost as exciting as the feel of throbbing meat goring his tender asshole.

As he fucked himself, he allowed the truth to settle in. The Jew behind him, with the gentle golden eyes, was one of those who had become Hellenized. Over the years, many Jews had embraced the Greek lifestyle of their Seleucid conquerors. They had continued to worship as good Jews in all ways, including circumcision, but had become set apart from the radical element embodied by Jochanan's High Priest father and brother.

The world was turned upside down in these last few days. The miracle of the Holy Oil was occurring. The sanctity of the Temple was restored.

His ass was full of prick, a gift he had never expected. He reveled in it. He humped that hot spear, driving his hefty buttocks into the heaving lap behind him. He massaged that pounding tool with his tight anal muscles. He drove them both to orgasm.

The sputtering torch spit its last, and darkness descended just as the Jew behind him let loose a river of spunk to flood his willing guts. His own cock erupted for the second time. The orgasm gripped both his spewing cock and his convulsing asshole. In the darkness, he took seed inside and welcomed it with a rapturous joy.

Even as that darkness enveloped them, Jochanan was comforted by the belief that there was still light in the Temple. He had faith in that. Faith.

In that stygian darkness they groped for each other and embraced. Pricks dripping they kissed deeply. Hands explored beneath robes. Tongues tangled.

Three miracles had occurred in that tunnel. First had been the surprising willingness of the man he'd thought was Greek to take his prick up the ass. The second had been the shocking revelation that the Greek was a Jew. The third had been the discovery of his faith, and the surrender of his ass to this same Jew.

But it was past midnight, and now the fourth day.

In awe, he only wondered what the next days would bring.

# # # # #

Later that night in Joch's trendy Montreal apartment, away from his family and the traditions he'd grown up with, he and Ariel finally came together. Joch tasted Ariel. His tongue explored beyond the crooked, full lips, delving into the hot mouth. He sucked on pert nipples, licked flat abs and tongued a deep navel. He slobbered over warm armpits. He gobbled up a thick cock dripping pre-cum and then sucked in a fat ball-sack.

He tongued down between spread thighs, licking crack until his lips latched onto the pouting ass-lips between the firm cheeks upended and parted for him. He'd never felt a hole open so wide for his tongue. Slurping and slobbering, he ate ass as if it was manna from heaven.

They fucked each other, not once, not twice, but three times to celebrate the miracle of Hanukah. Each time they came, both would shout, “It’s a fucking miracle!” to breathless hoots of shared laughter.

As sweaty and wild as the sex was, somehow they shared more that night. The connection went deeper, beyond one night, beyond the miracle of the Festival of Lights. A shared past, ancestors who might have done the same, explored each other shamelessly and fiercely and lustfully, that and more.

And there were five more nights to come before the celebrations were complete!

It was a good night to be a Jew.

A JEW FOR ALL SEASONS

By Milton Stern

For Sammy, Christmas was his least favorite time of year. The season always annoyed him, for he felt bombarded by reindeer, snowmen, Santas, elves, stockings and everything else that made the season unbearable. He remembered the other kids teasing him about being Jewish when he was growing up in the South, but what he hated most was being asked, “Is Hanukah the Jewish Christmas?” He would always answer, “No. Christmas is the Jewish Christmas. Jesus was Jewish, Mary and Joseph were Jewish, and at least one of the Wise Men was Jewish. That would be the one who brought the fur.” He would then go on to tell them that Christmas was not Jesus’s birthday as he was born during the month of *Elul*, which falls in August or September, depending on the lunar calendar cycle. But, the goyim weren’t interested in education, and he would be beaten up by a gang of them during this time of peace and holiness, for ridiculing their yuletide cheer.

So, it was ironic that during the recession of 2008, Sammy, would find himself grateful to have a job as a department store Santa as he had been almost nine months without full-time employment. He was also grateful for Christmas Eve as that marked his last day in the red fat suit. December 24 also marked the last day he would have to work with Marvin, the ornery elf they assigned to him for the prior month. To make the day even more special, the last kid to sit on Sammy’s lap lacked bladder control.

Both Sammy and Marvin had similar features, dark curly hair cut short, piercing green eyes, olive-toned skin and full lips, but that was where the similarities ended. Sammy was over six-feet-four, and Marvin was a little over four feet.

Sammy walked back to the dressing room that was reserved for Santa and his helpers to change and quickly stripped himself of his costume. He no sooner had put on his jeans and sweatshirt when Marvin walked in and began to strip.

“Fucking brats,” the holiday elf said as he took off his green felt shirt.

Sammy didn’t bother to look at the little guy because his attitude was a turn off, nor did he respond.

“I’ll bet you’re glad this gig is over,” Marvin continued.

“Yeah, but I do hate to lose the paycheck,” Sammy answered.

“Me, too. It’s been tough finding a job.”

Sammy wanted to comment on Marvin’s attitude being a hindrance to finding gainful employment, but he just was not in the mood to get into a conversation with him, and now that this job was over, he didn’t have to.

“You want to get a drink?” Marvin asked.

Sammy, who had his backpack over one shoulder and was heading out of the dressing room, turned around and gave Marvin a look of disbelief.

“Well?”

“It’s just that you’ve been pretty much an asshole this past month, and you haven’t said two words directly to me since we started. Now you want to go out for a drink?” Sammy asked.

"Yeah. Look, I hated this gig, and besides you tall people always get to play Santa while the real elves," and Marvin gestured to himself as if on display, "don't get to play the jolly ole St. Nick. So, forgive me if I am not such a happy leprechaun. I also don't care too much for the goyim or their spoiled kids."

"You're Jewish?" Sammy asked.

"My name *is* Marvin Minkoff."

"Who knew? Mine is Sammy Sagman," he said with a smile.

"I know. I looked at your application after they hired you. What do you know? Two members of the tribe celebrating *their* lord and savior's birth," Marvin said as he put on his jacket.

"Which took place during *Elul*," Sammy said. "What the hell? Let's go get a drink."

Marvin grabbed his backpack, and they headed out of the department store and down the street looking for a bar that might be open. Sammy knew of a leather bar around the corner, but he wasn't sure if Marvin swung that way. They walked a couple of blocks before Marvin stopped.

"There's the Falcon, Down Under's, the Garage ... pick one," Marvin said.

Realizing Marvin did swing that way, Sammy picked the Garage as it was the only one quiet enough to allow a conversation. Sammy suggested they put their backpacks in the trunk of his car, so they doubled back to the parking lot, ditched their backpacks, and walked the four blocks to the Garage.

As it turned out, Marvin was not the jerk Sammy thought he was; he just wasn't happy about his employment situation, and being a little person made it that much harder to find a job as many potential employers did not take him seriously when he came in for an interview. Sammy couldn't quite figure out what Marvin did for a living, but it sounded a bit like an assembly-line supervisor or a social worker. And, Sammy didn't bother interrogating him too much. Sammy was a print production manager before the company where he worked went under.

Around 11:00 pm, they decided to call it a night. They walked back to Sammy's car to retrieve Marvin's backpack before Sammy drove home.

"Do you need a ride?" Sammy asked as he closed the trunk.

"That's OK, I can catch the bus."

"Don't be ridiculous, besides, it's Christmas Eve; where are you going to get a bus at this hour?" Sammy asked.

"It's just that ..."

"Get in the car," Sammy insisted.

Marvin climbed in, and Sammy asked where he lived. Marvin only gave him cross streets.

When they arrived at the destination, Sammy saw a rundown motel offering weekly rates and efficiencies. He was heartsick. In the few hours he had spent with Marvin, he had grown a little fond of him, and he didn't like the idea of his having to live like this in what was essentially a crack house offering weekly rates.

"Is that where you live?" Sammy asked pointing to the motel across the street.

"Yeah, and don't give me any lectures. I had a nice time tonight and thanks for the ride ..."

"Not so fast," Sammy interrupted. "Go in and get your things. I have a two bedroom apartment. My roommate moved out a while ago, and I need help with the rent. No arguments, you can stay for as little or as long as you want," Sammy said and he was surprised at how quickly he offered Marvin a place to stay. This was so not like him to let just anyone into his home; however, Sammy was a compassionate person, and he knew he would not be able to sleep nights knowing Marvin was living in these conditions.

"Look, I don't need looking after ..."

"I know, but I am not leaving you here. I don't care how long you've lived here. This isn't safe, and I'm not leaving until we get your things and you come with me. End of discussion," Sammy said as he pulled up to the front of the motel. "What room is yours?"

Marvin stared at him for a second then resigned himself to the fact that he was not going to win this one. "Eight-H."

They gathered Marvin's things, which didn't take long as he pretty much sold everything he owned before moving into this dump. After packing them up in the trunk, Sammy drove them to his apartment. While he did not live in luxury or even the best neighborhood, Sammy's place was a far cry from where Marvin called home.

They carried Marvin's few boxes upstairs, and Sammy directed him to the spare room, which had a dresser, a bed and a nightstand with a lamp. The place was not that large, and they would have to share a bathroom, but Marvin did not complain. He unpacked his things while Sammy puttered around his bedroom getting ready for bed. He took off his shirt as it was unseasonably warm for this time of year and exchanged his jeans for some sweatpants, sans underwear.

He went in to check on Marvin, who had settled in very quickly having put away almost all of his stuff.

"Don't be shy. Help yourself to anything you want in the fridge, and ..." Sammy stopped talking when he noticed Marvin was looking away and apparently had been crying. "Marvin, what's wrong?" Sammy asked as he sat next to Marvin on the bed and put his arm around him.

Marvin wiped his eyes then looked up at Sammy, "I'm sorry. It has just been so hard these last few months, and I was a total dick to you while we were playing Santa and the elf, and here you go and open your home to me ... I ...."

"Please, it's my pleasure. I'm sure you would have done the same for me," Sammy said as he rubbed Marvin's back. "Now, don't say anymore about it. I'm going to take a shower and go to bed. I suggest you do the same. Tomorrow, if anything is open, we'll go and get some groceries and maybe go out for Chinese food." Sammy stood up and winked, and Marvin smiled back. Marvin also took in Sammy's form. Little did anyone realize that under the red fat suit was a hunk of a man, standing six-foot-four, around 225 lbs, and tight with muscle. He also noted how the sweats hugged his round butt as he walked away. Within minutes, Marvin heard the shower running.

Once Sammy was done and out of the bathroom, he called to Marvin to let him know that if he needed a shower, the bathroom was free.

Marvin stripped down and went into the bathroom and turned on the water. Sammy, wearing only a pair of white briefs, reappeared and startled him.

"I'm sorry, I just realized you may not be able to reach the shower head to adjust it," Sammy said as he looked over Marvin, who although a little person around four-feet tall, had an incredible body.

"That would help," Marvin said, "could you just detach the handheld, and I can take it from there."

Sammy detached the handheld shower and let it hang down and stared at Marvin again.

"Excuse me for staring, but you are really built ... I didn't realize ... I mean ..." he stammered.

"That midgets work out?" Marvin said with a chuckle as he stepped into the shower and closed the curtain.

"Yeah," Sammy said as he stayed put while Marvin bathed himself.

"There's a lot you don't know, and besides, a guy has to workout to make it in our world, or he'll never get laid," Marvin said with a laugh.

"I guess there is a lot I need to learn," Sammy said as he exited the bathroom.

After a few minutes, he heard Marvin turn off the shower, and he realized he forgot to put out a towel for him. Sammy immediately jumped out of bed and called out, "I forgot to give you a towel." He grabbed one from the linen closet, and he entered the bathroom right as Marvin opened the shower curtain.

Sammy handed him the towel and looked over Marvin's clean wet body. As his eyes scanned down, he noticed something else about Marvin. He may have been a little person, but that was all that was little about him. He was sporting a beautiful hard-on that was at least eight inches long, maybe longer, and very thick with a mushroom head.

"Sorry, guy, I've been kind of horny lately. I would have polished it off in the shower, but I didn't want to use up all your hot water."

Sammy didn't say a word. He just dropped to his knees and took that big dick into his mouth and started sucking as if he were starving for air and Marvin's tool provided oxygen. Marvin didn't stop him; he just moaned and placed his hands on Sammy's head.

Sammy reached back and removed his underwear to free up his own hard cock, which was an inch shy of Marvin's and not quite as thick. Once naked, he grabbed Marvin's full balls with one hand and felt up and down his compact, muscular body with the other. The whole time, Marvin was still standing in the tub. Sammy didn't care. His cock was heaven, and his pre-cum tasted sweet, very sweet, and there was plenty of it. Sammy couldn't get enough of his cock or the pre-cum he was being fed, and Marvin was not about to stop him. Sammy felt Marvin's balls tighten up and his cock swell even more, and he knew it wouldn't be long. His own cock was throbbing and bobbing and leaking.

"I'm gonna come down your throat if you don't stop," Marvin declared. Sammy just kept at it, sucking that big thick leaking cock as if his life depended on it, and the more he sucked, the more turned on he was. "Here it comes, buddy!"

The first blast went straight back, and more and more cum filled Sammy's mouth, and he didn't lose a drop of the sweet cream. In fact it was the sweetest load he ever tasted. He just kept sucking and sucking to be sure he didn't miss a drop, and tasting that sweet load brought him over the edge with a hand's free orgasm that blasted the side of the tub. Sucking on Marvin's dick was the greatest sexual experience he ever had – so far.

When they were spent, Sammy lay down on the floor on his back, his dick still semi-hard, and Marvin stepped out of the tub. Sammy licked his lips.

"Damn, your cum tastes just like … like … peppermint!" Sammy said with surprise.

Marvin didn't say a word, leaned over and kissed Sammy while he straddled his chest. The kiss was long, sloppy and deep, just the way Sammy liked it.

They broke away from each other, and Marvin had a glow about him as if he were being bathed in pink lights.

"You have been a good boy this year, Sammy," Marvin said.

Sammy thought he may have had too much to drink at the Garage, for Marvin was transforming. While his hot body and huge dick remained the same, his dark hair grew to his shoulders, and he grew a well-groomed beard.

Sammy was frightened at first until Marvin put a reassuring hand on his chest, which emanated a warmth he never felt before. They were still naked, Sammy on his back on the bathroom floor, and Marvin straddling him. The little man then sat on Sammy's chest, his cock resting on his sternum and pointing at his neck. His velvety balls felt so good against Sammy's skin, they made him tingle with joy.

"Who are you?" Sammy asked.

"My last name is not Minkoff, although I am Jewish," the now long-haired elf said. "I am Santa Claus's twin brother, Marvin Claus. Yeah, I know Claus doesn't sound Jewish, but our name used to be Clausenoffenberg before we changed it. The kids used to have so much trouble with Clausenoffenberg."

"But, Santa is a symbol of Christmas ... I mean Santa does not exist ... I mean ... Oh my God ... does this mean I have to convert?"

"Sammy, my son. The Christians high-jacked us a long, long time ago. We are just part of the Diaspora, who happen to be living at the North Pole. My brother and I are angels. We operate a factory and make toys, but we don't fly around with reindeer and jump down chimneys. That's the made up part."

By now, Marvin had reached back and was stroking Sammy's dick, which was springing back to life.

"Every year, Nick ... by the way, that is Santa's real name ... and I seek out a few individuals who have come into rough times and try to bring them some joy in the season. I have watched you since you were a child, always caring about other people, sacrificing your own happiness for others. You took care of your grandmother when she became ill with Alzheimer's and took her into your home, and you gave up your life for her. I knew your roommate didn't move out a while ago as you said. Your grandmother stayed in that room. Your grandmother died. While she was alive, your career suffered, but you didn't care as she was more important since she raised you after your parents died when you were a little boy," Marvin said as he looked at Sammy, who had tears in his eyes. "You took me in when you saw where I was living even though I was so mean to you these past weeks."

"Was this a test?" Sammy asked as he placed his hands on Marvin's muscular thighs.

"Actually no," Marvin said. "You weren't going to be my subject this season. I was actually looking out for David, the store manager, but his heart is cold and made of stone."

"So why were you crying earlier?"

Marvin looked away for a second, but his hand stayed on Sammy's now rock-hard dick. "Because I was so focused on David, I didn't realize how bad things had become for you since your grandmother's death. While you were puttering around in your bedroom and I was unpacking my things, I sneaked a look at your checkbook. You have only $8 to your name."

Sammy turned away in shame, but Marvin reached up with his free hand and turned his face toward him. "Sammy, you have nothing to be ashamed of. I have spent three thousand years looking for someone like you to join Nick and me as we seek out those needing help and understanding. If you let me 'join with you,' you will be able to join us and become 'one of the just,' who gets to pick 'the chosen'."

Sammy looked confused. "What do you mean *join* with me then *join* with you? Will I become like you? Like a vampire, the undead?"

Marvin laughed, and his whole body shook like a bowl of gefilte fish in jellied broth.

"What is so funny?"

"Sammy, you read too many horror novels. No, you will not live forever. You will live a regular life, but that life will be far from normal, as you will have a purpose and you will spread *simchas* and *nachas* to those who need it," Marvin said with a twinkle in his eyes. "So, shall we join in this purpose?"

"Sure," Sammy answered without hesitation.

Marvin then slid down Sammy's body until he was between his legs. He then lifted Sammy's legs until they rested on his shoulders.

"Aren't you going to use some lube?" Sammy asked as he attempted to reach into the vanity.

"No need, my cock will provide enough eggnog to make this very pleasurable," Marvin said with a wink, and he aimed his recharged dick, which he stroked a few times to coat with the copious amounts of pre-cum that was leaking from it, and aimed it at Sammy's hole.

"Wait ... what am I doing? I'm not a bottom!" Sammy exclaimed.

"You are now," Marvin said and drove his big cock in to the root without hesitation.

Sammy, who had braced himself for the pain, felt no pain, only bliss as Marvin proceeded to hump him for points. It only took a few minutes for them to come in unison, and it was the second hand's free orgasm of the night for Sammy. He shot so far that he hit is own face, and as he licked his lips, he marveled at how his own cum now tasted like ... like ... peppermint!

A BOY FOR CHRISTMAS
By Christopher Pierce

December 24, 2008

At last, everything was done.

Cards mailed, presents wrapped and given, tree bought and decorated, phone calls to out-of-state family and friends made. I poured myself a glass of eggnog and sat down on the couch in my apartment's small living room.

Whew! I almost sighed out loud.

I gazed at my Christmas tree, festively decorated with lights and ornaments. It was early evening, already dark outside, and the tree glowed warmly at me from across the room. Impulsively, I switched off the lamp next to the couch to enhance the effect.

It was nice.

At home in the dark with my Christmas tree.

I sipped my eggnog and tried to ignore the aching pang in my heart. Even though I knew it would make me feel worse, I leaned over and looked out my window at the busy city street below.

The neighborhood had been decorated for the holidays, and up and down the sidewalk couples strolled. Men holding hands, men arm in arm, one couple had even stopped under a streetlight and were kissing romantically. I sighed again, thinking how nice it would be if I had someone to share Christmas with. But I chided myself – I had much to be thankful for: a nice home, a good job, a car, friends and family who loved me; it seemed ungrateful to feel sorry for myself that I didn't have a lover of my own.

In any case, I resolved to have a nice time on my own. I had tomorrow, Christmas Day, off from work, so I'd have a whole day to relax and enjoy myself. The lights on the tree started to blur in my vision, and I realized the hectic pace of the past few weeks was getting to me. I drank the rest of the eggnog and set the glass on the table with the lamp.

Pulling a blanket over myself, I decided to take a little nap there on the couch before heading off to bed. It was so nice there, with the tree glowing softly and the eggnog in my belly. I snuggled into the blanket and closed my eyes.

"Merry Christmas ..." I whispered to no one in particular.

# # # # #

"Merry Christmas ..." I heard in my head. At first, I thought it was an echo of my voice, but as I slowly woke up, I realized it was not mine but another's voice. It was much deeper than mine, with a jolly warmth to it, and somehow in the back of my head, I heard jingling bells when it spoke.

"Is it Christmas?" I asked.

"Almost," the voice said. I sat up on the couch, and what to my wondering eyes should appear but a very large, very sexy man standing in my living room!

Was I dreaming?

If I was, it was a very good dream – the man was tall, at least 6'3" or more, burly and muscular, dressed all in red with white furry trim and big black boots on his feet. But instead of an old man, this man was probably in his forties, with a full brown beard and mustache that matched his twinkling eyes. Over his shoulder was slung a big green sack, full to bursting.

“Santa?” I asked.

“The one and only!” the man said with a hearty chuckle.

“But you’re so hot ...” I said. He roared with laughter and swung the sack down off his shoulder. He rested it at his feet, and I swear I thought I saw something moving inside it!

“I appear differently to everyone,” Santa said, “in the way that best pleases whomever I’m visiting. This is how I look to gay men.”

“It’s an honor to meet you, sir,” I said. “Can I get you something to eat or drink?”

“No, thank you,” he said, “I can’t stay long. I’ve got many more people to visit tonight. I just wanted to stop by and give you your present.”

Suddenly, I felt embarrassed.

“Oh, sir,” I said, “there’s lots of other people who deserve presents more than I do ...”

“Do you presume to tell me ...” Santa said, his voice growing hard, “who deserves presents and who doesn’t?”

I lowered my head, hating the fact that he seemed displeased with me.

“Of course not, sir. I’m sorry, sir.”

“That’s better,” he said, and putting one gloved finger under my chin and lifting my head so that we were looking right into each other’s eyes. I felt my body grow limp in the power of those blazing eyes.

"Now," he said, "let's see, you bought toys for your local orphanage, donated money to the Salvation Army, clothes to Goodwill, did volunteer work at your Gay & Lesbian Center, gave food to the food bank and fed people at the homeless shelter." He grinned. "And that's just this month."

"But I didn't do those things to get rewarded!" I said.

"And that is exactly why you deserve a very special present this year."

He knelt down next to his huge sack and unlaced the knotted gold drawstrings. As soon as it was opened, a very handsome young man popped out of the bag like a jumping jack! His shaggy hair was blond, his eyes were ice blue and his body was tanned and hairless. He looked about twenty years old, and he had the most brilliantly white smile I'd ever seen.

He pointed at me with delight.

"Is he my new owner, Master Claus?" he asked.

"That he is, my boy," the big man said, "that he is."

The young man was bare except for a tiny thong made out of the same red material with white trim the big man's suit was made of. He walked over to me and jumped into my arms. He smelled like Christmas trees.

"I'm Billy!" he said. "I'm your new toy!"

I looked at the big man with a surprised grin on my face.

"For me?" I asked in disbelief.

"Just for you," the big man said.

"I can keep him?" I asked.

"He's yours," he said, "for as long you want him. If you ever get tired of him, send me an e-mail and I'll come and get him." Santa then handed me his card.

Billy's hand found its way to my crotch and started fondling me through my shorts. I got hard real quick.

"No, sir," I said, "I can't imagine getting tired of this present any time soon."

"Well," the big man said, closing up his sack and hoisting it over his shoulder, "I'd best be off. Lots more presents to deliver tonight."

"Goodbye, sir," I said, "thank you so much!"

"'Bye Master Claus!" Billy said, waving.

"You be good, Billy," he said, then winked at me. "And you enjoy your present."

There was a bright twinkling light and the big man in red was gone. For a second, I was afraid that this was all a dream and that Billy would disappear, too, but no, he was right there, sitting in my lap, rubbing my cock through my shorts.

"Well, Billy," I said, "I think you're the best Christmas present I've ever gotten."

"But you haven't even tried me out yet!" he said, laughing playfully.

"I just have a feeling," I said, "now stand up. Let me look at you."

Billy obeyed me and got off my lap. My dick ached where he'd been stroking it. He was certainly a choice piece of merchandise, lean, small, cute as hell. I reached out and pulled his thong off, letting it drop to the ground. He had a nice-sized cock under there, and it was nice and hard.

He giggled as I took his dick in my hand.

"That feels good, sir," he said as I started fisting it.

"My name's Jeff, Billy," I said.

"Oh, I'm supposed to call my owner sir, sir." he said.

I realized that I liked him calling me, sir.

"Okay, we'll stick with that then."

"Yes, sir."

"C'mere," I said, and pulled him in for a kiss. His mouth was warm, his breath fresh and minty. I stuck my tongue in his mouth, and he took it happily, moving his own tongue out of the way, so I could explore.

He reached under my shorts and took my cock in his hand again and started jerking it. We just stayed like that for a few minutes, kissing and stroking each other. Then I broke it.

"Your mouth is so hot, Billy," I said.

"Thank you, sir."

"I'd like to feel it on my cock."

"Yes, sir!" Billy said and dropped to his knees. He carefully pulled my shorts down to expose my raging boner, and with a sigh of happiness took it in his mouth.

It was electric, like no blowjob I'd ever received. His mouth was like fire, like ice, like velvet snow seen through the window on a warm winter evening in front of a fire. I leaned back and luxuriated in Billy's oral service, loving and cherishing every second of it.

But, I couldn't hold out for long. Before I knew it, I was blowing my load down Billy's eager throat, and an intense orgasm was flooding through me. The boy slurped up everything I gave him and licked his lips.

"Mmm," he said, "you taste like eggnog."

I laughed and pulled him up from his knees onto the couch with me. Wrapping my arms around him, I spooned him with his back to my chest and my cock to his butt.

“You feel so good in my arms, Billy,” I said.

“You too, sir,” he said, “I’m going to like belonging to you.”

We lay there in silence for a few minutes, watching a few stray snowflakes fall outside the window. I must’ve dozed off because I woke up suddenly to a very pleasurable feeling in my crotch.

Billy was rubbing is naked ass against my hard-again dick. I squeezed him, crushing him to my chest.

“Now this is the only way to wake up,” I said drowsily. I noticed it was still dark outside, so I couldn’t have been napping long.

“Sir?” Billy said breathlessly.

“Yeah, boy?”

“Please fuck me.”

“Now there’s something I don’t have to be asked twice,” I said, gently pushing him off the couch and standing up myself. Normally, I’d have a guy do some oral service on me to get me ready for fucking, but the memory of Billy’s mouth and the reality of his butt on my dick were more than enough to get me ready.

I grabbed Billy, faced him away from me, and bent him at the waist over the arm of the couch. Jackknifed in that position with his ass in the air, he looked good enough to eat. Spitting in my hand, I slicked up my cock.

I used my hands to pull Billy’s butt-cheeks apart and saw his beautiful little hairless rosebud of an asshole. Unable to resist, I stuck my face into it and licked, loving its sweet taste. Using my tongue to open it up a little, I gave Billy a quick tongue-fuck to warm him up for me.

Pressing my cock against his asshole, I slowly entered Billy. He moaned, sounding almost like an animal in his need. Gently pushing back against me, he took me in farther than I'd thought I'd get on first thrust. It was amazing, in the same way his mouth had been, yet different and better. It was like he was made of heat and light and now I was becoming a part of him. Billy spread his arms out and grabbed a hold of the couch. With him anchored, I knew it was time.

I fucked him.

It felt so good; it was as if the top of my head was going to blow off. I thrust into him, then pulled out almost all the way, then pushed back in. Grabbing him by the hips, I held him in place, not that he was going anywhere. He took it well, grunting in time with my thrusts. I threw the boy a hard fuck, but he took it like a man.

When I felt myself getting close, I reached around and took Billy's dick in my hand. It was hard and dripping.

"You gonna shoot for me, boy?" I asked him.

"But sir, the couch!" Billy said.

"I don't give a crap about the couch!" I snarled. "Are you gonna come for me?"

"Yes, sir!"

"Good, 'cause I'm shooting now!"

I jerked him hard, and as my second orgasm of the night roared through me, I shot my load deep inside him. I groaned with release and pleasure, and I felt the boy shudder.

"Oh, sir!" he said, and I knew he was shooting his own load all over my couch.

"That's it, boy, yeah," I growled above him.

He cried out and slumped underneath me. I lay on top of him until we both could catch our breath. Gently, I pulled out of him, then laid him down on the floor, so he could rest. I got towels, blankets and pillows from the other room and sat down next to him. I wiped us both off (the couch, too) and then snuggled next to him on the floor next to the Christmas tree.

Billy was already asleep when I wrapped my arms around him again and pulled the blankets over us. With his back to my chest, I held him close, and soon enough, his deep breathing lulled me to sleep.

# # # # #

Christmas morning was bright and shiny through my windows. I untangled myself from Billy and sat up, stretching. It was a beautiful morning. I was so glad to have him to share it with. Billy yawned and sat up, blinking his eyes sleepily.

"Is it Christmas morning?" he asked.

"It sure is," I said.

"Did you get what you wanted, sir?"

I stood up and pulled him to his feet. Then I picked him up and tossed him over my shoulder. He laughed in delight.

"I did, Billy," I said as I carried him to my bedroom, happy that I was not going to spend the holiday alone after all. "I got exactly what I wanted. This is the best Christmas ever."

THE YULE GOAT
By David Holly

December 17, 2008

The fall quarter at Lithia College had moved like a snail making tracks over a glacier – creeping to an inexorable finish. I staggered away from the classroom, exhausted following the most grueling history examination ever conceived by any mortal being. The sadistic Professor Gulinyan had stuck it to us, no doubt of that.

When I had entered the classroom, dragging after an all-nighter with the course textbook, the day was already the coldest one of the year. The temperature had dropped further while I struggled through the exam. Trudging toward my campus residence in Leek Dormitory, I pulled my winter coat around me. Snowflakes stuck to my shoulders. I tried to appreciate the first snowfall of the season. The flakes were outsized and sodden, sculpting the firs and spruce that overtopped the campus into fantastic shapes.

When I reached my room, I sighed with relief. My roommate, Zak Noodleman, was out, probably *schtupping* his girlfriend. I got my sneakers off and dumped my wet coat onto the floor. My jeans and shirt followed. My socks were wet, so they went onto the pile, too.

Wearing nothing but my carnelian-colored briefs, I glanced at the long mirror we'd attached to the door. If it is possible to appear both haggard and puffy at the same time, I was managing nicely. I looked so shitty that I amazed myself. I lurched toward my bed and dropped. My mind was in a whirl – I must have tossed and turned for forty-five seconds before Morpheus claimed me.

I awoke briefly, aware that three hours had passed. I wanted to get up, take a leak, and drink a glass of water. However, I didn't have to pee that badly. I rolled onto my side and drifted off again. That's when the dream assailed me.

I was in a cabin surrounded by tall trees and high snowdrifts. Half a tree was burning in a massive fireplace. The floors were smooth trimmed spruce. Snowflakes frosted the window glass. Like Adam, I grasped that I was naked. The guys surrounding me were attired in form-adhering tights of fairy-like hues. Their doublets complemented their tights, as did their striped shoes with bells on the points.

"You're the Yule Goat, Alex," one boy told me. He was wearing silvery tights that made his ass look more naked than naked and a pouch that emphasized his cock and balls. To my horror, my naked body passed through stages of arousal. Flushed and excited, I tried to hide my growing erection, but the act of hiding revealed everything.

"No," the boy assured me as if he were answering a question. "The Yule Goat does not give gifts. He demands them." I could not recall my demand.

"Let me give the Yule Goat my gift," another boy said, fingering his hardened cock.

I knew what that gift would be. To my horror, I felt that I had asked for it. My heart thundering, I leaped up, naked and erect, and ran from the guys. An open hallway stood before me, and I raced down it, the pack at my heels. My bare feet slapped the pale floorboards that clung like thick mud, and my erect cock weighed me down. My ass wiggled, enticing the pack to greater effort.

Before I reached the door, they were on me. Strong arms held me, sweet lips kissed my own, thick cocks brushed my ass. I felt a big one sliding into my cleft. It was so slick that it easily parted my buttocks. The boys holding me bent me forward, forcing my ass back to take the cock.

Sweating like a rutting goat, I awoke with a huff. My pillow and bedclothes were drenched with sweat. My cock was bullet hard and twisted uncomfortably in my briefs. I stood, almost wobbling, and freed my cock. My briefs were sweat-soaked, but I hadn't pissed them. I hadn't ejaculated either, which was a relief.

I pulled the sheets off the bed and put them in a basket with my water-soaked clothing. I would drop them off at the college laundry in the morning. Letting my bed air, I wiped the sweat from my body with a used gym towel. I grabbed a clean pair of bikini underwear – forest green this time – a fresh bath towel, and sauntered down to the community bathroom.

I used the toilet before I climbed into the shower, and the intense dream-induced priapism abated. Then I stood under the hot spray and tried to wash away my feelings. I soaped my body, cleaning every nook and cranny. I massaged the herbal scented shampoo onto my scalp. I tried to clean everything away as I let the hot spray beat down upon my head.

I come from pioneer stock. My ancestors came to Eastern Oregon in 1852, claimed a gigantic tract of semi-arid land, and ruled it with a gun in one hand and the Bible in the other. Their descendent, my father, was a throwback to the family hardiness. My father had one tune, which he iterated doggedly: "God's purpose for sex is making babies. Sex for any other reason flouts God's law."

All my life, a repressed part of my psyche had flouted God's law; in fact, it had flaunted the lust that my father most specifically condemned. The male form drove me wild with desire. The female form aroused only mild appreciation. Around guys, hot surges rushed through my body, but when I dated girls in high school, their most passionate kisses hardly moved me. I tried to suppress my feelings. I prayed to be normal. If there was any Supreme Being out there, he/she/it wasn't listening, wasn't buying – as if the creator of the universe wanted me to be a flaming homosexual.

"Alex," a delicious masculine voice tinkled. I had been showering with my eyes shut, but I recognized the voice. It belonged to Llew Bobbin, a guy I sat beside the one time I attended a meeting of the campus Gay & Lesbian Alliance. "Nice to see you."

"Nice," a second voice echoed with an intonation that made me flush. His name was Dan Crow. Dan was a Native American: his ancestors had belonged to some tribe or other, and he was the gayest guy on campus. He was the elected chair of the Gay & Lesbian Alliance and other gay groups. He wrote gay erotic stories on the side – for actual money – and he had part ownership in a gay bathhouse. When Dan said the word nice, it carried connotations, innuendo, implications, and blatant ribald flattery. That I was naked while Llew and Dan were fully clothed did not ease my mind.

"Hi, guys," I said, turning off the spray and reaching for my towel. For the first time, I noticed that I had selected a hot-pink towel.

"Alex," Dan asked. "What are doing for the holiday break?"

The question alone made me feel funny all over. I had been planning to go home to Eastern Oregon to spend Christmas with my family. Not that the prospect of Christmas with those people sounded attractive – nights and nights of evangelical church services, followed by family prayers and quarrels.

"My plans aren't that firm," I lied, inviting whatever offer they had in mind. While I waited, I rubbed my body with my towel and pulled up my underwear.

"My family owns a cabin in the mountains," Dan said, eyeing my dick, which was rapidly disappearing behind the forest-green nylon-cotton weave. "It's remote. Our group plans to spend the break there. We'll see out the old year in the snowy wild realms, so to speak."

"Alex, you're invited," Llew clarified. "If you want ..."

Visions of horny naked gay boys shucking Christmas in a remote cabin flashed before my eyes. I listened for the still, small voice that our pastor spoke of, the voice of God speaking to my soul. I really did listen, but I heard only an anthem of acceptance. Choirs of angels sang, 'This is the EVERLASTING YEAH, wherein all contradiction is solved,' and I heard God thundering, 'SAY YES TO IT, ALEX.'

"Sure," I gulped. "I'd love it."

December 20, 2008

We left late after Dan's last final exam. I had called my father the day before to tell him that I wouldn't be home for Christmas. He was furious, manipulative, and controlling. "Are these boys HOMOS?" he finally yelled when I tried to explain why I wanted to spend my holiday in the mountains with a bunch of guys.

I fibbed. "It's a cabin up in the snow county," I assured him. "We'll be skiing. Hiking with snowshoes. Stuff like that. It's healthy."

My father didn't relent, but I left him no choice. I was shaking by the time I disconnected. My roommate, Zak Noodleman, shook his head. "You should tell your father that you're gay," Zak suggested. I could only stare open-mouthed at Zak. Did everybody read my secret thoughts?

Our destination was situated on the Continental Divide. We spent the whole day on the road, me riding the single rear seat in Llew's Honda Element. The other back seat had been removed, so we could stow our gear, food, booze, DVDs, and other paraphernalia. Our skis and snowboards were secured in a rooftop carrier. Dan's ragamuffin mutt He-Dog rode beside me for the entire journey. The trip was lively, however, because Dan was steeped in Native American lore, and Llew was a student of religion. He knew tales from every myth ever recorded, and by the time he had related all the flood myths, I was coming to the profane insight that Christianity really did embrace an entire pantheon and that Jesus Christ (not his real name) was merely a latecomer in a long series of resurrecting gods.

We climbed the final bit of snow-choked hill just after midnight. Two vehicles stood before the cabin, Ed and George having arrived separately and waiting with a late supper. The cabin was more of a lodge than a cabin. It had only two bedrooms, but the living area was gigantic. A generator provided power, while the fire in the fireplace provided additional heat. He-Dog promptly found the hearth, turned three times, and went to sleep.

We were exhausted after the grueling drive. Ed and George turned in while we were eating. After our light supper, we were also ready for bed.

"You'll be sleeping with Ed and George," Dan told me. "Keep your briefs on. No jerking off tonight."

I crawled into the double bed beside Ed. George lay on the far side. Brushing against Ed, I felt his cock stir in his silk boxers and wondered why Dan had cautioned us against sex.

In my dream, I was running in the snow. I was wearing nothing but wren-colored briefs, but the snow did not freeze my bare feet. Wearing reddish bikinis, which revealed their thick cocks, the boys searched for me. "We're hunting the wren," the robin redbreasts shouted. "Catch him and uncover his secret." I concealed myself in the ivy bush, bright with holly berries, but my slinky ass stuck out.

Laughing at the way I'd revealed myself, the robin redbreasts touched me with their thick birch rods.

Their rods became cocks, erect and dripping, and I knew that the robins were destined to fuck the wren. The robins seized me, lifting me into the air. The robin named Ed slipped between my legs, and his thick cock rode along the crack of my ass. I felt the sticky wet of his cum in my cleft and on my lower back.

I awoke with Ed's boner rubbing against my ass crack. I jumped out of bed and headed for the bathroom.

Llew, Dan, and a guy who'd arrived pre-dawn had already claimed the kitchen.

"Here's a cutie," the new guy said, eyeballing me.

"Alex, this is Millard," Dan told me.

"Call me Mill," the new boy urged stretching out his arms. I fell into his embrace, but I didn't expect the hot kiss on my lips. The kiss was ripe with promise. My cock stirred.

"Hey, save it, boys," Llew remonstrated.

They had made hot cocoa, tea in various flavors, and coffee. I grabbed a cup of thick coffee and a blueberry muffin sopping with butter.

"Save room," Mill urged, patting my stomach. He sounded prissy as hell. "We're cooking eggs, corned beef hash, and waffles."

The eggs were scrambled in butter and sherry, the corned beef hash really was a hash of shredded corned beef, onions, baked potatoes, and a cupboard of spices, and the waffles were two inches thick with melted butter and New Hampshire maple syrup.

Following our morning repast, we spent the day playing winter sports until we were physically exhausted. He-Dog particularly enjoyed the sledding. My muscles were crying for relief when we dumped our snowboards, skis, and show shoes, and climbed out of our snow-soaked winter clothing. I was showering and trying to warm myself when I heard the excitement.

"The guys are coming," Mill shouted. "Artem is sloughing up the grade with Vick and Ricardo."

I jumped into my trousers and ran to the door. A decrepit burgundy Saturn was making its way up the mountain road, the chains on its front tires clawing the snow during the last steep climb. When it finally dragged its weight onto the level ground before the cabin, three guys leaped out. A hot Latino boy latched onto me, hugged hard, and caressed my butt. "That's Ricardo," George informed me. "He's a lusty fag."

"You've got a curvy booty, Alex," Ricardo breathed into my ear. "I want to stuff you with my cock. This week, I'm gonna shoot a quart of cum up your ass."

"Alex, if you bend over to pick up a penny within a hundred miles of Ricardo," Ed interjected, "the horny butt fucker will stick his cock up your ass so far it will stick out your mouth."

George wasn't fazed by Ricardo's behavior or Ed's comments. He continued with, "Here's Vick. You saw him the time you attended our club."

I remembered Vick. He sat on the far side of the room during the queer meeting, looking shy and saying nothing. A swishy guy crawled from behind the driver's seat. "I'm Artem," the fairy boy said, exuding a gentle manner and a girlish disposition.

The nine of us crowded around a table for a dinner of bloody steaks, cheesy potatoes, garlicky salad, sizzling round bread, seasoned olives, festering cheese, dried nuts, chocolaty dessert, and thick red wine. He-Dog worked his way around the table, begging shamelessly. Everybody accommodated him. With our dessert, we watched the long version of *The Wicker Man* with Edward Woodward and Christopher Lee. After we watched the movie, we dropped into our beds. Llew lay beside me. He pressed against my back so that I felt his thick cock nesting against my ass. I wanted it, but feared it. I sighed whether in relief or disappointment when Llew whispered into my ear. “Not tonight, Alex. We’re suffering through the final days of continence before the new year’s outpouring.”

I wanted to ask Llew what he meant, but the wine, the rich food, and the strenuous physical sports had drained me. I fell into a deep sleep that carried me into another dream.

Vick, Artem, George, and Ricardo hung red bows and draped sparkling lights on the spruces and firs that towered over the cabin. Llew and Dan were dangling seed cakes from the boughs while Ed and Mill were setting mugs of hot cider around the trees. Strangely, the boys were naked. When they finished their task, they turned toward me. I saw that each boy was erect – hard and dripping cum. Llew, Dan, Ricardo, Artem, Mill, George, Ed, and Vick regarded me as the Yule Goat. I was an animal decked out for fucking.

Looking down, I saw that I was naked in the snow. I knew that they were going to push their hard cocks into my mouth and into my ass. I turned to run, but I stumbled and crouched on all fours, my outstretched ass making a tempting target.

Their hands were on me, hot hands that warmed me through. When Dan sprawled upon his back, the boys pushed me onto him. I felt his hard cock push into my asshole. His slick cock slid in easily. “There’s plenty of room,” he crowed. I raised my ass, and when I lowered it again, a second thick cock rode in alongside Dan’s. I felt only bliss.

My heart pounding, I awoke with a hand shaking me. "You were about to have a wet dream," Mill said. "I had to stop you before you got off."

December 21, 2008

We decorated the cabin. For the first hour, I believed that we were decorating our tall tree for Christmas. We cut the tree and hauled it in. We hung wreaths and garlands of holly and mistletoe, dragged in a gigantic log for the fireplace, and set up red and green candles, He-Dog under-foot the whole time. When Dan, while helping Llew erect an altar, referred to the mistletoe stems as the phallus of Zeus and the white berries as drops of his semen, I realized that I was involved in something less Christian than Christmas. We weren't celebrating the birth of Christ, but the old pagan Yuletide holiday, the Winter Solstice, Midwinter, Alban Arthan, Finn's Day, the Festival of Sol, the Great Day of the Cauldron, the Festival of Growth, and the Roman Saturnalia.

We passed the day in preparation for the night's revels. Mill, Artem, and George spent the whole day cooking while the rest of us completed the decorating. We ate a light lunch and snacked around five. Afterward, Llew demanded that everyone shower carefully, so we would be cleansed for the ritual. I had no idea what he meant, but I followed his orders. Dan even bathed He-Dog. We also took a nap, four to a bed, until Dan awoke us and told us to dress.

Our costumes consisted of colorful tights, worn sans underwear, a snug short doublet with a fringe of tinkling bells, and buskins. My tights were pinkish, and when I pulled them over my bare haunches, they looked positively lewd. My ass looked more naked in those tights than it did bare!

The living area had been transformed into a place of magic. My heart leaped up as I entered. Llew conducted a short pagan ritual, which we followed with a Morris Dance. I danced between Mill and Ricardo, my lust growing. I was not alone. Every cock was stretching its tights by the time we stopped.

"Now we choose the Yule Goat," Dan announced.

"Me," Mill shouted.

"No, I want to be the goat," Artem argued.

My heart was thundering. Fear and desire warred in me, and when I spoke, my voice came as a squeak. "I have to be the goat," I managed.

"Why, Alex?"

I told them about my three dreams, not all the details, but enough to convince.

"You understand what is going to happen to the boy who plays the goat?"

"Yes." My cock stiffened harder. "I want it."

"Then I decree Alex for the Wild Hunt," Llew proclaimed. "When we catch the goat under the mistletoe, we fill him and each other."

The boys began to leap, stomp, and fling. I ran around the table laden with rich foods. Two boys chased me. Vick headed me off. I ran for the hall, but Artem blocked me. Dan, Llew, and George tackled me, but they had to release me since there was no mistletoe over my head.

I ran around the table again, laughing at my pursuers. Ricardo and Mill blindsided me, and as Mill held me tight, Llew shouted, "Look!" Directly above my head, a clump of mistletoe hung from the rafters.

Mill held my chest while George and Ricardo lifted me. Dan and Llew pulled off my buskins. Ed's hands caressed my ass before he pulled down my tights. My cock, swollen to bursting, popped free. Once my tights were off, my feet touched the floor again. Vick held a tight grip on my dick, Mill stroked my ass, and Ed unbuttoned my doublet.

While they undressed me, the boys dropped their own clothing. I saw Ricardo slipping a condom over his cock and lubricating the outside. His eyes sparkled as he said, “Me first. I made Alex a promise.”

“First he must perform the ritual kiss,” Dan insisted. “Only after, may the Yule Goat receive his gifts.”

Dan brought his lips to mine. His tongue entered my mouth and warred against mine. Then he turned and offered his ass. “You must kiss my asshole,” he said.

If my father saw me touching my lips to a boy’s ass, he would either die on the spot or murder me. As it was, my audience applauded when I kissed Dan’s asshole and licked it more than necessary to fulfill the ritual. He-Dog yipped in appreciation, a well-known ass sniffer himself.

After I kissed his asshole, Dan turned again, so I could kiss the end of his cock. I mouthed it, kissed it, licked it, and let the head ride along my tongue. After a time, he pulled away and let Mill take his turn. I kissed each mouth, ass, and cock until Ricardo’s turn came. He had waited behind me the whole time, and he celebrated the moment by pressing his cock against my asshole.

“I claim privilege,” he said.

“Granted. Fuck the Yule Goat.”

My asshole opened as Ricardo pushed his thick cock inside. I had imagined that the first time would hurt, and I was pushing to allow him easy entrance. He slid in deeper and deeper, but I felt no pain. I felt an overpowering contentment. I opened for him, so he took me.

“Oh, Alex,” Ricardo moaned. “You’re a natural. Your ass was designed to take thick cocks.”

"Yes," I said. "I'm built to take it. And love it."

Ricardo thrust, pulled back, and thrust again. That's all it took. "Oh, my god," Ricardo shrieked. "I'm going to come. So quick."

My asshole was milking him off faster than anything he had experienced in his wildest dreams. He cried aloud as he filled the condom.

Once Ricardo ejaculated, all the boys were free to embrace the pagan night. I ended up sucking Mill's cock while Dan sucked mine. He-Dog danced around us in a frenzy of delight when I exploded my seed into Dan's mouth. Then Ed fucked me, his second orgasm of the night, but his most intense. I stroked his cock with my asshole while the deep pleasures rippled from my rectum to my cock. Lying on my back while Ed humped me, I felt my climax approaching. He banged my ass, and the motion sent tingles to the head of my cock. Then I was coming on my stomach and chest and onto Ed as well, while he howled and filled the condom in my ass.

Our orgiastic revels lasted until we were all drained, filled, and sore. Wobbling to our feet, naked and decorated with semen, we embraced and wished each other a fruitful Yule. Then we turned to the table, which groaned under the weight of roast pig, goose, potatoes, squashes, fried apples, salads, crusty bread, moldy cheese, and bowls of nuts, candies, and fruits.

Pressing my fresh-fucked ass against Mill's naked hip, I tippled oatmeal stout and devoured goose and pork along with a stinky Roquefort, parsleyed peas, creamed cucumbers, and sliced pears with raspberry glaze. When we turned to the cakes, pies, ice creams, and candy, I whispered to Llew, "Happy Yule."

"Blessed be, Alex," said he. "Blessed be."

SECOND TIME NAKED

By David C. Muller

Judah unrolled a map made of parchment across a wooden table, "This is where the garrisons are; here, here and here," he pointed. "If they need reinforcements, they're likely to come from here and maybe from some of these other places scattered all up in here. Based on Shimon's head count, we only know of some of the soldiers, but certainly not all of them. I imagine there are probably twice as many soldiers around Jerusalem, if not thousands more, we just can't see them. Simply put," Judah explained, "we'll just have to find out where all the barracks and forts are and how many soldiers are stashed away there."

"Oh that'll be easy, sure," Yochanan said sarcastically.

Judah said, "It's not that easy to hide tens of thousands of foot soldiers, no matter how dumb Antiochus thinks we are, and each one of us has our specific niche, as it were." Judah looked at his brothers hovering around the wooden table, "Meidan," he pointed to one of Mattathias's younger sons[1], "you're good with knives and slingshots. Asaf, you're good at turning things

---

[1] Famously it is written that there were only six Maccabees: Judah, Jonathan, Yochanan, Simeon, Eleazar and their father Mattathias the High Priest, but in reality there were more like twelve or thirteen Maccabee brothers, if not more, as well as several hitherto unnamed and unnumbered Maccabee daughters. In ancient times, Jewish families with the last name of "Cohen" were, much like today, generally not known for being small or compact. This historical discrepancy can potentially be attributed to a series of rabbis or scribes who, over the centuries, continuously altered biblical texts, editing out various characters they erroneously considered to be too insignificant for the cannon.

into fire. Daniel, you're good with money and finance, and let's face it, weapons we can't steal from the Egyptians we'll have to buy from the Babylonians. Yoni; you're the dissembler and Elazar, you're a self-described zealot, and the twins," Judah turned to Rotem and Tomer, "you're both exceptionally good at diversionary tactics. That'll come in handy when we lay siege to the Syrians up at Pisgat Ze'ev, but that comes much, much later."

Shimon said, "What we all need to do now is canvas the areas around the city, places down in the valleys and along the roads to Ashdod and Yafo, before we make any sort of move. Our immediate goal is find out just how many Hellenic soldiers are within striking-distance of Jerusalem."

"Nachon," Judah said, "so we each need to go out and, in our own special way, gather some intelligence. In particular, we need to know exactly how many troops are hidden away here, at this place," Judah pointed to a spot on the parchment, "Sivuv Moza, located just west of the city gates down the hill around near Bet Zayit. What exactly are they doing down there?" He looked among his brothers, "Who wants to check that out?"

The brothers turned to each other with tense, questioning chins and shrugging shoulders. Most of them were not all that eager, not at this point at least, to go snooping around the Seleucids on their own trying to get an accurate estimation of their local military might. The Seleucids were morally and ethically corrupt, and they took to killing the natives as sport, especially the ones from rural backwaters. At first, when Antiochus took over some time after the demise of Alexander the Great, things were fine, but then, over the years, the king started going after the Jews, enticing them to adopt Hellenic culture, inveigling them to ditch their religion in favor of Greek gods and statues. Adding injury to insult, the monarch from east of the Orontes eventually ordered pigs to be slaughtered on the altar in the Temple in Jerusalem.

Considered unclean and un-kosher and thusly ill-suited for theological sacrifice, the blood of swine on the altar of the Temple had been the final straw for the Maccabee family clan, and as a result, they'd snuck out of Modi'in, their village on the rocky edge of the coastal plain, to scheme and plot a rebellion against their foreign rulers.

Naveh, one of the older brothers rumored to be aged twenty-five to thirty-five years old, held up his hand and said, "I'll do it."

They looked at Naveh tirelessly and Judah said, "*Tov*, but," he held up his finger, "you mustn't tell anyone who you are or what you are doing. The circle of trust is slim, tight, and difficult to penetrate."

"Sort of like an o-ring?" Naveh asked.

"Exactly! This firmness must be maintained. Now," Judah went on, "one of you needs to go down to the desert to negotiate with the Moabites; we're running dangerously low on *pomelo*, and later on, much, much later, we'll need a halcyon border to the south, so some *lehitchanef*-ing[2] is in order. Who wants to volunteer for that?"

The twins, Rotem and Tomer, scoffed.

Meidan sneered, "Inbreeders."

Asaf said, "Oh hell no, dude. Fuck that, I'd rather slide down a drain pipe."

"Come on, guys," Judah sighed. "Somebody's got to go down there and at least talk to them. It's just a courtesy call. Yoni?"

"Uhn unh," Yoni tsked, "I ain't going nowhere near no damn Moabites."

---

[2] *Lehitchanef* – Hebrew word for "brown-nosing," also "ass-kissing," in transliteration

“Elazar,” Judah asked him, “maybe you can go? You’re good with animals.”

Elazar held up his hands, “But who will watch my birds?”

“Fine,” Judah rubbed his temples, “Yochanan, you’ll go down to the desert to Moab.”

“Oh dear Moses, no!” Yochanan said, “Anyone but me, please!”

“Quit your bitching, bro,” said Judah, “you’ll ride down on the white horse.”

# # # # #

Naveh set out from Latrun the next day hours before sunrise, heading east. He bought a donkey from an Arab in Abu Ghosh and rode up to the peak of Tzomet Harel by daybreak. Disguised as a Philistine, Naveh wandered among olive trees and sheep, secretly spying on the garrison at Sivuv Moza down below in the valley just west of Jerusalem.

Sivuv Moza was alive with early morning madness and Naveh found it easy to move down the side of the rocky slope unnoticed. He watched foreign soldiers come and go in and out of several low lying structures built with golden Jerusalem stones cut out of nearby mountains. As he got closer, Naveh saw that Sivuv Moza was a transit point, a supply post and a stable for horses.

Naveh the Philistine, (the enemy had no clue that he was really a Jewish spy), sauntered right on up to the Greek facility and rambled around like an Arab persona non-grata; no one, not even the commanders, stopped him or questioned him. Upon closer inspection of the personnel, Naveh heard the soldiers speaking with Cypriat accents.

Seleucids and their outsourcing, Naveh thought to himself, that explains how I could get so close. By and large, many of the soldiers were young boys, and Naveh reckoned some of them to be as young as fifteen or so. These people aren't known for being the brightest stars in the galaxy.

One of the soldiers caught Naveh's eye: one that was tall and muscular with fair and creamy Mediterranean bronzed skin, a Byzantine nose, broad shoulders, topped off with flowing straight blond hair and a pair of sparkling diamond topaz blue eyes. Naveh had seen this particular soldier before; he even knew the soldier's name: Jason Menelaus. As a Cohen, Naveh was a frequent visitor to Jerusalem, and he knew his way around the massive Temple Mount complex. That's where he'd first spotted Jason Menelaus, not three days older than nineteen, on guard duty a fortnight earlier.

It was well known in Judea that the Greek sentry assigned to brood over the Temple were forbidden to make eye contact or to mingle with the Jews, and in an effort to annoy them, fat obnoxious children would point and giggle, calling them names and spitting on their sandaled feet. Not known for their patience, many a young boy incurred the wrath of the Greek sentry who beat them down for any minor grievance, sometimes with swords.

This incapacity for patience did not deter young teenage girls from toying with the young men. The Temple long ago desecrated, women from regions well beyond the city walls; from places like Beer Sheva in the Negev and Haifa in the North; came to the Temple with fathers and older siblings dressed scantily like hookers and harlots. On many other occasions, secularly Hellenized Jews, such as bored and shamelessly uninhibited housewives venturing out from rich, upscale Jerusalem neighborhoods, would stare at, point at, poke, flash and flirt with the young guards of the Greek sentry. Among the youth of Judea, it was considered a thrilling rite of passage for teenage girls to grope a foreign soldier in the hopes of getting a rise out of him, causing their flimsy Greek togat to sprout up like a Saharan pump tent.

Two weeks prior, however, at the start of the second week of the month of Kislev, Naveh had returned to the Temple in Jerusalem from a hunting expedition out to the wilderness of Ein Gedi and the ruins of Sodom. He came in to one of the eastern courtyards tired, thirsty and dirty. Jason Menelaus had been the lone guard in that same eastern courtyard. Without realizing it and facing Jason Menelaus, Naveh had stripped naked to wade into a steamy tub of water that had been brought out for the men. Upon wiping soapsuds from his eyes, Naveh caught Jason Menelaus staring inquisitively at his *brit milah.* Naveh thought Jason Menelaus was cute and accordingly made no attempt whatsoever to hide his circumcised penis from those dazzling pair of Greek eyes. Naveh noticed, likewise, Jason Menelaus's very own brewing erection suddenly forcing his dark red dress-robe of a uniform to rise involuntarily like the flag of a far-off republic.

"Mmm hmm," Naveh delighted in catching the young blond Greek glancing at his crotch. Naveh laughed, moving laboriously slowly that day in the tub, showing himself off to Jason Menelaus, as he bathed among other Jewish men, all of them splashing around naked in the winter sun.

Naveh had not forgotten about that moment, he'd also never later pursued the soldier of the Greek sentry ...

... until now ...

Naveh spied Jason Menelaus at Sivuv Moza training with an archery specialist and thought, 'Good thing I've got this Bedouin garb on today.'

Naveh kept an eye on Jason Menelaus, shadowing him as the Greek sentry hiked up toward Givat Shaul heading to work a shift of guard duty at the Temple just over the hill. Naveh took an estimated stock of the manpower and supplies available at Sivuv Moza as well, and somewhere along the way, he shed his Philistine costume, reassuming his role as a rural Jew. Naveh was hardly a novice, and he knew what he was after as he followed Jason Menelaus all the way into the Temple.

Evidently ordered to guard the southeastern edge of the complex, Jason Menelaus maintained a disinterested and indifferent gaze as he took his position standing at attention in a mostly empty courtyard linked to an outer wall via a marginalized colonnade. Meanwhile, to make himself sufficiently dirty, Naveh wandered first through the Temple marketplace, abundant with greedy money changers, filthy leather merchants, pungent spice traders and whorish girls of a Judean persuasion who, at this time, place and era in history, (and indeed until today even), were excitedly interested in sampling the quintessential Hellenistic, uncut, Eastern Mediterranean cocks that stood, literally and figuratively, in contrast to that of the Jewish men of ancient Israel. Then, sufficiently soiled, Naveh, a Cohen, requested a bathing tub be brought in to the same mostly empty courtyard where Jason Menelaus stood guard stoically. Naveh, as the son of one of the High Priests, pulled rank and expelled everyone from the courtyard so that he could bathe; everyone except for the Greek sentry who was duty-bound to remain at his post unmoved for the next seven hours.

"Hey," Naveh immediately addressed Jason Menelaus, "you saw me naked with all the other hunters after we got back from that *tiyul* down to the Dead Sea. Do you remember me?"

Jason Menelaus moved his head ever-so-slightly, as if trying to make his neck more comfortable whilst doing his best to stare sternly and blankly at the wall opposite.

"We're a shy one, are we?" Naveh came to stand between the guard and the tub of warm water, "Maybe you don't remember me, hmm?" He tore the band off his head, tossing it into a corner, "We'll see now, won't we?"

Jason Menelaus coughed slightly, clearing his throat.

Naveh threw off his clothes, suddenly appearing a second time naked before the youth. He caught the Greek shifting his eyes to look upon him and yanked the silver chain from round his neck before turning around. Bending over to untie the leather sandal straps laced half way up his calf, Naveh knowingly exposed his soft pink and inviting wet hole buried deep between the smooth twin crevices of his ripe round Semitic ass. He took his time with those sandals; finally barefoot, Naveh, pulled apart his rump, opening his dirty dark little secret like a thick book of schlock fiction.

Still bent over, Naveh reached past his testicles and fingered his anus. "Any of this look familiar?" He glanced up at Jason Menelaus from between his legs and saw a pair of Greek lips part with anticipation. "I'd love to feel your rod deep inside. You want to hoist it on up in there?" Naveh jimmied his forefinger and his thumb into his rectum, pumping into himself for a moment, letting each finger pop slowly out of him. He flipped around and moved quickly over to the Greek sentry and lifted up his robe.

"Well, well, well," Naveh smiled down at a rising erection, "what have we here?" He reached out and stroked the cock of Jason Menelaus. Naveh was impressed with the Greek penis; stocky girth, bulbous, short and uncut, "This won't hurt a bit."

The Greek dropped his shield and growled, "You ... Jew," Jason Menelaus' panted, his voice creaking, "Jew ... you let go of me!"

"Shh," Naveh aggressively clutched the Greek's jaw and face with one hand while stroking his cock with the other, "don't speak. Let me do all the talking, alright?"

Jason Menelaus tried to move his javelin against Naveh, but Naveh gripped the guard by the wrist fast and quickly, sharply pinching the carpel tunnel ligament, forcing the hand of the Greek sentry to fly open, dropping the javelin.

Jason said, "We shouldn't be doing this."

Naveh said, "We are doing this."

The Greek squirmed then and reached for his gladius, fumbling impotently with the ornate scabbard.

"Oh stop," Naveh pulled Jason Menelaus' hand from his sword, "You're enjoying this."

The soldier let out a groan, yet still he fiddled with the dagger pinned to his waist belt, arguing physically, but with lessening resolve, with the rural Jew. "I ... uh ..."

Naveh tugged on a string and the dagger fell to the floor. He moved closer to Jason Menelaus; they were face to face, nose to nose, as Naveh rubbed under the robe, playing with foreskin, "Not so shy anymore, are we?"

Jason Menelaus started breathing heavily; he licked his lips. Only centimeters away from Naveh, he inched in for a kiss, devouring the Jew with his mouth and tongue. Naveh did not back away; he kissed him back hard and looped the palms of his left hand around the back of Jason Menelaus' head. His right hand pushed robes further out of the way, pressing the cut and the uncut together for the very first time. Jason Menelaus melted forcibly into Naveh; he wrapped his arms around him, his fingertips gently gliding down his spine, seizing his perfectly round behind squarely in his bronzed muscular hands. The Greek sentry pulled the Jew closer to him, spreading apart his cheeks, flattening his tight hole.

Naveh rolled his ass up and out as Jason Menelaus guided his middle finger to the cusp of his rectum. He slowly snaked his middle finger directly over Naveh's hole like an eclipse, pressing firmly onto his dark secret with a small, subtle circular motion. Gently, and with reticence and restraint, Jason Menelaus inserted his digit into Naveh's back pocket, eagerly pushing and pulling at the hole.

"You Greeks are real direct about it, aren't you?" Naveh lifted himself off Jason Menelaus's middle finger.

"I want to fuck your ass," Jason Menelaus grunted.

"In due time soldier, in due time," Naveh caressed the Greek lovingly. He kissed him on the lips and pushed him down onto his knees, bringing him eye-level to his groin. Naveh held his circumcised manhood, gently swabbing it around Jason Menelaus' mouth and chin, rubbing the mushroom head around the tip of his nose. "Patience is a virtue you will learn, young lad," using his penis, he pried open Jason Menelaus's tight pink lips, "you will learn."

Jason Menelaus closed his eyes and sucked down hard on Naveh's cut cock. The Jew nodded appreciatively; the rumors were true: Greek boys were notoriously easy. Then the Greek soldier gagged, and Naveh took hold of Jason Menelaus' ears.

"Open your eyes," he said. "Look at me."

Jason Menelaus opened his diamond-blue eyes, brimming with tears, as Naveh clutched at his flowing straight blond hair and said, "I can tell by your accent you're not a native Aramaic speaker," before thrusting his dick past a set of tonsils.

Jason Menelaus deep-throated the penis, making a loud slurping noise, slathering the manhood with his warm saliva.

Naveh said, "I bet you're from Cyprus," as he fucked the Greek soldier in the face.

Jason Menelaus ceased oral activity, and the penis flopped out of his mouth, "How did you know?"

Naveh looked down and, grabbing him by the back of his head, he turned around quickly and pulled Jason Menelaus's face into his butt, "Tongue-fuck me, lick my hole."

Jason Menelaus complied, he grunted.

"This is probably your first time abroad," Naveh said, "you're far away from home. You're lonely ..." Naveh pushed his anus onto Jason's face, "more importantly, you're horny." Naveh held open his ass, enjoying the feel of Greek tongue on the rim of his sphincter.

Jason Menelaus grunted and slurped at Naveh's hole; slapping some glute, he growled, "Let me fuck that ass." He slid his hand down the crack of Naveh's backside.

Naveh looked over his shoulder, "You've done this before, haven't you?"

The Greek panted and groaned, he poked Naveh's ripe hole with three of his fingers, "You're ready for it."

Naveh flipped around and pulled Jason Menelaus up off his knees; he kissed him hard and violently, lustful. They pressed their bodies together and Naveh lifted his right leg, providing Jason Menelaus easy access to his waiting and expectant cavity. Naveh undid the waist belt and tossed clothing over a shoulder. He took in the sight of a nubile nude Greek soldier, young and golden smooth, ripped with taut musculature and perfectly symmetrical eight-pack abs.

Naveh gasped at the beauty and clutched tightly to Jason's hard and strong uncut cock; "You do a lot of fucking, do you, with this big tool? You and your Greek soldier friends?"

"Hhhnffgh," Jason Menelaus grunted, pressing into Naveh.

Naveh took hold of Greek shoulders and leaned Jason Menelaus up against the tub. He dropped to his knees, blowing on the uncircumcised Hellenistic penis. "You like to fuck them?"

"Yes."

Naveh licked the base of the cock, "Do you fuck them hard?"

"Yes."

Naveh darted his lips across the shaft, "Do you want to fuck me?"

"Yes."

"Mmm hmm," Naveh then went down on Jason Menelaus; he swallowed the Greek cock, opening his jaw far and wide, delighted to taste, for the very first time, the flavor of the Greek sentry.

Jason Menelaus loudly received the oral pleasure; he panted, he groaned and he moaned with full voice; even Naveh had been taken aback by the volume of his ecstasy. Jason Menelaus nearly shouted, heaving, as Naveh lapped his lips around a dangling pair of mildly hairy balls.

"Your pole is magnificent. You must fuck me with it. You must fuck me hard like when you fuck another soldier." Naveh said, "I want to feel what it's like to have the Greek sentry inside me, to ride you. I can ride you?"

Jason Menelaus grunted and jerked his hip, causing his penis to smack Naveh, still down at his heels.

Naveh pointed towards an archway, "Let's go over to the alcove. I'll want something to lean on." He wrapped his hands around Jason Menelaus' sex and towed him by the rod over to the side of the courtyard. Jason Menelaus followed along obediently as Naveh wrapped his hands around the youth's sweaty testes. "So," Naveh gently squeezed Jason Menelaus's balls, "when you fuck the other Greek soldiers, how many do you fuck and where do you fuck them?"

"Up the butt," Jason Menelaus grinned and panted, "I fuck them in the ass."

Naveh rolled his eyes and squeezed the balls tighter, "Do you fuck them in the barracks or at the garrison?"

Jason Menelaus grunted; he lightly grabbed at Naveh's wrist and smiled, "I fucked some of them on the boat, I haven't been up to the barracks or the garrison."

"You haven't?" Naveh eased up on the balls a bit. "What's going on down there at Sivuv Moza?"

Jason Menelaus said, "Troops fresh off the boat."

"I don't follow?" Naveh twisted the balls around dutifully.

This brought the Greek to the top of his feet; he moaned passionately, "The barracks and the garrisons are more up near Nablus, on the way to 'Gido."

"As in Megido?"

"That's right," Jason Menelaus nodded, and Naveh yanked on his balls again; Jason Menelaus exhaled noisily.

Naveh asked, "How many soldiers are up at the garrison in Nablus?" He squeezed on some nuts and they had to stop walking.

Jason Menelaus perspired anxiously, "I don't know, four legions, five."

Naveh clutched more sharply, "How many legions are passing through Sivuv Moza these days?"

Jason Menelaus growled, "I cannot say."

Naveh stared at the Greek skeptically, squinting his eyes; he got back down on his knees and, with hands still firmly clasped round a treasure of flesh, blew softly and wetly on the frenulum. "You can, too, say," Naveh pulled back Jason Menelaus's foreskin and temporarily barred the tips of his teeth, running them across the protrusive lip of his cockhead. Naveh smirked and raised an eyebrow, tightening his grip on those balls. "You sure about that?"

"Uh ..." Jason Menelaus tried, if only for a second, to push Naveh off him, but in his naïveté, he relented and said, "I don't know, maybe no more than three legions, two going, one coming."

"Only," Naveh put the penis in his mouth, "one," he sucked on the penis, "legion," he licked at the piss slit, "coming," he swallowed the shaft, "in." He pulled the cock from his jaw, "And you're saying four, maybe five legions up in Nablus?"

"Yes," Jason Menelaus grabbed the back of Naveh's head, "something like that, maybe six legions. Now," he impaled the Jew's face with his erection, "suck my dick."

Naveh went to town, slurping, sucking, licking, tonguing; going down on Jason Menelaus, tasting the svelte texture of his intact foreskin.

"Oh yeah," the Greek snarled and took hold of chin and neck, spearing his penis down Naveh's throat. "That feels good."

Naveh tasted pre-cum warmly oozing out of Jason Menelaus as he sucked on the penis; he'd never tasted Cypriot nectar before; and again intertwining his fingers around sweaty testes. He pulled lightly on the flesh as if they were knots at the end of a rope.

Jason Menelaus wrenched his cock away from Naveh, "I'm not allowed to fornicate with Judeans."

"We've made it this far; we may as well finish each other off, *echad le'shani*," he said, spitting into his palms, wiping his own saliva like lubricant on the prick and on his hole. He turned around and bent over, propping out his butt like they were pillows. Naveh said, "Be gentle with me, you brute."

Jason Menelaus, of course, grunted and then drilled his rod down into the Jew.

Naveh immediately started sweating. He said, "Good morning!"

# # # # #

Later on, Judah asked his brother, "*Nu?* What did you find out?"

"There could be as many as six Greek legions north of Jerusalem." Naveh, this time, unrolled a map made of parchment across a wooden table, "This area here," he pointed at a spot on the map, "Sivuv Moza; it's just a transit point, two legions going, one legion coming. There're also horses."

"That gives Elazar something to do." Judah asked, "Anything else?"

Naveh said, "I think the Greeks have soldiers on the road to Megido. I think we need to worry about keeping hold of the North."

Judah nodded, "We'll look into it."

They stared at the map together.

Judah asked, "How'd you get this information?"

Naveh smirked, "I met a guard, some kid really. They'll just about put anyone up at the Temple these days."

Judah raised his eyebrow, “He told you all of this?”

“Well, I … ,” Naveh gestured absently, “you know … told him ‘I understand’ and all of that bullshit. He was … you know … really young, a boy who still needs his mother. I sort of had to … convince him I was worth it.”

“Looks like your trick worked.”

“No worries.” Naveh folded his arms across his chest proudly, happy to help the rebellion. He said, “We should clean the Temple up later on anyway, just hose the place down, make sure everything is kosher again beforehand.”

“Mmm.” Judah nodded whilst staring at the parchment map.

Naveh said, “It’s really dirty in there.”

KWANZAA COUPLING

By Troy Storm

"What the hell is Kwanzi, anyway?"

"It's Kwanzaa, you white, politically-incorrect dork!"

"Zee ... zaa! It's just an excuse for having a black Santa Claus and giving a bunch of presents day after day after day just like the Jews!"

"There is no such thing as a black Kwanzaa Claus!" Dewayne scrambled up from his cushion to his full six-four height, clinched fists on hips, towering over the low coffee table and glowering down at his unimpressed adversary seated opposite.

Shit. My little matchmaking Kwanzaa dinner party wasn't going quite as I had hoped. Dewayne may be big and black and beautiful, but he was sort of defensive about his color and his race; and Warren, who wasn't quite as big, but was tanned and gorgeous, just tended naturally to be sarcastic and not very tradition-oriented.

Somehow, I thought they might hit it off.

"C'mon, guys," I pleaded, hauling my sorry host ass up from the floor to try and mollify Dewayne while not antagonizing Warren any further, "it's just a little seasonal get-together to get to know each other a little better. Let's not get into ... uh, specifics."

Dewayne icily turned on me. "And you've got a Christmas tree over there! It's not a Hanukah bush, you Jew! There's no such a thing! You're both ..." He sputtered. "Blasphemous! You oughta be ashamed!"

His beautiful black biceps bulged inside his shirt, and his shapely forearms tensed as he swung his massive arms up to cross in front of his magnificently sculpted pecs and turn in a huff to stalk across the room.

Sigh. And I had such other plans for those arms.

Faced with his broad back, however, there was nothing to do but drool over his gorgeous, tight ass. Normally Dee's magnificent assets were encased in an impeccably tailored business suit, but after hours, 'slumming,' he wore immaculately fitted jeans and designer polo shirts that he had altered to just skim his broad tapered back and narrow waist. Not tight. Nothing that obvious. Just skimmy.

I sighed again and sucked the saliva out of my mouth, hoping my dick wasn't gonna get too leaky for my jocks. Looking to Warren for some sort of help in rescuing the evening and being sourly rebuffed with a look of pure condescension through his expensive rimless glasses, I scurried around to plead with Dewayne.

"Dee, I'm sure Warren didn't mean to offend you. He's the secularist among us. And, you know me ..." I did a little shuffle hop. "Ta dah! I celebrate everything!"

Dewayne twisted to glare at Warren who was watching us as if we were recalcitrant children refusing to believe there was no Santa Claus. "Snot nosed, smug, superior white boy," he muttered under his breath. "And Kwanzaa is a secular holiday. Even you don't know the difference." He humphed and glared back at Warren. "I'll bet he gives his mama and daddy great pain."

"His mama and daddy are no longer with us, Dee," I whispered, hoping for a bit of empathy, "but, he's a smug, superior, really good-looking white boy, and I know how appreciative you are of masculine beauty. You ought to see him with his clothes off. That's why I thought you two might ..."

He cut me off with a vicious hiss. "He probably drove his beloved parents to the grave and you make me sound as shallow as he obviously is. I'd like to secular his white ass."

"I heard that," Warren grunted from his place at the low table, forking in another bite of my glorious Chicken Veronique – which was slowly coagulating on my prized dinnerware as they wrangled – into his languid, pouty mouth. "I don't understand it, but I heard it. I prefer up-front transparency to twittering self-congratulatory snidisms."

"Twittering self-con ...! What the fuck?" Dewayne spun to stalk back toward Warren.

"Dee! He's a lawyer! They talk like that."

"And I am a very successful corporate executive! And I will not be condescended to with racial stereotypes. You white male, stuck-up, smug ... white boy!"

I quickly dashed into the kitchen to grab the desert. "Plum pudding time! Plum pudding!" And raced back to find Warren glowering up under his eyebrows at Dewayne's very formidable crotch looming menacingly over him.

Dewayne saw it, too. He slapped his big hands together in front protectively. "Don't you dare give me that, 'he's probably hung like a fucking horse ... they all are' look!"

Warren rolled his eyes. "As if ..."

I plopped the beautifully prepared *piece de resistance* between them.

Warren's baleful look rolled to the dish. He was resisting it very well. "And why do they call it a pudding? It's a goddam cake," he muttered.

Dee's hands tensed. I suddenly had the horrific vision of him pushing Warren's face into my beautiful desert. I snatched my piece away.

"Uh, you're right. It's a cake. And I forgot to pour the liquor over it." I hustled to the kitchen. "We'll have it later. Any more chicken, anyone?" I called out, hopefully. "Or veggies? Bread? Refresh your drink? Wine ... liquor ... formaldehyde ...?"

I galumphed back in, defeated.

Warren snickered. Dewayne looked puzzled. Then he, too, smiled. Barely.

Hope springs eternal in the matchmaker's heart!

And it was the season to be ...

"What about we watch some porn?" Me, bright-eyed, hopeful.

"Are you kidding? Now?"

"That's disgusting"

"In front of the Hanukah bush?"

Me, defeated, encore. "Well, we could go into the bedroom ..."

"Your subtlety, mine host, is about as delicate as that grotesquely decorated seasonal symbol." Catty Warren.

Dewayne guffawed outright. "He's right. It looks like you hired my six-year-old cousins to see who could throw on the most stuff. Yes!" He turned to Warren, defiantly. "I have a lot of siblings and cousins. We procreate profusely!"

"Fortunately," the pretty white boy spat back. "We will provide, if you can't."

"Oh, please, not politics, too!" I wailed. "Our president is black!"

"That crack was not politics! It's racism!" Dewayne lunged. Warren threw up his hands and caught the big black man right in his impressively protruding crotch.

They both jerked back. Both shocked.

"Oh!" "Uh!" "Sorry!" "Uh! I ..." And blushing.

Well, there did seem to be a bit of civility left somewhere buried under those embarrassed scowls, after all. I cleared my throat. "I have little gifts for us, but I don't think this is the time to give them. Maybe later, when the liquor has soaked into the pudding ... and if you're good little boys."

"Being a good little boy has never gotten me anywhere ... not since I was six, anyway." What a surprisingly heartfelt comment from Warren.

Dewayne seemed slightly mollified, too. Slightly. "Well, being a bad big boy couldn't make you all that beloved of your clients, either," he needled, glowering. But not so angrily. He slowly settled back into his place.

I had thought that seating us on cushions around the coffee table where we would eat would get us closer to the floor – closer to being prone more quickly, if the occasion arose. Now, all my clever planning seemed to be doing was emphasizing how we were all having more difficulty maneuvering up and down as we ... matured.

But at least there seemed to be a break in the hostilities.

No porn, no presents, and small talk seemed to be an instant invitation to baring fangs.

I had tried the theatre. We had all seen *August: Osage County* at the Steppenwolf.

"What an utter piece of drivel," Dewayne announced belligerently. "Another dysfunctional family tearing at each other's throats. August Wilson has already done that to absolute death! And much more entertainingly!" August Wilson is an African-American playwright.

Warren's eyes blazed, all but steaming his rimlesses. "I was profoundly moved. It was an impeccable piece of theatre."

I quickly tried the movies. "What about that *Revolutionary Road*? I just adore Kate and Leo. I still get all quivery when I think of *Titanic*."

Dee had gasped. "Oh, god, I agree. What an amazing, painful experience. I was in fucking tears."

Warren's eyebrow almost disappeared into his thinning hairline. "A pitiful take on *American Beauty*. Mendes should have been ashamed."

"Mendes directed *Revolutionary Road*," Dee said, puzzled.

"Exactly," Warren snorted.

End of the arts discussion. I didn't dare bring up Keith Urban's latest.

Where was my copy of *100 Ways to Keep Your Kids Amused on a Rainy Day* when I needed it.

I'm in publishing.

Silence. In the kitchen, the brandy was slowly soaking into the Christmas pudding/cake. No plums.

"You wanna play a game," I suggested, without much hope.

Surprisingly, they both looked interested.

"I like games," said Dee. Probably his competitive spirit. *Combative* spirit.

"What kind?" Warren was wary but appeared to be willing.

"Well, uh," I improvised. "Since my presents aren't appropriate right now and since no matter what you celebrate around this time of year does seem to include giving gifts, why don't we play a little gift game?" I hopped up and went to the Christmas tree/Hanukah bush to rummage among the packages underneath. Most of which I had bought for myself.

They were both sitting up straight, poised, ready to do battle, when I returned.

"Now, take these ribbons, go around the apartment and find something that you think is appropriate for the other two, then come back and we'll try to guess why. You can't keep the stuff," I hurried to clarify. "It's just a game." I wasn't about to give up any of my precious *tchotchkes.* If I had thought about it in time, that would have been a great way to get rid of some junk, but ... well, next time.

Instantly, their beady little eyes darted around. Smirking, they both jumped up and stalked the place with a little bit more intensity than I had expected. I began to get a little nervous. Maybe this wasn't such a good idea after all.

Warren disappeared into the kitchen. Dewayne into the bedroom.

"Ah ha!" Warren returned triumphant. I hadn't even had a chance to start looking.

"Uh, should we wait 'til ...?"

"No, let's go right away," Warren said as Dewayne returned. "We can keep score or something. Keep presenting presents until ... we don't want any more."

"Uh, well, okay, I guess. Is that okay with you, Dee?"

"Whatever." He was empty handed.

"Then I guess I'll go first." Warren smirkily presented us with our gifts. He had tied a ribbon on a pot, which he gave to Dewayne and another on the half-empty bottle of brandy, which he gave to me.

"The pot is black," Dee noted, apprehensively.

"Right on!" Warren gave a thumbs up. "You're always calling the kettle black, so to speak, so ...?" He indicated the pot. "So there you are."

Dewayne looked at the pot, trying to put it all together. "You're the kettle and I'm the pot? But that means ... I'm calling it like it is. And we're both ... That sounds kind of like an apology ... sort of."

Warren shrugged. "Sort of. In the spirit of the season. All I could find was a stainless teakettle or I would have gifted our host with another black cooking utensil, too. Instead," he handed the liquor bottle to me, "here's your half-full bottle. I, normally, would see it as half-empty. You are a credit to us all."

Well, gee. Things were beginning to look up.

Dewayne broke into a huge smile. Big gorgeous grin, blinding molars, shining chocolate eyes. My shorts were struggling to keep up with my leaky dick.

I grinned back. All the way around. "Okay. Who's next?"

Dee hurried back to the bedroom. Warren, visibly more relaxed, started looking around the living area. I sighed. He was really a good-looking guy. Lean build like Lance Armstrong, thinning hair cut short, great skull, the glasses were really sexy. He had a way of looking at you like dessert. Which he loved. I thought about the plum pudding. And my shorts.

"I'm ready." It was Dewayne, from the bedroom. "Sit down. Let me know when."

I indicated the couch to Warren. My knees couldn't take that cushion stuff much longer.

We sat down. "Okay," I called.

Dewayne came back in.

Stark naked.

Warren and I both stared, chins softly brushing the carpet. My shorts gave up trying.

There was a ribbon tied around Dee's little toe. He approached me.

"Do you know how important this little sucker is to balance?"

"Un ungh." I tried to focus on the toe he was indicating, but my gaze was still glued to the massive monster ding-donging between his legs as he strode forward. Not excessively massive, you understand. Just perfectly massively proportioned attached to his huge frame. With mouth-watering balls cling-clanging underneath to match. Giants. Bolo balls. I made my eyes slowly cut to Warren.

He had managed to close his mouth. His eyes were narrowed on Dewayne's dyno dick stick, too. But there was no other ribbon in sight for him.

"The little toe is important," Dewayne said. "And, we can learn to balance without it. But, it's harder. And so," hands on hips, Dewayne bent his knees and lifted his massive leg in my direction to present me his toe. "I want you to know how much I appreciate your helping me to keep my balance ... by reminding me not to sweat the small stuff." He cut a mischievous eye toward Warren. Warren smirked back.

I giggled and took the ribbon, popped off my loafer and sock and slipped the ribbon around my own little toe. I was feeling all warm and cozy. Quite the good host. And my crotch was all happily gloppy with precum. Warren gave Dee another thumbs up. But not as enthusiastically as the first.

"Or maybe I should give a little finger up," he suggested, giving a small smile. Resigned to no present.

And then Dee did the most extraordinary thing – especially for a big muscle guy. He was still balanced on one foot. He put his arms out and slowly revolved, shoving his heel around to do so, concentrating like mad to keep his balance, tongue between his moist, thick lips. And as he turned, he swung his lifted leg down and back, his foot pointing at his ass, which, when it came into sight, had a ribbon hanging out of it. He looked over his shoulder at Warren.

Quickly leaning forward to pull the ribbon out of the puckered orifice and read what had been hastily scribbled on it, Warren read, "Kiss my ass."

With a grateful huff, Dewayne swung his leg down to plant his foot solidly on the carpet, back still toward us. "Man! I haven't got the balance I ..."

Warren pushed off the sofa onto his knees, planted his palms on the big man's butt cheeks to pry them apart and buried his face in Dee's butt.

Dee gasped. "Oh, wait ... I ... didn't ..."

Warren's tongue stroked long, slow, lavish licks up Dee's crack as the big guy's handsome face melted, and he slowly bent over to put his palms on the carpet with his butt high. He slowly pushed back against Warren's gaping mouth.

His big ding-dong stopped ding-donging to harden and rise and plaster its huge self against his belly. His cling-clangers tightened and clutched the butt of his bone.

I barely had time to get my pants and soaked shorts off my quivering ass before grabbing my belching meat and ending up with a fistful of cream.

Dewayne opened his heavy eyes and grinned at me in response to my appalled whimper. "Sorry you didn't make it around front." He licked his lips. "I could have sucked down that load."

I came again.

He grinned sexily. "While Mr. Lick Master is doing his thing back there, waddle around in front here and let me do my thing on your thing."

I did so. And he not only swilled down the manjuice coating my dick but whistle-cleaned my ticklish palms as well. Hee haw! I was ready for the next round.

Dewayne was hee hawing himself and 'oh-man'-ing mightily from the gnawing of his hole he was getting from Warren. He growled toward his rear end, while writhing above me as on my knees I tried to tackle the black oranges knocking at my nose. "You are making my ass mighty hungry back there. Got anything you can feed it?"

Holey holidays! The big black dude was ready to take it up the butt?! And the privilege was going to my buddy ... and not me ... the host!

Warren, who was more than ready to ram in his wand and make magic, was still amazed that he had been invited. "I ...? Hell, yes, you Black Beauty, that is one gorgeous hole I have been mashing my face into."

Now you have to understand that though we gay men are often prone to fuck at the first hello, Dewayne did not often give that permission. He was a romantic dude, and even if he and Warren had hit it off from the get go – which they most definitely had not – I still expected the big, beautiful man to want a bit more wooing.

Warren I knew was a slut when the scent was right.

Me ... I just hoped for the best and was mostly disappointed.

But I was turning out to be a great matchmaker!

Dewayne popped his big ole gagging gonad out of my mouth and turned to Warren. "Looks like I'm gonna have to do a little persuading that maybe the worm has turned." He folded the white boy into his arms and planted a mouth-to-mouth resuscitation on Warren that sent the drool running down my chin and the dick goo draining onto my freshly shampooed carpet ... again.

Warren came out of the clinch, eyes shining like Christmas morning confronted with the package of his dreams.

He swallowed. "Okay if I fuck you from the front, Dewayne? I want to see your face."

Dee's face was softer than I ever remember seeing it. "You can bone me from any direction you want, Warren." He didn't take his eyes off his dreamy well-kissed bro. "Wrap him up for us, will you, Mr. Hostess with the Mostest, so we don't have to take our eyes off each other."

His broad back went onto my getting-it carpet, massive thighs wide and high, his phenomenal ass rolled up high and wide open, its moist, purple-black pucker trembling with anticipation. Warren kind of sighed as the big man pulled Warren's shoulders down and locked lips with him again, while keeping his ass high to allow me to hustle to grab a pre-lubed Large and roll it onto his wonder pole.

Then it sank from sight into Dewayne's butt, and I was left to my own devices as their sweaty selves made an absolute mess of my clean carpet.

Warren's beautiful butthole kept winking and blinking at me as he fucked himself silly in Dewayne's devouring rectum – all the while sucking on Dewayne's massive pole – Warren being a very flexible corporate type.

That seemed to delight Dewayne so much – being fucked and sucked at the same time – that he insisted Warren do it again. Second time round, Warren was on his back, or rather on his butt, as Dewayne squatted on his boner, pumping himself up and down, and Warren stretched up to get almost a third of Dee's monster pole in his mouth.

It seemed a little tacky to just watch and jerk off ... so I ran to get my video camera and taped the whole holiday happiness. From every possible angle. And got some amazing close-ups! Even to this day, I ... but I'm getting ahead of my little bringing-together party.

When they finished blowing their loads, both just cuddled in each other's arms while they caught their breath and waited to bone up for the third time.

They waved at the camera and acted like horny teenagers, Warren pointing out each and every one of Dewayne's fabulous assets and carrying on about what a fabulous lay he was while Dee just grinned foolishly and snuggled and stroked and plucked and tweaked and licked whatever he could reach without having to exert himself too much.

They were really into each other.

I was a successful matchmaker.

I was fucking not getting any!

That's okay, I tried to convince myself. I hadn't planned on a three-way, but you know how us matchmaker types are, always hoping to be rewarded for our bringing-together. Just a little prezzie, maybe. A fuck or two. A thank-you blow job.

What I got was Warren announcing it was now his turn to be fucked by Dewayne.

"Uh, baby, no," Dee protested. "Honey, I am a big, big boy. I would never in the whole wide world hurt that beautiful golden-tanned bottom with my big ole black fence post."

"I want to straddle that fence post and slide up and down it until I've got cum coming out my ears."

Fetching vision. Warren did have a way with words, and he always did want to be a trial lawyer rather than a corporate hack. But Dewayne was right. Warren would never be able to take Dee's dick up his tight ass. I knew. I had been there, and it was always a hassle to get my not-quite-as-formidable meat up Warren's butt. He seemed to have totally forgotten that, in the euphoria of having the gorgeous black man bounce up and down on his.

Warren would not be deterred. He leapt on Dewayne.

It was a disaster. The XXL X-tra Thick X-tra Slick condom double doused with Super Grease couldn't begin to penetrate that desperate dude's tight hole. He was pissed. He was angry. He was sarcastic. He sniffled, heartbroken, his dream of becoming one with Dewayne's dong unfulfilled.

He was not a happy fuck toy.

Toy! I ran to my toy box, grabbing the "Kiss my ass" ribbon on the way and returned with a selection of festive anal probes. Various bright colors and shapes graduated from piercing the tightest bunghole to butt plugging the most accommodating. As I said, I had been there, and with a lotta help from my toys had progressed from somewhat painfully accepting a slightly under-sized six-inch bone to welcoming with open ass a much more substantial member.

Warren looked a little concerned at the array of probes; Dewayne, too.

"Suck on Dewayne's pole while I prepare the patient," Dr. Host announced authoritatively. Then I dove in, smirking at their surprise, and applied mouth to hole.

Truthfully, I wondered why Dewayne had somewhat perfunctorily slid his tongue over Warren's butthole before attempting penetration, especially since Warren himself had done such a spectacular job of kissing Dewayne's ass as per the Kwanzaa ribbon. But maybe getting his dick inside of Warren seemed such an impossible task he didn't want to prolong the inevitable.

For whatever reason, I gave Warren's ass my best. To be honest – transparent – Warren and I have a history, as I said. We've been fuck buddies for years, and I know that ass inside and out. I knew what he needed to open up, and I hoped Dewayne would pay attention.

I stroked, I sucked, I licked, I finger-fucked his pretty little hole, I nibbled on his beautiful butt cheeks, I sucked on his perineum and his big dick and big nubby balls. He took the pink gel tickle tube with no problem; he took the thicker purple prostate prober with no problem; and when his ass gobbled up the black rubber butt plug I figured he was ready for the real thing. I crooked a finger at Dewayne.

He had been taping the whole thing!

But in an instant, he put the camera aside and slid behind Warren to take my place.

"Whisper sweet somethings," I whispered. "And he loves a tongue in his ear."

Dewayne snuggled against Warrens' back, big hands reaching around to stroke his dick and his tits while sexily gutturally purring into Warren's ears. Warren's ass melted around Dewayne's huge dick, sucking it balls deep.

They didn't even fuck, they were so thrilled. Dewayne stayed plugged all the way in while Warren slowly ground his ass, both of them panting and growling until they were right on the verge. I was so fascinated, I just watched, both hands gripping my meat.

"Get over here!" Warren suddenly barked as he pushed himself up on his knees. "I want to fuck your ass!" Dewayne was totally gone, gripping Warren's body, his stubble scraping Warren's neck and shoulders, his big butt pressing forward hard, keeping himself impaled in the white boy's butt.

I hesitated for about a second and a half. Another second and a half and Warren was sunk up my ass. "Aw, fuck, yeah! Happy Fucking Holidays!"

I reached back to hold the three of us locked together, Dewayne reached around to grab my dick and my tits. Warren raised his hands over his head, screaming, "Come! Come! Come!"

I silently added, all ye faithful, but that seemed slightly blasphemous, so I kept it to myself.

The faithful came.

And came.

And came.

A couple hours later when we had to give our sexual organs a rest – which pretty much included our entire bodies, we were all cuddled together on the bed in my beautifully decorated bedroom polishing off the remainder of the plum pudding and swilling down egg nog.

"Kwanzaa is a fine festival," Warren agreed, pouring nog into the tiny black curls at Dewayne's crotch and sucking them clean.

"It's all about family and tradition." Dewayne stretched his giant arms wide and held us close.

"We're family and we're starting our own traditions." I plucked at Dewayne's thumb-sized tits.

Everybody murmured agreement – in the spirit of the season.

It lasted 'til Easter when an even more beautiful black man showed up from Kenya.

Oh, well, for us matchmakers, there's always another holiday.

SPIN THE DREIDEL

By Troy Storm

"Is this okay?" Tony asked, hesitantly, looking at the small four-sided top. "I mean, it's not like being irreligious or something?"

"No, no," I answered brightly. "It's a kid's game. Except kids play it with money ... or candy. We won't be using money ... or candy."

"What will we be using?" Stewart, lying on the rug across from Tony, smugly asked.

"Well ... I thought we might use clothes."

"You mean, like strip poker?" Tony shook his head, horrified. "That sounds bad. I don't want to offend anybody."

"Oh, c'mon." Stewart rolled onto his back, arms stretched over his head, chiseled pecs straining the knit of his polo shirt. Tony's eyes widened at the very impressive sight. "We promise not to let the nuns know you were playing with a Jewish kid's toy."

My gaze landed on another taut section of Stewart's clothing, lower and even more impressive.

Tony's full lips pulled into a pout. "I just don't want to do anything wrong."

"The rabbis used it to teach kids about the Torah," I explained, lightly, "but at Hanukah the kids use it to grab some *gelt*. I'm the only Jewish kid here. I promise you won't be offending me."

Tony still didn't seem convinced, but he didn't get up and leave. Stewart and I glanced at each other. My parents were away for the weekend – we had the house to ourselves – and we were hoping to make the best of our holiday time to get the hunky on-the-fence, straight-but-maybe-interested dude to come and play in our persuasion for a few days before we all headed back to our respective colleges.

Straight-but-maybe thoughtfully examined the dreidel then twirled it on the plate I had provided in the middle of our little circle. We all watched it topple. "What does that mean?"

"That's a letter called a *Hay*. You win half the pot."

"*Hey*! *Hey*!" he grinned. "Where's the pot? *Gelt* is money, right?"

"Right."

"But you're gonna use clothes?"

"Uh ... yeah ..."

Tony twirled the small toy again. "What's that?"

"That's *Shen* and you lose everything ... in the pot."

"But I got nothing to lose. None of us have got nothing to lose." He snickered.

"Oh, I wouldn't say that." Stewart shoved a hand under his polo and stroked his very flat, very six-packed abs.

Tony carefully watched Stew, then again thought for a minute. "No offense, Jared." That's me, Jared, the gay Jewish kid. "But I don't get how you're planning to get us naked with nothing in the pot."

"What?"

Stewart shoved himself up on his elbows, suddenly very un-languid.

"Well ... I mean ..." Tony shrugged. "Say, we put half our clothes in the pot, then if I win half the pot or all of it, I've just got more clothes, right?"

"Uh ... yeah."

"And if we start off with all our clothes in the pot, then we're naked to begin with, right?"

I shrugged. "I guess maybe I hadn't thought it through." Which was true. The thought of getting Tony naked in itself was enough to blow my concentration on exactly how it was to be done.

"I mean," Tony continued, pedantically, as Stewart's beady eyes narrowed. "We're here to have sex, right? That's the whole point of us getting together, right? To, like, share our experiences from college."

I looked dumbfounded at Stewart, who was looking a lot less smug. The bulge in his Dockers was showing that the evening had suddenly taken a very quick turn for the more interesting.

"Well, yeah," I confessed. "But I ... we weren't sure you'd go along. I mean, you being ... straight and all."

"Well, I tell you," Tony sighed, resignedly. "It's true. I got me a lot of freshmen pussy." He shook his head. "I don't know what it is. It must be my smell or something. They are all over me."

"It could be because you have turned from a geeky high school nerd to an incredibly hunky dude," Stewart noted quietly, sitting up, his laser gaze all but burning the threads off Tony right then and there. "Can I suck you off first?" He reached for Tony's crotch.

Tony laughed. "Sure, man. I could use a good blowjob. The girls mean well, but they just don't have the suction, you know what I mean? And they're either giggling or acting slutty. Not a great turn-on."

I slapped Stewart's hand away. "What is this 'first' shit? It's my house. I thought up this party. I should give Tony head, first. My suction is spectacular, man." I looked imploringly at the now-hunky dude.

"Well, damn, it sure is nice to be hassled over by you two. You were my idols in high school, and you wouldn't give me the time of day."

"Idols?" I couldn't believe my ears. "You were with that nerdy group with the all As. I didn't think you knew we lesser mortals were even alive."

"Hell, you know how it is." Tony leaned his back against the den sofabed, stretching his arms along the cushions. He had a pretty damn good-looking stretch, too. "Gotta run with your peers or you get cut out. When I realized I was jacking off to the sight of you and Stew in the showers as well as the glimpses I got of panties and thongs under those short cheerleader dick teasers, I thought I might be a little more 'flexible' than just being plain straight. So, I decided to give myself freshman year to find out."

"When did you turn into such a hottie?" Stewart pulled off his polo shirt.

"Great definition." Tony took in all of Stew's upper torso assets. I yanked off my shirt, too. "Excellent. You two still look superior. That's what did it for me. I figured if I was gonna score, I should look better than I did, so I signed on to a weight course. Turns out I've got the right genes." He slowly unbuttoned his plaid while Stewart and I licked our lips and waited as he pulled it out of his pants and shrugged it off.

"Holy shit," Stew murmured approvingly. "Dibs on the tits."

"Dibs on nothing," I panted, reaching to test the merchandise. Stewart slapped my hand away.

Tony stood, obviously pleased at our response to his slow unveiling. “Wait'll you see the rest. I'm fucking gorgeous.” He took off his pants.

Sure enough ... damn ... he was. Not only chiseled chest and abs, and trim waist, but flaring thick thighs and knotted calves. In his tighty whities, he was a wet dream. And I was wet. Half way there.

Stew looked pretty impressed, too – his Dockers sure as hell were – mixed with just a tinge of envy.

“And I've got a great butt. You queers are really hot for butts, right.”

“Right,” I croaked, hoping against hope. And sure enough ... damn ... he turned and dropped ‘em. Slipped right out of his jocks, naked ass beaming right at us. The play of his glutes and the sneak peeks of his pinky, pursed button hole hidden between as he bent to yank off his socks, and the fleeting dark shadow of his ballsac and dick swinging heavily in front was too fucking much.

I was in pain. I scrambled to rip off my jeans and get out of my underwear and ball up my boxers to jam against my bubbling dick before ...

“You look really good, To ... Tony.” Please turn round. Please turn round.

He wiggled his ass. Giving us a little show. Stewart pulled out his meat and started savagely whacking it.

“Now don't expect too much,” Tony said, still facing away, sounding a little nervous. “Us straight guys, it sometimes takes a while to get a good hard-on from just talking to other guys about sex.” He was obviously tugging and pumping it up to make a good first impression. “Man, I remember how terrific you guys looked naked in the locker room ... I was so ...” He gave a funny cackle that caught in his throat, then heaved a resigned sigh ... and turned around.

I came ... doubled up over my balled up shorts.

"Holy shit," Stew muttered at the sight of Tony's dick. He stopped pounding and just stared. "And you're not even fucking hard."

"Damn thing," Tony groused, slapping the seven or eight inch slab of detumescent meat back and forth. "I was kind of hoping to blow you away. It can get really big ..."

"Dibs on the blowing." I hoarsely whispered as I came a couple of more times. "Uh ... don't hurt it, Tony." I would have leapt forward to grab the thick semi-soft shaft and protect it from harm with my life, but I was a little weak in the knees at the moment.

Tony looked at me more closely. "You okay, Jare? You look a little ... pale."

Stewart smirked, propped himself on one elbow and resumed beating his meat. "You just scared the cum out of him, T."

Tony finally got the picture of me being naked and having just blown a wad and Stew lying there half-naked slamming away on his pork.

"Well, gee," he grinned, looking back and forth, then beginning to pull on his pork, "looks like I might have gotten the ball rolling."

"Considering the pair of low hangers you've got swinging underneath that cobra, I'd say you got a pair of balls rolling," I noted, dryly.

Tony snickered. "They're not so much when I get good and hard. They just pull right up under my dick."

"Oh, do show us, please, sir." Stew always gets sarcastic when he feels his load building. I think it's to keep from screaming out how damn good he feels. "Oh, yeah, do show us your hard dick, Tony, my boy. Show your old buddies ... how ... fucking phenomenally ... well hung you are ... oh, man, am I gonna come good ... oh, fuck yeah, it's gonna be a gusher ... oh sweet holiday spirit slam one ... HOME!"

Since he was beating hell out of his dick, it wasn't a straight projectile. The first was a spiral rope of cum he shot a couple feet in the air that looped and splattered back down onto him and the surrounding indoor/outdoor. The next was an arc that hit Tony in the foot and the next few were a bunch of squirts that he tried to catch with his hand, but that ended up all over his Dockers and his bare flat abs. Falling back, hand still gripping his burping exhausted organ, he cooed, "Oh, sweet friends, that was awesome. I hope I will be able to repeat that totally cool experience to make my life richer and more whole before we part." He blinked and looked around, sloe-eyed. "Hopefully without the encumbrance of sodden garments. I'm a fucking mess. Sorry about the carpet." He fell back, spread-eagled, eyes closed, smiling the smile of the well satisfied.

It was quite a show. Tony gaped, his fist frozen, choking his beet red boner. I got up, finished mopping myself and tried to will my half-hard flopper back to full-hard readiness.

"Stew is fucking huge," Tony noted, admiringly. "Just like me." Stewart's sizable shaft seemed to be the inspiration Tony needed. He resumed whacking his whack stick and, sure enough, within minutes it grew into a full, flushed, rock-hard gut-choker.

Stewart slipped out of his Dockers and 2(x)ists. He and Tony beamed happily at each other.

"Wow." Two buddies in my den with giant boners just begging to be drained, I thought. The holidays were good. I finished dabbing at my recently-emptied organ and was pleased to note that the warm glow whizzing through my midsection was truly indicative of the blood gushing back into my fuck stick and rapidly turning it into a proud fuck pole.

“Hey, we've all got big dicks!” Tony stepped over Stewart and came toward me. Stewart instantly dumped his louche languidity and hopped up to get in on the inspection.

Grabbing my meat, Tony felt it up good. Really good. Really, really fine. “Yeah, man. Hard, too. You wanna feel mine?”

“I do.” Stewart clutched Tony's dick as the straight-but-now-more-than-willing dude laughed. I hustled to get in on the action, and soon we were all standing in a tight little circle pulling and milking and otherwise testing the respective singularities of each other's excellent manhoods.

“That feels fucking great,” Tony purred. “You guys are getting me hot.”

Stew snorted, cutting his eyes my way. “Since it's your house, why don't you drop and blow him now, so I can eventually get a gut full before our hot stud runs out of sophomore seed to shoot into our orifices.”

I could think of several reasons why not to be so blatant – being more the romantic, than action hero – but the look in Tony's eyes as he listened awestruck to Stewart's pontificating made me feel I had better move my ass if I wanted to get my share before Stewart carved up tasty Tony and devoured him whole. I instantly did as Stew had so crudely suggested.

“Aaaah!” Tony was pleased. I drove my head into his crotch, forcing him backwards to sprawl his ass onto the sofa, muscular thighs wide. My nose drilled into the patch of pale blond curls half-circling the root of his meat. His giant dick was mine. Its huge purple head safely snugged into the back of my throat.

I've never known exactly how I've been able to suck the biggest, hardest dick all the way down to the root and still breathe as my suckee writhes in ecstasy under my mouth's marauding ministrations until he finally blows a gorgeous gob of goo into my gut. But I have. And I am grateful for the gift. Must be my name: Jared – he who descends. Yeah.

Stewart watched, grinning expectantly. He had been there many times, in Tony's place, and he may be a smug and self-satisfied steaming hot prick, but he knows a great blow job when he gets one and, I might add, is appreciative. He sure as hell knows how to say thanks.

Tony muscular legs shot straight out as I hauled him into the home stretch. "Ohmigod, ohmigod, ohmigod!" and then he blew a load so deep in my throat I could hardly taste it. Damn. Oh well, the evening was young. Plenty of time for manwine tasting later.

"That was fucking fantastic, man!" He bellowed, ready to announce my oral facility to the whole world. "Has he sucked you off, Stew? He's fucking amazing."

"Many times," my smug fuck-buddy grinned. "I am in awe of his abilities. He has even greater gifts, Tony my lad. Show him your butt, Jare. Isn't that magnificent?"

Tony stared at my ass. "Uh ... yeah ... I guess."

Stewart and I both gasped. "You do not revel in the joys of butt-fucking?" Stew's voice dripped with sadness. "I would have thought the first thing a straight guy would want of a gay dude was to invade his ass."

Tony looked properly crestfallen. "No, man. Pussy is what I invade. A guy's ass seems ... I don't know ... a little messy."

I guffawed. "Ha! Damn, right, man! It sure as hell can be, if you hit it wrong!" Stewart glared at me. I snickered. No reason to go into gories for the newbie's edification. "But when you get it right ... like a perfect pussy that just sucks you in and gobbles you up ... it can be awesome."

"How the fuck would you know about a perfect pussy?" Stewart smirked.

"I read a lot."

"Well ... that does sound interesting." Tony mused, staring at my hole.

"Wait a minute! Wait a minute!" Stewart pushed us apart. "First you get to blow him and then you get to fuck him? What about a little sharing in this fucking joyous holiday season?"

"I was talking about him fucking me," I snapped.

A little too straight-forward for the straight boy. "Oh ... uh ... like I said, I'm not really into ..."

"Are you for fucking real, T.? Fucking Jared's ass is one of the great experiences a dick can have. You should be on your knees praying to have his butt spread open between 'em. Hey, babe," Stew swatted my butt – he was already pulling on a rubber, heavy duty – "let me show the dude what he has in store."

I love being fucked by Stewart. The man is a master. I turned back around, dropped to kneel on the rug, and cradled my head in my arms, blissfully ready, on the sofa cushion, knees wide on the rug.

"C'mon, suit up." Stew handed a condom to Tony. "Two tongues are better than one."

Two magnificent meats creaming my colon. Didn't I tell you Stewart knew how to say thanks?

From my curled-up arm, I could see Tony looked slightly hesitant, but when Stew put mouth to hole and started swathing my pucker button with his tried-and-true tongue and I nearbouts passed out from pure pucker-hole bliss, moaning and croaking whole-heartedly, our virginal butt-buddy leaned in real close to check out the action.

Stew being a true pro at preparing for penetration, Tony learned plenty, and along with my progressively rapturous response, his empathetic excitement grew by leaps and bounds. By the time Stewart was reaming me royally with four forceful digits, Tony was puncturing his own bottom with his own determined digits.

Growling into my gaping butthole, Stewart moved his mouth up my ass to my backbone to my neck to my trembling ears. As his hot breath toasted the top of my head, his massive meatpole pushed way past where his four fingers had stretched my sphincter wide and dug for my anxious interior.

I tend to be vocal when I'm having a real good time, and even more vocal when the going gets better. Stewart fucked me slow and solidly, and I all but ate the sofa cushion before I realized there was much better fodder to be ingested. Awkwardly, I reached out to grab the nearby newbie, my grip fortunately landing on his rigid dong. I dragged Tony's prong around into my mouth, his bumbling beautiful bod following behind. By the time he had managed to arrange himself on the sofa, my face was buried between his spread-eagled thighs, suckling steadily on his rock-hard shaft.

Soon Stewart's fucking and my sucking morphed into a steady rising rhythm that built to a phenomenal climax on everybody's part.

Happy Happy Hanukah!

After we caught our breaths, Stewart started getting snippy 'cause I had sucked off Tony twice and he hadn't even laid a hand on the freshman fuck toy, so in order to keep the peace, Tony offered himself up to Stewart to play catch-up. I grumpily thought that was being a lot generous until I found myself nosing around Tony's butt while Stew was blowing him and realized Tony had reached back with both hands to lock my face in place. He wanted me to eat his ass. And bone him.

And bone him I did.

Tony liked being fucked. A lot. His fine hole was made to be filled with dick. He particularly liked being fucked and sucked at the same time that he was sucking, so while we sixty-nined on the rug, Stewart happily plowed his ass a couple of times, and then for good measure crawled around behind me and plowed mine.

Until we were all even.

Nothing left in the pot.

The next morning as we all sat naked around the breakfast table, Tony played with the dreidel.

"I've got it figured out," he announced. He spun the top. "What's that?"

"*Nun* ... you lose your turn."

"Okay." He passed it to Stewart. Stew spun.

"That's *Gimel* ... you win all the pot." We both looked at Tony questioningly. Surely he wasn't counting the maple syrup, stack of pancakes, butter and jelly in the middle of the table as a pot.

He grinned. "That means: the guy spinning can do anything he wants with the other two. Now give it to Jare." I spun. "Hey! Hey! It's *hei*. You get half the pot. You can do anything you want to with one of us. While the other guy does whatever he wants." He took the dreidel.

"*Shen*. You lose everything?"

"That means," Tony announced triumphantly, "anybody can do anything they want with you. Don't you think that's a great game?"

We did. Better than *gelt* anytime.

HOME
FOR THE HOLIDAYS
By Ryan Field

Nathan Carmichael was a quiet young man who tended to avoid direct eye contact with most people. He owned the only video store in the small town of Martha Falls, MD, and lived upstairs on the second floor. When an attractive man walked up to the counter to rent a video, he didn't just stare down at his lap and smile casually as he did with most people, he clenched his fists and bit the inside of his mouth.

He wore thick, black eyeglasses, plaid short-sleeve shirts and baggy, lifeless jeans that sagged in the back. Though he was six-feet tall and had strong, wide shoulders, he tended to stoop forward when he walked. His reddish brown, curly hair fell to his neck in long chunks, and he parted it too far to the right. And his black gum-soled Oxfords were weathered and scrappy because there were no shoe stores left on Main Street in Martha Falls, and he hated shopping in large, crowded malls.

The only people who knew he had the naturally well defined body of a swimmer were the men he met at the rest stop along the interstate. There were no gay bars in Martha Falls, and the only openly gay people he knew about were too outrageous to take seriously. So he kept his sex life simple and discreet and safe; but he didn't abstain from enjoying men altogether. When he needed a man, he cruised the rest stop on the highway or the glory holes in state park men's rooms. And there was always the adult bookstore twenty miles north. He kept a full supply of lubricated condoms in his car at all times (even though he was always the bottom), and never exchanged bodily fluids with strangers. It was furtive and dark in those places. You didn't have to look anyone in the eye, and you could remain anonymous.

He liked his small video business, and he was happy with his life for the most part, but Christmastime was always so long and arduous. He hung little white lights around the entrance and the front window and placed a small, plastic Christmas tree (pre-decorated from the drugstore) on the counter. He didn't go overboard with wreaths and ornaments as so many other shops in town did. But he did stay open late on Christmas Eve for several reasons. One was that he was performing a public service, for people who wanted to buy a DVD to give as a last minute gift – even though few ever did. People rented DVDs earlier in the day (to get them through the holidays), and by five in the afternoon, business slowed down to practically nothing.

The second reason he kept the store open was that cruising for sex on Christmas Eve was pointless. The rest stops on the highway were empty because all the guys who normally would have been cruising were home with their families celebrating the holiday. Nathan didn't have any family left in town. He had one brother who lived in California, but he couldn't just pick up and leave the store once a year. He was the only one who worked there.

The third reason he remained open late on Christmas Eve was because of the Martha Falls Annual Christmas Eve Pageant in the town square. All the shops stayed open late, and it wouldn't have looked good if he'd closed. The pageant wasn't exactly a religious event. The gazebo and the shrubs were lit with colored lights; a huge plastic wreath with fake poinsettia leaves hung from the bronze statue of the town's original founder, Col. Jeremiah Martha. The high school band would bang out secular Christmas music, the library sold butter cookies and small cups of warm cider, and Santa always arrived with an elf to take photos with small children. Bucky Johnson, the president of the Chamber of Commerce, was always Santa, but you never knew about the elf. One year it was the fat little man with missing teeth who sat in front of the convenient store scratching dollar lottery tickets all afternoon. The year before that it was the short, pushy woman with red hair who was always late returning her DVD rentals. Nathan didn't even look out the front window to watch. The only thing about the pageant that ever changed was the elf.

So, it came as quite a shock one Christmas Eve a few years back when Santa's elf walked into the store and tugged on the sleeve of his red plaid shirt. "I need a last minute gift. I'm so glad you're open late, man."

Nathan's eyebrows went up, and his chin dropped. This year the elf wasn't the little fat guy with missing teeth or the pushy red-haired woman or any other local freak show. It was a cute young guy, with reddish hair and blue eyes, wearing green tights and a green velvet jacket that stopped at his waist. "Take your time," Nathan said.

When the elf turned and crossed to the back of the shop where the latest DVD releases were, Nathan looked up from his book and stared. The green tights hugged his muscular legs and round bubble ass. They were so tight they rode up his ass-crack and created a deep trench. His black boots with three inch heels clicked against the wooden floor; his legs were slightly bowed and his hips wiggled. And when he turned to the side, something large and oval bulged from his crotch.

Then someone else walked into the shop, and Nathan quickly lowered his head to his book. But, his eyes went up, and he saw everything. The guy who had just walked in was about Nathan's age and good looking in a rough, athletic way. He was staring at the elf with glazed eyes. Clearly, he'd followed him into the shop, and now he was cruising him. He crossed to where the elf was choosing between an action adventure DVD and a romantic comedy and pretended to read the DVD covers. Nathan saw him stare at the elf's ass and lick his lips. He looked as if he was ready to throw him down and pounce. When the elf finally decided on the romantic comedy, he gave him a quick smile and said, "Excuse me, sir," so he could cross back to the counter and pay for his DVD. Nathan saw the guy grab his dick and whistle back. The elf was oblivious to all this. But, the guy followed him back to the counter and shoved his hands into his pockets to adjust his dick.

The elf placed the DVD on the counter and said, "I hope my girlfriend likes this. She's really hard to please. And my mom is going to go nuts if I don't get back to the car soon." Then he pulled a smashed twenty dollar bill from his elf jacket and handed it to Nathan.

When the elf referred to his mother as "my mom," Nathan smiled. He looked as if he could have been in his mid-twenties, but now he sounded so much younger. And when the guy standing behind the elf heard this, he took a deep breath, sighed out loud, and stepped back a few feet. Evidently, he'd thought the elf was older, too. Nathan wanted to laugh out loud; the poor guy looked so disappointed. But, he didn't laugh. He just put the DVD into a bag, handed the elf his change and looked down at his book again.

The elf wished Nathan a Merry Christmas, then wiggled his innocent ass out the door, so he could catch up with his mother and disappeared in a flash. The other guy licked his lips again and shook his head a few times. Then he stepped up the counter and asked, "Do you have an adult's only section? I'm home visiting family for the holidays, and I don't have an account here."

This all happened around nine o'clock that night; besides the elf, there hadn't been a single customer in the store since seven. Nathan had naturally assumed that the good looking guy would leave when the elf left. But there he stood, an attractive young man, with large blue eyes, dark brown hair and a wide smile. He wore a sleek black leather jacket with a long red scarf; he had that out-of-town look. "There's a section in the back," Nathan said, and then pointed to a door with a sign that read 'Private: Adults Only.'

"Do you have any private booths?" the guy asked. He leaned forward slightly to look into Nathan's eyes, but Nathan kept staring down at his own knees.

"Ah well," Nathan said, "No; just rentals, is all." His voice became abrupt; he wasn't running an 'adult bookstore' in the middle of town. But he did wonder how this guy was going to watch porn while he was home visiting his family. Did he sneak down to the family room when they all went to bed? Maybe he had a small DVD player or a laptop.

"That's cool, man," he said. But he stood there staring at him and rubbing his jaw. He tilted his head back and asked, "Do I know you? You look very familiar. What's your name?"

Nathan gulped and stared at the red scarf. "Ah well, Nathan. Nathan Carmichael," he said. His voice was low, and his hands felt a little shaky. The guy sounded a lot like someone he'd once known; but that was so long ago.

The guy smiled and shoved his hands into his pockets. "I thought so," he said. "Don't you recognize me, man? We went to high school together."

Nathan lifted his head slowly and stared at the guy's handsome face and dark brown hair for the first time since he'd entered. But when it finally occurred to him that he did know who this was, the guy's face wasn't the first thing he remembered. He had a flashback of his high school days, and he remembered this guy's long, floppy dick bouncing around in the boy's locker room. Nathan had attended a Catholic High School, and he'd worked late every Tuesday and Friday night after bingo with this person. Nathan was in the chess club, and this guy was on the football team. They had nothing in common other than the fact that they were the guys who took down all the folding bingo tables in the school gym. And then one night, after all the tables had been folded and stacked, the guy asked Nathan if he wanted to get stoned in the locker room. One thing led to another, and Nathan wound up sucking dick for the first time in his life – big, thick football player dick, too. And all this continued on Tuesday and Friday nights for the remainder of their senior year. It began with Nathan sucking him off, and by the time the school year ended, he was nailing Nathan into the locker room floor. It wasn't as if they became best friends and started hanging out. There was no talk of a relationship; this guy was dating one of the cheerleaders the whole time he was screwing Nathan.

"It's Lance Roberts," the guy said, "We were in the same class, and we worked bingo on Tuesdays and Fridays."

"Ah well, Lance Roberts," Nathan said. He reached out to shake his hand and smiled. Then it all came rushing back – the adolescent drama and excitement he used to experience when he saw Lance walking through the gym door in a pair of tight levis on bingo nights, and then the dread and disappointment he'd experienced when he watched him walking through the hallways with his cheerleader girlfriend on his arm. "It must be ten years at least," he said.

Lance smiled and started to rock back and forth on the balls of his feet. "You haven't changed much at all, man."

Nathan wasn't sure that was a compliment. But he smiled anyway and said, "Neither have you." But Lance had changed a little. Now he was even better looking; he'd filled out and gone from being a scrappy looking teenage boy to a strapping twenty-eight-year-old man with a strong, wide jaw line.

Lance laughed out loud and shook his head. "Of all the people to run into while I'm cruising one of Santa's elves and looking for porn on Christmas Eve," he said. "It's just that coming home for the holidays is rough since I came out of the closet. My family accepts me being gay, but there's this silence all the time, as if they don't know what to say."

"A well, there you are," Nathan said. He wasn't sure how to respond. The last thing he'd expected to hear that night was that Lance Roberts from high school was gay. He'd never kept up with anyone from high school. As far as he knew, he was the only one in his class to move back to Martha Falls after college. Everyone else had either moved to Baltimore or some other big city. "I guess that's family," he said, shrugging.

"Do you own this place?" Lance asked. He looked the store up and down for a moment. Then he stared at a sign that read, 'Video Boutique.' "It's nice," he said.

"My parents died while I was in my senior year of college, in a car accident. And I decided to move back here and open a small business. Since there weren't any video stores, I figured I'd give the town something it needed. And here I am," he said. He quickly stared over the counter at Lance's jeans. They were tight and hugged his solid thighs; he remembered the salty taste of his cock after football practice on days when there hadn't been time to shower before work. Lance had always been so eager and needy; and Nathan had always been so willing to please him.

Lance told him he was sorry to hear about his parents, and then he went on to quickly explain that after graduation he'd gone to college in Baltimore, majored in

Criminal Justice and become a State Trooper. Then he said he'd been married for a few years and that he had a daughter who now lived with his ex-wife in Florida. He shrugged his shoulders and said, "One night, after we'd come home from a party, I just blurted it out. I told my wife, 'I'm gay. I'm sorry; I tried as hard as I could, but I can't do this anymore.'"

Nathan opened his eyes wide and asked, "What did she do?" He'd never actually come out of the closet to anyone. He'd figured it was no one's business after his parents died.

Lance smiled. "At first she was shocked, of course. But then, after she thought about it, she said it all made sense to her. We'd been having problems for a while, and there hadn't been much sex at all the last year of the marriage. It's not that we fought with each other; we lived like best friends ... roommates. I think she was actually relieved to know it wasn't her fault."

"Well, there you are," Nathan said. He'd heard a few stories like this while cruising for sex. Every now and then one of his tricks would open up and feel the need to purge. But he was starting to relax now. His hands weren't shaking anymore and when he spoke, he looked into Lance's blue eyes without thinking twice.

"Hey, why don't we go somewhere for drinks tonight," Lance said, "What time do you close?" He pressed his large hands on the counter and leaned forward.

Nathan blinked a few times and tilted his head to the side; he smelled spicy and leathery. "I can close anytime I want," he said, "but there's nothing open in Martha Falls on Christmas Eve this late." But when he saw how Lance frowned after his comment, he added, "We could go upstairs though. I live on the second floor."

Lance smiled and rubbed his palms together. "Cool, man. I'd like that."

When Nathan crossed from behind the counter to lock the front door and lower the lights, he brushed against Lance's black leather jacket by accident. He smiled and said, "Excuse me," but when he looked down he saw that Lance's tight low-rise jeans were bulging forward in the groin area. Then he remembered that Lance once wore a pair of red bikini briefs at Christmastime, with the silly image of a black and white milking cow printed across his groin. The cow had a green Christmas wreath around its neck and gold balls hanging from its ears. When Lance walked around the locker room in that underwear, his dick was so large and his balls were so heavy the cow looked as if it were jumping up and down. Nathan felt a pull in his own groin, and his dick began to grow. He wondered if Lance still felt the same way about him. Back in high school, though they never took any of it very seriously. Sometimes, Lance couldn't wait to get his pants off. There had been nights when he'd been so horny he'd actually begged Nathan to suck his dick.

After the lights went out, Lance followed him to the back of the store, past the 'Adult's Only' section, and through a door that lead to a narrow flight of pie slice stairs. The building was actually an old Victorian house on Main Street that Nathan had renovated completely with money he'd inherited from his parents. The narrow, circular staircase opened up to an expansive second floor that had a loft-like feeling; walls had been taken down and oak floors had been refinished with a high gloss coating. The walls were pure white now, and the few pieces of furniture were sleek and modern, with simple straight lines and solid angles. Nathan liked things precise and orderly, and he despised anything that reminded him of his grandmother's attic.

Lance looked around and said, "This is really nice. You've worked hard on this place. The floors are so shiny they remind me of the high school gym where we used to work bingo." And without being asked, he removed his leather coat and the red scarf, then rested them neatly on the back of a brown leather club chair near the fireplace. "It's unexpected," he said, "it's all so modern."

Nathan smiled and shrugged his shoulders. "I hate old shit, is all," he said, "I wanted to live in a city loft, but didn't want to move to the city." He noticed that Lance was wearing a tight black sweater; his chest muscles rounded through the wool and the sleeves were pulled up to his elbows. He still had those large, solid forearms Nathan had always loved. There had been times back in high school when all he had to do was stare at Lance's forearms and he'd get an erection.

"But it's not very Christmassy up here," Lance said.

"I do my part for the holidays downstairs," Nathan said. Then he asked, "What can I get you?"

"A vodka martini," Lance said. He ran his palm across the arm of the soft leather sofa and smiled.

Nathan extended his arm and said, "Make yourself comfortable." Then, he crossed the room to a long kitchen area and stood behind a massive center island that was covered with a highly polished slab of black granite. He reached for a remote control that was resting on another black granite surface behind him and turned on his favorite jazz station. It was the only station that wasn't playing the expected Christmas songs that night. They played a few jazzed up holiday songs every hour; but it wasn't constant. He didn't have anything against Christmas songs, but he'd been hearing them since Thanksgiving, and he'd had enough by then.

When he returned with two martinis, Lance was on the brown leather sofa. He was leaning back; one arm was stretched on a cushion, and his legs were open wide. He placed Lance's drink on a coaster that was already in place on a square, black marble coffee table and sat down at the other end of the sofa.

Lance's eyes grew wide when he leaned forward to get his drink. "Ah, I need this, man," he said. Then he raised his glass high and said, "To bingo."

"To bingo," Nathan repeated, raising his glass, too. But he wanted to say, 'To boy's locker rooms and big dick.'

Nathan took a slip, but he saw that Lance swallowed back almost half the drink at once. He smiled and said, "You were thirsty."

Lance stared at him for a moment. A deep, intense stare; there was a half smile on his lips, and he raised one eyebrow. "Do you mind if I take off my shoes and get comfortable?"

"Ah well ..." Nathan said.

But before he could say anything else, Lance was kicking off his shoes and stretching his long legs across the length of the sofa. Then he lifted his large feet and rested them on Nathan's lap and said, "Why don't you take off my socks," he said. His eyes were glazed now and he was smiling. "C'mon ... for old time's sake. We don't have to worry about getting caught now. That is unless you're married or have a lover."

Nathan lowered his head to Lance's large feet and sighed. "No. I live alone."

"I can't tell you how many times over the years I've thought about our bingo nights in high school," Lance said then he reached down and adjusted his dick. "I'm really glad that cute little elf in green tights decided to buy a DVD tonight. If I hadn't been following him, I never would have met up with you again."

Nathan remembered how much Lance had always liked to have his feet massaged, especially after he'd gone through a rigorous football practice. He used to stretch out on a locker room bench naked, close his eyes and moan while Nathan would rub and squeeze his sore feet. And by the time the foot massage was over, his dick was always rock solid and ready to be drained. So Nathan took a gulp of his drink, placed it on the table and slowly removed Lance's black socks.

Lance rested his head back and whispered, "Ah yeah. That feels so good."

Nathan bit his bottom lip and began to massage his feet. They were large and strong, with small patches of black hair on the toes. He squeezed and rubbed for a while, and then Lance said, "Do that thing you used to do ... please." His eyes were closed, and his voiced was soft and deep. And between his legs, you could see his erection popping through the denim fabric.

Nathan knew exactly what he was talking about. So he leaned forward and started licking the bottoms of Lance's feet. He didn't have a foot fetish; he'd never licked anyone else's feet like this. But with Lance, he didn't give it a second thought. He'd always thought every part of his body was sexy. If Lance had begged him to lick and rub his ear lobes instead of his feet, he would have done that, too.

"Ah, man," Lance moaned, "That feels fantastic. No one has done that for me since high school." He reached for his drink, swallowed it all, and placed the glass back on the coaster.

Nathan licked between his toes and all the way up to his in-step. He licked gently, with the tip of his tongue, and continued to massage the bottoms of his feet with the tips of his fingers. "Is this okay?" he asked, with his lips pressed against Lance's big toe.

"Yeah, man. But hold on for a second," Lance said. Then he unzipped his jeans and quickly pulled them off. He lifted his arms and pulled off his sweater, too. He wasn't wearing underwear, so he was now naked. "Ah man," he whispered, "Do it like you used to do it ... please."

He didn't even have to say please because Nathan's man-hungry tongue was already licking his ankles and working its way up his strong, hairy legs. When he reached the inside of Lance's thighs, he opened his mouth all the way and sucked Lance's huge ball sack inside. His cheeks bulged with large, salty balls; he sucked and swallowed and took deep breaths through his nose. He could smell the damp, tweedy aroma of Lance's cock while he gently rolled his balls in slow, even circles.

Lance spread his legs wider and said, "Ah man, yeah." Then he grabbed a handful of Nathan's hair and lifted his head up a little. "Get naked, man. I wanna see that hot ass again."

Nathan's head went back, and Lance's soggy balls slipped from his mouth. He stood up, kicked off his over-sized shoes and stepped out of his baggy jeans. His dick was hard and jumped a few times. It wasn't as wide as Lance's dick, but it was just as long. His legs and his ass were shaved smooth because the guys he'd been with had always told him how much they liked that. And there was a small patch of hair, neatly trimmed, above his dick shaped like an arrow.

When he removed his plaid shirt, he kneeled down on the sofa again between Lance's legs. Lance smiled and said, "You look great, man. Now turn around and spread those legs, so I can see that hot ass."

Nathan turned toward the back of the leather sofa and arched his back. He pointed his firm, round ass in Lance's direction and wiggled it a few times.

Lance reached forward and slapped it gently. Then he bit his bottom lip and said, "Suck me off now."

Nathan smiled and turned around. He remembered that Lance had always whispered things like this under his breath, but he'd never actually been bold enough to talk dirty out loud. He pressed his palms on Lance's thighs again and opened his mouth. When he wrapped his lips around the head of Lance's dick, Lance moaned, "Suck it, man. Suck that dick."

Nathan took the entire shaft all the way to the back of his throat. He was a more experienced cock sucker now, and he was ready to prove it. When he pressed his tongue on the bottom of Lance's dick and began to suck it in and out of his mouth, his cheeks indented. It was still as thick and meaty as he'd remembered from high school, and it still tasted salty and tangy. He took a deep breath through his nose and closed his eyes; he liked a man's dick to taste and smell like dick; not soap or cologne. He knew Lance was ready to blow a load; his pre-cum oozed, and Nathan swallowed each sweet, clear drop.

When he finally released the big sopping cock, he reached down and massaged his balls a few times. "You want me to finish you off like this?" he asked. He didn't mind being submissive with Lance. That's what had always been so special between them. The lines between top and bottom were clearly drawn from the start. This was something he'd taken for granted in high school because Lance had been his first man, but when he'd started screwing around with other guys after high school, he was amazed at how boring sex can be with two submissive bottoms.

"I wanna fuck you, man," Lance said, "I want to open those legs and slam into that hole now."

He hesitated for a second and then placed his palm on Lance's strong forearm. "I'm really serious about being safe, man." Then he lifted the lid of a small wooden box on the coffee table and pulled out a lubricated condom. He shook the small package a few times and said, "Is this cool?" His eyebrows went up and he shrugged his shoulders.

"I'm HIV negative and disease free," Lance said, "But feel free to put the condom on my dick. I think it'll be hot watching you cover my cock with a rubber." Then he grabbed his dick and banged it against Nathan's leg a couple of times.

Nathan smiled. He remembered that Lance had always liked being treated like a king – the man in charge, but at the same time pampered and babied and adored. So when he slipped the condom over his dick, he did it gently and methodically as if he were performing delicate surgery. Normally Nathan liked his sex fast and anonymous, but this Christmas Eve with Lance it occurred to him that he only wanted to be tender and articulate. There was something about the way Lance stared at his ass that turned him on so much he wanted to fall on his knees and beg for dick. So when Lance slapped his ass again and asked, "Can I fuck you now?" he nodded yes.

Then Nathan climbed on top and straddled the rock-solid dick. It was pressed up against his ass crack; he arched his back and licked his index finger, and then shoved his wet finger inside his hole and moved it around a few times; even though the condom was pre-lubricated, he wanted Lance's dick to slip right in as easily as possible so that when the sensitive nerve endings at the head of Lance's big dick felt the inside of his soft, warm hole, Lance would gasp. Men always did that when they entered his ass; they raved about how soft and tight it was.

He pressed the tip of Lance's cock head to the pink opening and slowly pushed it past his tight anal lips. When the head was inside, Nathan arched his back and sat back slowly so the entire shaft could slide into his body. As Nathan had predicted, though Lance's eyes were closed by then and his brows were knitted together, when the big dick reached the bottom of Nathan' ass, Lance began to moan and sigh out loud. "Fucking hot, man," he said, "I remember how fucking smooth and tight that ass is. Ride my dick, man."

"You wanna come inside?" Nathan asked. His teeth were pressed together and one foot pressed on the floor for support. He never talked out loud during sex; this was a first. But he was so excited and so into Lance's dick, he couldn't help himself. "You wanna slam that fucking load into my hole?"

"Yeah, man," Lance said, "I wanna come inside. I wanna blow my load into your tight, fucking hole, man." He grabbed Nathan by the waist and pressed down hard.

While Lance held his waist, Nathan slowly began to rock and rotate his hips in circles. He squeezed the lips of his hole and tugged on Lance's cock as if he were jerking him off with his hand; he went up and down fast so that each time Lance's dick slammed up his ass there was a loud slap. Lance started to buck his hips with the same rhythm Nathan used to ride the dick. In no time, Nathan was riding the big dick so viciously and with such intensity his head was flying in all directions and his eyes were rolling backwards. He couldn't seem to get enough; he backed into Lance's dick so hard he had to grab the back of the sofa so he wouldn't fall off. He shouted, "Fuck me, Lance. Fuck me hard."

"I'll fuck that ass, man," Lance said. He bucked his hips harder and closed his eyes.

Lance began to wiggle his large feet and move his legs around, and Nathan remembered that's what he used to do right before he was about to come. So Nathan grabbed his own cock and started to jerk it off.

"I'm close, man," Lance shouted, "I'm fucking close ... ready to blow soon."

"Go, Lance," Nathan said, now jerking his own dick, so they could come at the same time.

Lance leaned forward to squeeze Nathan's round chest muscles, closed his eyes tightly, and shouted, "Fuck, man ... here it comes ... fuck, man ... ride that dick." Then his entire body started to jerk around; his hairy legs stretched all the way out and his toes curled back. When he came, he bucked his hips into Nathan's ass and filled the condom. And Nathan hardly had to touch his own cock; and he came with Lance's big dick buried all the way up his hole. He shot a load over the arm of the sofa, past Lance's head, that landed somewhere on the wooden floor.

Lance grabbed his waist again and sighed. "Man, that's the best fuck I've had since high school." Then he bit his bottom lip again and slapped Nathan's ass hard a few times.

Nathan pressed his ass harder against Lance's dick and tightened his hole. He wanted to keep it inside as long as he could. "I needed that," he said. His hair was sticking up all over and his lips were swollen from the cock sucking.

"Come here," Lance said. He reached forward and pressed his wide palm to the back of Nathan's head and pulled it toward his face, so they could kiss. He stuck his thick, warm tongue all the way into Nathan's mouth and rolled it around a few times.

Nathan pressed his lips to Lance's and sighed while they sucked tongues. Even though they'd fucked all through their senior year, this was the first time they'd ever actually kissed. Lance's dick was still up his ass and he was moving his hips in slow circles; the big dick filled him completely.

After the kiss, Nathan slowly stood, and Lance's dick slipped out and hit him on the stomach with a slap.

Before Nathan crossed the room to get a clean towel and a warm, wet wash rag, he leaned forward and slowly removed the used condom from Lance's dick.

Nathan was kneeling on the floor beside the sofa, massaging his balls with the wet rag. His eyes were closed and his legs were spread wide. "I'm glad I stopped in for a DVD tonight. I never would have hooked up again with you if I hadn't."

Nathan smiled. "I guess you have to get back now," he said. Then he ran his other hand up and down Lance's hairy thigh and sighed.

"I'm a big boy," Lance said, "I can stay out as long as I want."

Nathan smiled and squeezed his balls a few times with the warm rag. "I'm curious. Do you still have the cow underwear? The red ones with the Christmas cow?"

He laughed and said, "You really liked them from what I remember. All I had to do was walk around a little, and you were down on your knees milking that cow with your mouth." He slowly rubbed Nathan's ass and said, "I threw them out years ago."

Nathan reached between his legs and grabbed his dick. It was soft now, but still a handful. "It wasn't the cow I wanted to milk. It was what was behind the cow that made me thirsty." Then he opened his mouth, stuck out his tongue, and started licking the soft shaft. It was warm and spongy and smelled like his bathroom soap now.

Lance placed his hands behind his head and sighed. "If I sleep here tonight, I can give you a really good Christmas present in the morning."

He looked up and jerked his head; his mouth fell open for a second. He'd expected Lance to do what he'd always done after fucking: put on his pants, pull up his zipper, and say, 'Thanks ... I needed that ... see you next week.'

"That is if it's okay to spend the night," Lance said. He spread his legs a little wider and adjusted his position on the sofa.

Nathan pressed his lips together and squinted his eyes for a moment, and then he pressed his palm to his throat and said, "Of course it's okay to spend the night. Because I may have a Christmas gift, or two, for you."

Lance laughed and scratched his balls a couple of times. "I'll bet you do."

Outside and in front of Nathan's home, the elf who led Lance into the store, looked up at the second floor window and smiled. Then he scampered away and disappeared in a flash.

THE LAST SATURNALIA

By Jay Starre

Galla Marcus Flavius upended the silver-encrusted beaker to pour out a liberal portion of Italian wine for his slave Felix. He half-hoped the blond giant would guzzle it all and pass out before the festivities became even more raucous.

Galla's naked amber ass jiggled then flushed bright pink as a hand whipped out to smack one round cheek. He wore an elaborate leather cuirass, borrowed from one of his own gladiator slaves, but nothing else. From his narrow waist downwards, his handsome body was exposed to the gawking view and hooting derision of the feasting crowd.

It was the eve before the final day of Saturnalia. All this nonsense would thankfully end tomorrow, on the day the Christians were now calling Christmas, a celebration of the birth of their god-king the Christ.

Felix smirked up at him from his lounging position on the couch, Galla's own couch. The slave's white toga stretched across ludicrously-large muscles and tented at the crotch where an obvious erection actually twitched and leaked to cause a gooey smear on the expensive gown, Galla's own gown.

"Serve the other guests as generously, Master, and wag that delicious ass of yours for all to enjoy. Later, I have plans for it and your sweet, tight manhole as well!"

The vulgar Celt guffawed, displaying fine white teeth between full red lips, surrounded by a curling honey-gold beard. The man was a barbarian brute, large, coarse, and supremely fit for his occupation of horse-training in Galla's stables.

The crowd joined in the laughter at his expense, regardless of the fact this was his own home, perched on a slightly elevated and desirous hillock overlooking the rest of Ravenna. In this year of 454 CE, surrounding marshes protected the relatively new capital of the Western Roman Empire from marauders.

Situated in the northeast of Italy, the Alps loomed not far away from the city, and a taste of winter air wafted in from open balconies and windows. This cool breeze mingled with the herb-scented smoke from a dozen braziers and the redolent stench of cooked meats, honeyed delicacies, and spilled wine.

Acutely conscious of his bare ass and dangling prick and balls, that reeking breeze seemed to insinuate between his thighs and lewdly caress his nude body. His prick stiffened slightly, testament to his own mixed feelings.

It was his doing, this reversal of the usual. Saturnalia traditionally lasted for eight days, from December 17 to 25. Feasting, carousing and all sorts of gluttonous, ribald activities took place. This was expected, and here in Ravenna, they were yet good Latins enough to carry on these traditions, even with the puritanical Christians barking at their door.

But there was one more ancient custom less often practiced. The reversal of roles. Master would become slave, and slave become master.

It was only the previous evening at another dinner party when he proclaimed he'd honor this tradition. Eyes alighting on the hulking figure of his blond slave in the far corner, he announced to all, "Tomorrow eve, Felix the horse-tamer will be master at the feast. I, Galla Marcus Flavius, will be his personal slave!"

Galla had chosen Felix not only due to his hulking masculinity which he found quite attractive, but because he was a Christian, and known to be smug about the superiority of his religious beliefs. He'd half-believed the slave would refuse his offer, disdaining the pagan ceremonies as beneath him. But not so. The giant accepted instantly, with a bright gleam in his sky-blue eyes that sent a shiver through the Ravenna nobleman's slimmer body.

Drunk then, sober now, he wondered how much he'd regret that decision by the time the night was over.

The crowd he passed through on his duties of wine-serving were a brew of Ravenna's elite nobles and a fair number of slaves who'd been elevated to the positions of master, for this night only.

Hands slapped, groped and pinched his body. The rude intimacies ranged from assaults on his well-defined bare biceps, along his muscled thighs, and to his naked ass and freely-swinging balls and prick. Notwithstanding the cool winter breeze coming from outside, he flushed hotter and hotter as those warm hands came at him from all directions.

It was one of his own kind, a noble visiting from Constantinople itself, who dared the boldest of the insults thus far perpetrated upon the fallen master of the house. "Bend over, Galla Marcus Flavius. Spread those lush brown cheeks and show us your pretty pink sphincter! I have something here to offer that hole of yours!"

The Cypriot accent rolled from wine-wet lips as the nobleman gripped his crotch with one hand and leered. Galla might have been able to ignore the ribald suggestion if not for a pair of eager slaves turned masters who seized his elbows and turned and bent him at the waist right before the seated visitor from the east.

"Pig grease, fit for a pig-prince!"

This rude remark preceded the sudden insertion of a hand between Galla's rounded ass-cheeks. Fingers smeared pork drippings from the noble's own plate up and down Galla's crack, taking special care to lather up the snug lips of his asshole.

The jeers of the crowd deafened as Galla flushed from head to toe. The fingers in his ass were slender but insistent, rudely exploring as they coated his deep butt crevice with the gooey grease and tickled the tender entrance to his guts.

He shivered and bucked, biting his lip as his prick thrust up to stiffen between his thighs. His asshole quivered and pouted, afraid and excited all at once. He managed to bear it by remembering that this was Saturnalia after all, a wild holiday where anything might happen – and often did.

Felix rescued him, albeit for even lewder purposes of his own. The Celt loomed over him, slapping aside the less burly slaves holding his elbows. He seized the Constantinople nobleman's wrist to pull it from between his master's quaking ass-cheeks.

"Thank you, kind sir, for that generous greasing. But I have plans for Master Galla and his sweet butt and hole that may or may not include your noble hand."

The words were offered in Latin somewhat garbled by the Celt's barbaric accent, yet surprisingly refined for all that. His message, of course, was not refined in the least.

He was pulled upright by a calloused hand on his biceps then unceremoniously dragged through the chamber and out into the hallway. Hooting laughter followed their exit. The giant beside him loomed dangerous – and exciting. His ass-cheeks slid sensuously up and down, the grease slippery and warm as it dripped down to coat his dangling seed-sack from behind. His prick reared entirely upright, the crown slamming against the firm leather of the cuirass encasing his torso.

"Here. We'll await the first of your guests to find us."

The words were ominous, the voice deep and growling. Booted feet kicked his apart as he was dragged toward a marbled pillar in a shadowy nook where one of Galla's own pagan gods inhabited a shrine.

Leaning back against the pillar, Felix pulled the nobleman into his arms, placing his head under one brawny armpit and reaching around him to put each of his large hands on one of the Latin noble's smooth ass-cheeks. He pulled them apart to reveal the greased, pink hole between.

"Now, anyone passing can view what's offered ... your hole, slave, for use!"

He breathed in the stink of the Celt's pit, a heady aphrodisiac that only intensified the quaking of his limbs. What would happen next? What was about to befall his spread ass and greased hole?

The flickering of nearby beeswax candles illuminated the rounded smoothness of Galla's patrician butt globes, while glowing braziers added their own light to offer glimpses of the hole between those globes and the glistening grease coating it.

He shuddered with anticipation. His ass held open, greased hole on view for the first passerby, it was a novel and titillating experience he hadn't even imagined previously.

It wasn't long before a curious wanderer happened on them. The house was full of revelers Galla himself invited, all men that night as the women were banished to their own section of the sprawling mansion.

Galla realized someone was there by the sound of a loud intake of breath, followed by the growl of his burly slave.

"Lick noble ass. Eat the pig grease out of that patrician hole!"

A face, smooth cheeks sliding into his own hairless mounds, pressed between his spread thighs. Lips, then tongue assaulted him. He gasped, his own face buried in Felix's pit, wriggling back against the invading tongue that stabbed and slurped over his tender anus.

The horse-tamer's snickering was joined by another's laughter. He couldn't see who it was with his face pressing into that brawny armpit. A flush of additional embarrassment coursed through his body, especially since he'd just rolled his hips backwards and squirmed lasciviously into that sucking mouth buried in his greased ass-crack.

Not only was he on display, but he'd been caught in the act participating in his own nasty degradation. Willingly! He had only a moment to ponder that thought before a body slipped between his spread knees from in front, hands grasping his upper thighs, hot breath on his crotch. Hotter lips engulfed his stiffened cock.

Now, he really squirmed, caught between mouths assaulting both his anus and his prick, slurps and lip-smacking loud and nasty in that quiet corner. As if that wasn't enough, one of the calloused hands that held his butt-cheeks apart rose to clutch at the thick ringlets of auburn hair on the back of his head and yank him out of armpit. His face was turned upwards, his mouth gaping open in a loud gasp just as Felix's lips clamped over his.

The Celt's plump tongue invaded his mouth, slobbering, swabbing, stabbing. The brutal kiss mashed his own patrician lips cruelly, wine-soaked and hot and wet. Now, three mouths attacked him.

Knees weak, he writhed between the lips bobbing over his throbbing cock and the lips sucking his asshole inside out. His own mouth gaped open like a fish out of water, barbarian tongue swiping around inside. But still, there was more!

The other big hand on his butt slapped him once, the smack resounding in the alcove before it swiftly moved to grip Galla's own hand. The steely clasp forced his fingers forward and under the horse-tamer's toga. There, he discovered a throbbing column of Celt meat, his fingers forced to wrap around the torrid shaft.

That prick was long, yes, but more than that, it was thick. He pumped it experimentally, feeling the turgid flow of blood within making it pulse and swell. He slid up and down the length, amazed at how enormous it was within his wrapped fist. A colossus of a cock!

Now, he recalled the single most important reason he'd dared this Saturnalia reversal of roles experiment. He'd seen this prick before, on an occasion when the broad-shouldered horse-tamer had disrobed to bathe just outside the stables.

The slave's prick had dangled between his burly thighs then, not erect but still potent and wide as it flopped down there amidst harsh soap suds. Felix noticed his master eyeing him, and true to his smug nature, fondled that plump prong with his large hand, running fingers up and down the thick girth as he lathered it and pumped it. Galla watched transfixed before the smirking Celt turned away to rinse off, offering a final view of his solid, blond-furred buttocks.

That was then, and now the master had the slave's prick in hand, just as he'd desired. He shook all over as those mouths assaulted him and that prick jerked between his fingers. The thick meat pulsed, replete with vigor and full of promise. How would it feel in his mouth, or up his tender asshole?

He abandoned any final pretenses, relinquishing his ingrained role as master, noble, Roman amidst the modern elite of the new Ravenna, and surrendered to the pagan lust of his ancestors. Now, right now, he was slave to his history and his traditions.

The mouths he wriggled between were insistent and greedy. Whether it was slave or master, or slave turned master or master turned slave for the night, he couldn't have said. It hardly mattered. His asshole gaped open for the tongue invading it, his prick pulsed between the slick lips suckling it, and his own mouth yawned wide for the barbarian tongue conquering it.

Soft beard caressed his own smooth cheeks. Large nostrils exhaled heated air into his own snorting nose. They breathed together, slave and master. Galla was so incensed, he willingly thrust his other hand under Felix's toga and added it to the one already pumping the slave's enormous prick.

Felix's mouth pulled away with a slurp.

"Come, Slave Galla, I would parade you in front of our guests. Let them witness your night as a pagan whore. Let any who wish sample your wares – your sweet slave ass and juicy slave hole!"

The blond behemoth kicked aside the pair attached to Galla's nether parts, clamped a beefy paw around his neck and twirled him around to begin the parade he'd promised. The Ravenna noble was forced to release his two-handed grip on the barbarian's massive prick, but his fingers still tingled with the memory of it.

The sensual image of that pulsing prick remained with him as he was led through the labyrinth of corridors and chambers of his rambling mansion. Slender columns of the finest veined marble, tiled friezes depicting scenes of Roman soldiers in their conquests, exquisite wall hangings alive with the local scenery of winged fowl skimming watery marsh, and lovely vases and pottery from all over the Eastern and Western Roman Empire; all these trappings of wealth meant little to nothing as the Ravenna noble was led through them by his Celt slave. A giant hand clamped around his neck, his bare ass slick with pig grease and saliva, and his erect cock waving before him as a testament to his own depraved lusts.

Snickers, outright laughter, gasps of admiration and disgust, and hands, many hands, assaulted him as he passed through these halls and rooms. Hands snaked out to seize and pump his stiff member, or tug and tease his dangling seed sack. Hands smacked his bare, amber buttocks. Fingers slid into his butt valley and searched out his well-eaten asshole to finger and probe rudely.

He flushed bright pink from head to toe, embarrassed, titillated, exhilarated. The total availability of his lower body, naked and slick, was constantly driven home as Felix steered him through the candlelit rooms toward their next destination. They stepped outside into his central courtyard, a starry night clear and crisp above. Heat from the debauched festivities inside leaked out on all sides like the breathing of a depraved beast. Within the sheltering confines of another alcove dedicated to one of the nobleman's pagan deities, the Slave Felix thrust the Master Galla.

"Here we'll await the not-so-tender mercies of your guests. Time to offer them your sweet anus, slave!"

The deep voice rumbled in his ear as the Celt propelled him backwards, so his naked ass pressed against an iron grate that served as a decorative wall between the outer alcove and the inner corridor.

He was bent over at the waist by a big paw on his lower back, his bare feet knocked apart by a kick from the Celt's boots, and his ass mashed against that iron grated wall. The blond giant's calloused paws grasped his ass-cheeks and spread them.

In that ludicrous position, his hole was presented in lewd display within the square frame of the iron grating. Each iron square was half a foot in width and height, the space created amply large to allow exploration by any passerby.

He bit his tongue and moaned. Well aware of the sight he presented, the nobleman shuddered violently as he awaited the inevitable. He believed he could feel the eyes of those on the other side as they gawked at the nasty image of the mansion's master crammed up against the grated wall. Lush ass-cheeks pressed against the iron, with pink hole, wet and available, framed by the iron grate.

Breath heaving, Felix's big hands still clasping his bare butt-cheeks, Galla waited. Voices whispered nearby, on the other side of that wall. Would they take the bait? What were they waiting for?

He couldn't help himself. He wriggled his ass back against the iron grate. Moaning, he actually pouted his ass-lips, a drool of pig grease and spit oozing out. Another moment passed, and with no response from those on the other side, he let out a loud groan and a grunted plea.

"Please. My hole is so hungry. Please use it!"

The Celt laughed above him. The men on the other side of the iron wall whispered between them briefly before all at once, Galla felt something touching him.

A finger, light and caressing!

It slid over his distended sphincter, stroking the rim. He groaned and wriggled backwards, unable to move beyond the firm grate to provide himself any more satisfaction. The finger continued to stroke, tickling and teasing unbearably. Snickering mingled with appreciative sighs as he mashed his bare ass against that iron and pouted his asshole nearly inside out.

"Sweet hole. Hungry, we see," one of the voices whispered huskily.

The finger teasing him was no longer alone. Another digit began to slide along his palpitating anal rim. Both fingers teased, toying with the quaking lips, and then teasing the gooey entrance with little dips and strokes.

It was maddening! He shook all over as those fingers ran in circles over his slick butt entrance, toying but not entering. The memory of that enormous phallus hidden under Felix's toga reared up to taunt him.

"Please! Finger my hole," he begged.

All at once, one of those circling fingers found the center and plunged. Driving deep, past the knuckles, it probed and twisted. Galla's hole gaped open for that invasion, his gut churning. His mouth was wide open and drooling as he found himself clutching at Felix's thighs in front of him. Mad with desire, he burrowed his head up under the slave's toga.

"Suckle on master's prick, slave!"

The rough command came just as his face collided with that monster prick. Mewling, he snorted in the heady stink of barbarian crotch as his tongue came out to swipe at the fat slab of prick slapping against his mouth. He licked up and down it, searching for the crown in a crazed hunt for fulfillment.

Just as his lips clamped over the drooling head, another finger slithered into his gaping asshole. Two of them twisted and stabbed, sending waves of pleasure through his gut. He swallowed prick head and squirmed around those exploring fingers. More fingers dipped in and out, separate hands he guessed. Were there two men, three, or more assaulting his tender hole?

He imagined a group behind him observing his humiliation. The fingers probing and stroking his slick butt-lips and greased hole were relentless as they stretched and massaged. The gargantuan prick in his mouth throbbed and leaked as he suckled on it like a hungry calf at the teat.

Voices whispered lewd encouragement. Snickers and outright laughter reached his ears through the Celt's gown covering his head. His patrician head bobbed over that thick barbarian shaft while he wriggled madly back against the firm iron of the grated wall and the plunging digits of the men behind him.

"Enough! Time for master prick up slave ass!"

The announcement was immediately followed by rough hands forcing him upright and propelling him forward. Felix's white teeth flashed in the dim light as he dragged his noble slave back into the brazier-warmed corridors of his mansion.

His asshole throbbed, empty now but stretched and pulsing as he padded his way through a miasma of men in various states of disrobement, groping, fondling, and sucking and fucking in every nook and corner. The festivities had degenerated into a wild orgy.

Well aware of his vulnerability, he shuddered with delicious humiliation as he contemplated his horse-tamer's recent promise. He was about to get that elephantine prick up the ass!

"This is perfect. Saturn's couch for the ass-fucking of your life! And all your guests free to watch."

Felix propelled Galla into the atrium where the noble had created a shrine to his favorite deity, Saturn, the god of sowing – and seeding – which was entirely appropriate for this lewd occasion. The Celt barbarian was about to pump his seed deep in the bowels of the Ravenna nobleman!

A couch occupied center stage just beneath the statue of a bearded and majestic Saturn, naked and sporting an erect phallus, and of course an enormous ball-sack full of the spring's seed to be sown.

The blond behemoth released Galla briefly as he lifted his toga over his head and discarded it on the exquisitely tiled floor. His body was a work of art to rival the statue behind him. Flowing golden locks and curling golden beard, a smattering of blond down on arms and crotch, and muscles bulging, the Celt sprawled back on the couch and chortled.

"Come, mount your master's prick!"

Galla shuddered at the sight: the massive biceps folded behind the large head, the wide shoulders huge with power, the naked thighs massive and spread, and there awaiting his tenderized asshole, the monster prick he'd just sucked.

A score of herb-scented candles dripped at Saturn's feet, casting flickering light on the Celt's golden body. His big grin widened as he purposely licked his lips and beckoned his slave for the night forward with a crooked finger.

The nobleman obeyed, as he'd vowed to do the previous night, clambering up on Saturn's couch and spreading his thighs out on either side of the Celt's massive legs. His ass, slick with spit and pig grease glistened in the light, like smooth, warm amber, as he reached behind and grasped the column of barbarian prick thrusting up from Felix's lap.

Staring down into the bright blue eyes, he moaned out loud as he placed the dripping crown in the center of his ass-crack, on target to violate his palpitating anal maw. The broad knob pressed against fluttering ass-lips, straining the entrance. He bit his lip, arched his back – and sat!

In it went, burrowing past any resistance, stretching, probing, slithering deeper and deeper. Galla groaned, dropping his sleek ass-cheeks, meeting his own hands as they gripped the thick base rising up out of the Celt's heated crotch.

"Ah, so sweet, my nasty little slave! Swallow your new master's prick with your talented pagan asshole!"

The growled words rumbled in the massive chest Galla leaned against. His back arched further as he sat right down on the giant column to settle in Felix's lap, now entirely gored by Christian prick.

It pulsed inside him, hot and stiff. He wriggled, gasping as the monster flesh teased his prostate and strained his aching anal lips. He rose up off it, mewling as the fat shank rubbed his sphincter on the way out. After half of it had exited, he reversed direction and settled back down, swallowing inch after inch of enormous cock.

"Yes! Your guests are enjoying the nasty display. Show them how you take prick up your noble hole! Ride it!"

He obeyed, rising and falling in a grunting rhythm, swallowing and expelling his slave's fat meat, arching his back, wriggling his greased ass-cheeks, imagining the eyes watching him from behind as he fucked himself before the mighty statue of Saturn himself.

Felix's hands moved to clasp the leather cuirass encasing his torso. The mighty paws now aided him as he rose and fell, driving the heated prick in and out of his aching hole. Faster, harder, the squishes and smacks of his greased hole and his slippery butt-cheeks ramming against the Celt's downy thighs growing louder and lewder.

Then, the slave turned master let out a loud guffaw as his hands lifted and spun the writhing master turned slave. "Face your audience! Let them see your drooling lips and depraved joy as prick invades your pagan asshole!"

It was done. His body was raised, spun and turned so he now faced the leering audience of at least a score of his guests. That prick did not leave his tender asshole, spinning inside his guts until it was thrusting up inside him from behind now, curving up to pulse deep in his aching hole.

His thighs flopped wide apart, and although athletically muscular, were dwarfed by the mighty thews of the Christian slave. Flushed already, his entire body grew even pinker as he found himself riding that big prick again, this time watching those who watched him.

The massive meat inside him pulsed with torrid heat. He was stuffed! But that was not the end of it. The Celt's greedy paws gripped the undersides of his knees, pulled back and up. Galla was splayed wide open for the audience, prick stretching his ass-lips for all to see.

"Come forward, Nubian. Your master is in need of more prick!"

Was it possible? Galla moaned, his body shuddering as a Nubian slave emerged from the leering crowd. His own house slave, the black African was usually timid and obedient. Tonight, his obsidian eyes twinkled, his full lips pursed with relish, and his lengthy prick rose to full mast between his lean thighs as he strode toward the couch.

Naked except for a delicate golden chain belt around his slender waist, his dark body gleamed in the candle-light, his unbelievably lengthy prick rising straight from his crotch and aiming for Galla's already stuffed hole in front of him.

The lean, black body mounted the couch and engulfed Galla. All at once he was surrounded by hot flesh. The dark mouth came down to cover his, big pink tongue slithering beyond his lips just as the tapered crown of a second prick began to push past his straining sphincter.

He groaned around tongue as he willed his asshole to open. Pushing down and out, he managed to distend his stuffed sphincter, amazed and exhilarated as both pricks thrust into him simultaneously.

It was truly unimaginable!

The pair, blond Celt and black Nubian, began to fuck him. He flopped between them, thighs wide open and pulled back, hole distended and swallowing. The fat prick thrust up from behind, the slender prick gored him from in front. At first they pushed inward together, then they began to drill him in an erratic, counter-rhythm.

He sucked on the tongue in his mouth, riding that double-fuck like a ship in a storm. Totally conscious of the eyes watching his violation by his own pair of slaves, he surrendered all vestiges of pride and bounced and writhed over those heated columns pumping his guts so relentlessly.

The ache in his ass was a torrid pleasure that emanated throughout his body, swelling his own prick as it was rubbed against the firm leather cuirass by the Nubian's thrusting belly. That aching pleasure rose to a crescendo of sweet delight.

He felt orgasm approaching. His body betrayed him, flopping, squirming, riding, gaping open to the twin assaults on his asshole.

His churning sphincter massaged the pricks drilling it with rapid pulses. It was enough to elicit orgasms from the two slaves a moment before his own.

Cum flooded his innards. The pricks up his ass rammed balls-deep together, spewing in pulsing rhythm.

Galla sucked on the tongue between his lips and let loose with his own rapturous release.

It was midnight and Christmas Day by this time, and those Christians present were taken with a sudden religious fervor, dropping to their knees and praying to their Christ-God, even while the pagan master of the House was being sowed by his own slaves beneath the pagan statue of his own God, Saturn.

Regardless of the situation, Galla surprisingly retained a modicum of his wits. Even while he spewed cum to coat his cuirass and the Nubian's sleek black belly, he spit out the tongue in his mouth and shouted out a proclamation to the gathering.

"I have seen the Christ! I will henceforth practice the Christian religion!"

The following morning, with the return of the normal situation, the master of the house summoned his horse-tamer for a private audience.

"As you heard last night, I have renounced my pagan inclinations and am now a Christian like yourself."

They faced each other, Galla dressed in his immaculate white toga, Felix in his shabbier wool stable gown. They shared the same thought; Galla had become a Christian out of necessity. All the nobles of Ravenna, and the Empire were espousing the Christ's religion. It had been only a matter of time before he would have faced that choice.

But for now, his amber orbs gleamed beneath finely manicured brows as he stared down at his smug slave. "We are both Christians now. No more barriers between us. You may now perform your duties without fear of damnation, slave!"

With that announcement, Galla sprawled back on his own couch, lifting his muscular thighs and pulling up his toga. His already-greased ass-crack glistened, his prick stiff and leaking. His pink hole twitched, nicely stretched from the previous night's debauchery.

Of course the blond Celt understood.

Still, he couldn't help smirking as he strode forward to mount his master.

HOT DROPS
By Cliff Morten and Aiden Kell

"Don't spill a drop, or I'll discipline you," Shane drawled in a low voice while he filled the glass again. "I'll punish you hard ..." Luke shivered, but it wasn't out of fear. It was arousal caused by Shane's voice murmuring these words that was sending goosebumps up and down Luke's tanned skin.

Luke knew that Shane would never seriously hurt him, but there were a few words he loved especially to hear from Shane, words like 'discipline,' 'suck me,' 'I'll spank you,' or 'thrust' – oh god, yes, 'thrust,' that had to be his favorite! Even Shane reading out the income tax declaration would have done the trick as well, to tell the truth.

Luke was kneeling between Shane's spread legs, one hand braced on the mattress, the other holding a glass of red wine for Shane – mysteriously blinking dark red liquid, a color similar to that of the burning candle Shane held. The only source of illumination in their rustic cabin, softly flickering candlelight from pillars all around the room highlighted the deep amethyst in the goblet and the planes, curves, and shadows of the bent golden body on the floor. Shane picked the glass of wine from Luke's hand and savored a mouthful of it, enjoying the expensive taste and mentally preparing for his artwork. Then he handed back the glass.

"Bow down lower. Ass up," he ordered. Luke complied and settled into an even more humble position, head deeply bowed with Shane's erection level with his eyes, which made him feel like a supplicant of a primal phallus-god-worshipping religion. Holidays were spent in such rites. Both men had a week free, during which they would stop to sleep, take minimal food and drink, for the usual exchange of Christmas packages, and little else.

Sure enough, Shane gripped his hair and guided him toward his groin, slowly invading his mouth and pushing Luke down until half of his cock was enveloped by Luke's hot mouth. "Don't move or suck," Shane said. "Just hold still. I like to let it rest where it belongs – inside you. You will keep totally still," he added threateningly, though obviously he was more acutely in danger than Luke now.

Luke trembled with the realization of how important his obedience was. He was stunned at the confidence and trust in Shane's actions – Shane just had proved that he hadn't the slightest doubt of Luke's total obedience.

Holding the glass for Shane became a lot more difficult like this, and Luke flinched when the first splash of hot wax hit the small of his arched back and smoothly ran down the curve of his spine. But he somehow managed to keep the balance of the glass.

Shane leaned over him and thoughtfully stroked his left upper thigh. "I'll show you how I would mark you," he announced, and without delay he drew his signature in a writing of molten heat over the sensitive skin of Luke's thigh. Luke instantly recognized Shane's name in his handwriting, having seen it often enough to visualize it now from the touch, the letters appearing in front of his eyes while they burned on his skin.

It came lightning-fast, and Luke was frozen with heat for a second; then he jerked, but desperately tried to suppress the movement and keep as still as possible. A deep throaty cry wrestled out of him, but the only movement he made was a little shift forward, which made

Shane's cock slide a bit deeper into his mouth. The wax slowly cooled and dried, several single lines running down a few inches and then stopping.

"Good," Shane patted him very approvingly. His cock had swollen in Luke's mouth, but now he withdrew it. "Turn around," he demanded, taking the glass of wine from Luke and putting it down in the nightstand. When Luke did, he could see himself and Shane in the mirror opposite the bed; Shane made him kneel on the bed with his left thigh showing to the mirror.

"Look at it, Luke." Shane's name in red letters on his left thigh, irregularly sprinkled and with clotted droplets of red around it, looked a lot like he'd carved it in blood, and Luke shivered with the sudden desire for Shane to mark him like that with a knife. He imagined Shane cutting him, fast and cruel. The thought filled him with chilling excitement.

"Do you know what I'm going to do to you?" Shane ran his left hand up over Luke's muscular ass, then his flank, then back down. He slapped the pale flesh, watching the combination of the slight shock wave with Luke's surprised flexing. Both ripples faded in an instant. It was really a hypothetical question; Luke gave no answer but for a rumbling interrogative sound low in his chest.

"I've a mind to plug this tight little pucker of yours." A long digit strayed inward to that very place. Shane fingered the center of the guarded opening; it gave a little, then clenched in defense. Tapping several more times in a random beat, he smiled lazily over the involuntary flutters his little prodding touches brought forth. Luke was trying to hold still, but couldn't help a few tiny trembles. Sweat was starting to spring up along his spine, beautifully reflected in the candlelight.

Giving no other warning, Shane tipped the candle's brimming load of molten wax into Luke's crack.

"Aiahh!" bellowed the other man, snorting.

Shane laid a restraining hand on his hip. "Be still!" and Luke struggled to obey. At first, the red wax ran straight down, following the crease like a flash flood through an arroyo. A small stalactite of it dripped off Luke's balls. Soon, half congealed, it started to catch in the hairs and dam up on itself, and then it did what Shane had envisioned in the first place, covering the holy of holies in a thin scarlet layer.

'Break the seal' – the phrase bounced through Shane's mind as he tipped the drained candle back up. The shimmering wax was so inviting, not to mention what lay below. Almost immediately a thin skin formed across the surface of the seal, a small shift from Luke revealing it was still malleable, though not for long. As fast as he thought of it, for words would take too long, Shane stuck the candle back into its holder. He got up onto his knees behind Luke, grabbing his other hip, too, as both a command and warning.

The tip of his erection touched the warm, still almost hot, substance. Shane pushed through, into Luke's oiled hole below, and buried himself. Besides the tight ring of muscle, the added heat – almost too hot – greeted the skin of his shaft from head to base as he assaulted the gooey coating.

Luke's amused, cryptic voice floated back to him: "I've heard of wax dummies and sculptures, Shane, but wax cherries ...?"

"Izzat so? Well maybe I'll break it again." It would've felt so good to just stay and let the sex-love-fucking take over, but no, this time he would go for the artistic create and break. The slight sting from the initial contact of his glans with the hot wax confirmed – more of that!

He let the red stream flow down Luke's ass cheek and crack once more, idly remembering memorized paintings of the Last Judgment, with naked 'sinners of the flesh' swept away and drowned by orange-purple glowing hell-lava; he fucked through the soft warm layer, feeling the resistance, then heat again. He repeated the procedure several times in much the same way as he always played with candles and their wax when they lit the dinner table for decoration, dreamily exploring the pliant substance, kneading it into different forms in his hand, letting it cool on his fingers and peeling it off.

He didn't care when some of the splashes missed their destination, landing on the small of Luke's back or the outer zones of his ass cheeks. Without thinking about it, he pressed in thumb or second finger in the fresh plots, leaving his fingerprints visible on Luke everywhere, as if he was a sealed letter.

And yes, he realized, while he thrust forward through wax-skin into Luke's clenching hole for the seventh or eighth time – with some of the earlier layers already splintering and softly scraping his balls – yes, sometimes he'd like to have Luke sealed. Too bad this sexy hole served for more practical body functions, too, otherwise he would have closed it to the world with whatever kind of chastity device he could in times when Luke left him for longer periods.

He was jealous – oh so jealous, at times. The thought of Luke fucking someone else was bad enough, but the idea of Luke letting another man ...

Shane had forgotten about the candle in his hand for a moment and when he thrust forward suddenly with more rage and force behind it, the candle dipped, and a large sprinkle of wax shot over Luke's back. Luke flinched a bit – not from pain, but at the surprise. Shane fucked him harder now, not bothering to reinstall his virginity in between anymore.

Luke didn't care much about topping or bottoming, but he, Shane, did. He had had sex with men before Luke, but hadn't taken it up the ass from anyone but Luke, and he didn't want Luke to take it from any other man but Shane. It was that – that one thing he had with Luke and Luke had with him – that was a true match. He didn't want it to change. Ever. The fierce sense of ownership was the strongest it had ever been in him, with Luke, though it was hardly the first or only time he'd felt that way in a relationship. There was a certain freedom, too, in their mutual possessiveness because he knew Luke would never cheat on him, not in that one way they'd given only to each other.

Luke was his. Shane thrust in and noticed the letters of his name he had applied on Luke's thigh earlier were already breaking and half-way removed; he felt the gaps on the writing with the fingers of his left hand. He was still holding the candle with his right.

He didn't want his name extinct from Luke's skin, so he wrote it down again, this time squarely over Luke's back. And then at another angle, a bit smaller. He leaned forward with the next thrust, signing Luke's shoulder blades, rather shakily, but still readable. So he went on. He soon needed another candle, but luckily he had spare ones on the night stand. He didn't draw out while he lit the next candle, and seconds later continued to cover Luke's body with his inscriptions. He mostly wrote his name, but "love" and a heart appeared occasionally, too, and he went on as if in a trance.

"You're mine," he growled, looking at Luke's body all decorated with the name, Shane.

"Yes – take what's yours," whispered Luke, sensing the underlying need for confirmation in Shane's acting.

Now that he was in, embedded so far, the wax sealed them together. Shane hadn't planned it that way, and he should've foreseen it; the sticky, hardening wax glued them tight. It made Shane somewhat frantic, claustrophobic. When he was on top, he liked the long slides and heavy hitting, pounding thrusts. Every inch of his cock, going oiled in and out of Luke's gripping body was a sight to savor. The thudding of their hearts and guts when he rocked their strong flesh just so was like an earthquake in his head; he never wanted the earth to stop moving from his fucking.

The reality was that if he tried this, he was going to rip hairs and who knew what else with all the dried wax. It was built up in layers now around Luke's hole, covering his lower cheeks and the backs of his balls, running in the little stalactite and the rest, down the back of his thighs. Where Shane was touching him was stuck, too – the fronts of his thighs, his groin, and at least half his pubes were congealed in a mass.

"It's gonna hurt, as much as we're glued together," he grimaced.

Under him, Luke's muscles were starting to bunch. "Don't care ... need it, Shane. You need to mark me more, on the inside too." Luke was almost whining out of the depths of his lust.

Shane reacted to the words and the tone. Pushing Luke's head down roughly, he bent far over his long, sinuous back, letting the coils of his own lust start to unravel. At first, he concentrated simply on pushing his cock in as far as it would go, moving a half inch in and out at a time. Under the flare of the place where the crown met in a V from both sides, probably the most sensitive spot on his body, Shane felt the bump of Luke's prostate, and he sawed at it with all his limited mobility. It didn't take long before Luke was shaking, his hand trying to get at his own prick.

"No, Luke ... no you don't!" Shane forcibly removed the hand, replacing it with his own. He continued to hump at Luke from behind, rotating his hips, then squeezing his ass muscles tight to get far inside. He was getting frantic; he needed more leverage, more motion.

At last, other than his hand around the taut, leaking organ hanging below, Shane pushed Luke flat by simply falling on him. Using his knees, he pushed Luke's legs apart as far as they'd go. From what he could see, the other man's eyes were closed and his jaw pushed forward as Luke did when he was getting very close. "Just give it to me!" The surge in Shane's hand said the same thing.

Not being able to move as he wished was starting to make Shane more than claustrophobic; it was making him angry. He twisted his body like a weapon. Ramrod-hard from watching himself mark Luke over and over again as his own, Shane pumped with increasing speed and desperation, captive of the wax, frantic to come and mark his own in the way he'd been asked. Luke made high, keening noises; the pull of the wax had to hurt; it was hurting Shane and while he usually wasn't into pain, this time it only seemed to add. His cock was like living lead, needing to spew forth and fill the tight caressing mould all around it.

He'd not done it for a long time, but Shane found himself biting into Luke's neck. At first, the man stiffened; then his body flopped against the mattress and against Shane's trying to speed up the pace. Shane was only too happy to go along, as much as he could. The bite was a means to control, just as the wax was. Sanguine and salty, the muscle and skin between his teeth was still dotted with specks of candle wax. Shane grabbed on and rode, grabbed on and fucked, turning animal in the heat of it. He continued to stroke Luke's cock, wanting to know he'd set off his possession's release before he would take his own. By the feel of things, it would not be long.

Panting, bunching his spine, driving forward with his hips, Shane shifted his bite, spitting away chunks of red wax from time to time. He closed his teeth around the tail of an S or a ringed A, after a while, the only word in his head was Shane, there in front of his eyes, his identity, and fuck, the primal source of his existence. 'Fuck Shane

Fuck Shane Fuck Shane Fuck Shane…' before he knew he was grunting the words, and then Luke was, and then they were both screaming them.

When he felt the vibrating jerks of Luke's cock that meant he was exploding, then the manifestation of thick cream coating his fingers and puddling below, Shane allowed himself to come. The last gigantic, if muted, thrust sucked him in. Somewhere in the middle of, 'Fuck Shane' and his breathless entreaty to take it all, his howls of broken control and pulled hair from the contracting of his balls as they gushed his love in seed, the fact that his words and gestures and marks were not empty as a forced thing on his part, but gift of acceptance on Luke, struck him as it never had before. Shane went still, not only from the waning of his orgasm, but in a strange gesture of marking again, in doing nothing but just being there.

The next day, when Shane fucked Luke, it seemed to him the lines of his name-writings were still visible, faintly paler on Luke's tanned skin. Or maybe it was just an illusion, caused from the vivid memory. He followed the curvature of the largest "Shane" he had written; the image still was clear in his mind, more than any signature he'd put on cards and tags of the perhaps more tangible but less meaningful gifts.

Yes – his name was still there.

CABIN FEVER
By Stephen Osborne

I'm not sure what I expected. When Mike told me that his parents had a cabin out in the middle of nowhere, I had envisioned a small log structure with someone who resembled a young Abe Lincoln outside chopping wood. When we pulled up, I saw that it was indeed a log cabin, but it was hardly small and was obviously very modern. It was a bi-level house, built into the side of a hill, with a front yard large enough for a football field and a huge deck that took up one side and stretched around to the rear of the house. My mouth fell open as he turned off the car engine.

"What's the matter, Cary?" he asked, looking at me in concern. He must have misread my reaction because he quickly added, "Hey, it's got electricity. It's not like we're going to be huddled up next to the fireplace freezing our asses off."

In all honesty, I could think of worse ways to spend an evening than cozying up to a fire next to Mike, but I couldn't tell him that. We'd been friends since high school, where he'd been the star center on the basketball team and I'd been the darling of the theater department. Somehow, despite coming from vastly different school cliques, we'd managed to stay friends through high school and even into college. When I came out to him, his only reaction had been to shrug and say, "No problem. Just no tongues when we kiss, okay?" Mike had a joke for every situation.

I opened my car door, still unable to take my eyes off the cabin. "No, it's just that ... well, it's huge!"

Mike slid his long frame out of the car, pulling the hood of his parka up over his wavy blond hair. “Yeah, and the weird thing is we really don’t use it that much. After they bought it, my mother decided that she didn’t like the fact that it was so far away from everything.”

It was indeed isolated. The promised snowstorm had already started, but so far, it seemed more like a light dusting than a storm. Still, if we got the six to eight inches the weathermen warned, Mike and I could find ourselves trapped in the house for several days at least. I might not even be able to get home for Christmas.

Good. I mean, why would I want to see my folks over the holidays when I could be cooped up with Mike, yearning for something I couldn’t have?

Self-torture is a marvelous thing. I know I should fall in love with some cute gay guy and live happily ever after, but the first time I saw Mike’s muscles bunch up as he went for a jump shot I was lost. He doesn’t know, of course, that I yearn to get naked with him and rut like weasels. I’m not sure what his reaction would be if he did know. I knew, though, that I wasn’t prepared to find out.

Mike looked up at the sky. Several large flakes settled on his eyelashes. God, he had long lashes for a guy. “I hope we brought enough food,” he said. “If we get stranded out here I don’t want to have to resort to hunting for food. There’s no way I could eat Rocket J. Squirrel.”

Jokingly I said, “We might have to eat each other. The Donner party all over again.”

He eyed me with mock exasperation. “You’d like that, wouldn’t you? Me nibbling all over you?” He shook his head with a laugh. “Sorry, Cary. You’re too skinny. Not enough meat to satisfy me.”

“Oh, I’ve got enough meat for you,” I said, grabbing at my crotch with my thick-gloved hands.

It was a little game we'd engaged in ever since I told him I was gay. On his end, it was just a little harmless flirtation. For me it was daydreaming.

Mike and I grabbed the bags of food we'd brought, and he led the way inside. The place was furnished in a rustic style but had lots of elegant touches that made it feel very homey. The kitchen was all chrome and stainless steel. Somehow I had been expecting a wood burning stove and an old copper kettle. Even though the kitchen was roomy, we kept on bumping into each other as we stowed away the groceries. Finally, Mike suggested that I get our luggage out of the trunk while he finished with the food.

Back outside, I found that the snow had increased in intensity. There was little wind, so the flakes just drifted down, making a rather pretty scene. The cabin was surrounded by tall pine trees, which now looked custom made for Christmas with the boughs covered with snow. I quickly made a snowball and lobbed it at the closest tree, missing by a mile. Another snowball came closer but still fell wide of the mark. With two misses, I really concentrated on the next throw, which managed to barely hit the tree, leaving a little round snow blob to mark the spot.

Mike opened the front door, still in his parka. "I can see you're working hard," he said.

"The tree insulted me," I joked. "Had to teach it a lesson."

"Seems like you're the one that needs taught a lesson," Mike said as he launched himself off the porch. He tackled me, and we both tumbled into the snow. We laughed as we wrestled around, although it wasn't much of a match. He was taller and much stronger, and soon he was straddling my stomach, holding down my hands. I hoped he couldn't tell that I had a woody from tussling with him. Mike looked down at my face with an evil grin. "Say you give, or I'm going to hock one right in your face."

I tried unsuccessfully to buck him off me. "You wouldn't," I said.

A hoarse rumble came from his throat. "I mean it. You'd better give up."

"I give! I give!" I shouted between giggles.

Mike smiled but then shot a huge wad of spit out. It didn't hit me, but I still yelled in protest, and we ended up wrestling in the snow for another ten minutes or so, rolling around like little kids. By the time we finally got our bags, we were soaking wet.

Back inside we stood in the foyer and kicked off our shoes. Everything was sopping. Gingerly, I pulled off my socks and looked at Mike for direction. I didn't want to track water all over his parent's cabin.

Mike gazed at the puddle of water already forming on the hard wood floor around us. "We'd better just strip everything off here and get dry stuff out of our bags. Then I'll light a fire, and we can have hot chocolate around the fireplace!"

I gulped and hoped that I could keep from ogling Mike as he pulled his wet clothes off. I found as I yanked off layer after layer that even my underwear was wet. I looked at Mike. He had made a pile of soggy clothing on the floor next to him and was standing there in boxer briefs that were fairly dry. I guess since he'd been on top for most of the wrestling they had escaped relatively unscathed. He bent over to rummage in his suitcase, giving me a wonderful view of his ass. My dick, which had softened once the wrestling had stopped, resumed its quest to burst out of my briefs.

Mike grabbed a pair of basketball shorts and a T-shirt out of his bag. He glanced back at me. "You'd better get your underwear off as well. You've got a dry pair in your bag, don't you?"

"Um ... yeah."

A frown crossed his brow. "Dude, do you have a woody?"

There didn't seem to be any way to deny it. The damn thing was standing at full attention, pointing right at him like a sexual divining rod. I turned away, aware my face was beet red. "Maybe a bit of one," I said sheepishly.

He laughed. "You're packing more than I would have given you credit for, Cary. Just keep in mind I don't swing your way, dude. I don't want you crawling into my bedroom tonight for a taste of Big Mike."

I pulled the wet underwear off and retrieved some dry clothes from my suitcase. "You call yours Big Mike?"

Mike stepped in front of me and cupped his hand over his cock, nestled safely in his boxer briefs. "Nothing else to call it!" he said with a grin. I could see that it was indeed huge. Oddly it was semi-hard. Mike, it seemed, got a little excited by the wresting as well.

Minutes later, we were dry and huddled around the fireplace. Mike ruined the mood, however, by pulling out his cell phone and calling his girlfriend, reminding me in no uncertain terms that he was now and always will be straight as an arrow. I couldn't hear her end of the conversation, but the lovey-dovey talk on his end was enough to make me sick. At one point in the call, he assured her he'd be back before Christmas day so that they could be together. He just wanted, he told her, to spend a few days "roughing it" with his bud, Cary.

Ending the call, Mike groaned theatrically. "You're lucky, Cary," he said. "You don't have to deal with dating girls. You have to jump through all sorts of hoops to keep them happy. Guys aren't like that. We just want sex!"

That evening, I made dinner for us. I must admit I used all my culinary skills in an effort to impress Mike. He had three helpings and belched loudly when the feast was over. We were doing the dishes when Mike suddenly shouted and ran to the window. Wondering what startled him, I followed, asking, "What's going on?"

He didn't have to answer. Outside the storm had hit in earnest. In the time since we'd arrived, several inches had accumulated, and the snow showed no signs of slowing down. Already the car was just a white blob in the driveway.

I tried to speak with a worry I didn't feel. "We might just get snowed in."

"Shit," Mike muttered. "Jenny will kill me if I don't make it back by Christmas Day."

We stood there, watching the flakes fill the night air. "It's beautiful, though," I said.

"Sure is."

I wondered if Mike realized just how close he was standing to me. I had to stop myself from putting my arm around him and resting my head against his shoulder. I knew I could do it in a joking way – Mike wouldn't mind that. Somehow, though, I knew that would feel cheap and unsatisfying.

When we awoke in the morning, we found that the storm had ceased. However, it was obvious that we wouldn't be going anywhere for a day or two. We stood once again at the window, me dressed in gray sweats and Mike in a tank top and his basketball shorts, and surveyed the scene. Everything was covered in a blanket of snow. I couldn't even tell the long driveway from the surrounding lawn any longer. Some of the trees looked as if they might collapse under the weight they now carried.

"There's no way the two of us can shovel out that drive," I said. "It would take us weeks."

Mike shook his head. “My parents have a guy they use. He has a snowplow. I’ll give him a call later.”

After a hearty breakfast, Mike and I hooked up a game console to his parent’s television and got lost for hours in the game. During a break, Mike used his cell phone to call the snow plow guy. I could tell from the stony set to his face that the call wasn’t going well. “When can you get to it?” Mike asked after what seemed a lengthy debate. Mike finished the call with a sigh and looked at me. “He says we’re supposed to get another two to three inches tonight, so he’s going to be busy for the next couple of days. He doesn’t think he’ll be able to get to us until Saturday.”

Saturday was the day after Christmas. “Holy crap,” I said. “It’s a good thing we brought food for a week.”

“Your folks won’t throw a fit over you not getting home for Christmas?”

My parents would be in an alcoholic stupor, but Mike didn’t need to know that. “They won’t care,” I said.

“Well, Jenny’s is going to split a gut. I promised her we’d spend Christmas together.” He took a cushion from the couch and belted me with it. “Looks like you and I will be spending Christmas together.”

A pillow fight erupted, although it was short-lived. After I smacked a cushion across Mike’s face, he decided to forgo the soft weapons and simply sprang at me. He collided hard against my chest, knocking me off the couch and onto the floor. He fell with me, both of us howling with laughter. I feebly struggled against him, enjoying the feel of his weight against me. Suddenly, he stopped and released me. He stood and quickly walked to the kitchen. “I’m hungry,” he said. “Want me to make some sandwiches?”

I watched as he walked away. He was turned in an attempt to hide it, but I could see that his basketball shorts were tented! Mike had a woody from wrestling around with me!

I knew that even straight guys often got hard while wrestling. Hell, there were enough pictures on the Internet of wrestlers in singlets sporting hard-ons. Still, part of me hoped against hope that there was at least a little part of Mike that felt the same way I did.

That night started off with verbal fireworks as Mike talked to Jenny on the phone. I was in the kitchen, making dinner, and Mike was in the living room. An old *Seinfeld* episode was on TV, but the sound wasn't loud enough to drown out Mike's part of the conversation. After telling her that it looked as if we might be stuck in the cabin over the holiday, his voice got higher and more defensive.

"Well, I didn't make it snow! How was I to know we'd get nearly a foot in accumulation?" He paused as she responded. "Yeah," he went on, "like you can believe anything the weathermen say! They're never right! I think you'd be more concerned with Cary and me being stuck out here in the middle of nowhere! It's a good thing we brought plenty of food because there is no way the car is moving until a snowplow can get up here!" He listened again. "Yes, I've got tire chains. Chains aren't the issue here. The issue is that there's a foot of snow covering a long fucking driveway!"

He was silent for several minutes as he listened to whatever she said. I tried to make extra noise with the pots and pans to make it seem like I couldn't overhear.

Jenny must have finally paused for breath. Mike's voice grew angry. "Well, if that's the way you feel, go ahead and fucking spend Christmas with Terry Morris. He's a fucking ass anyway. Hey, here's an idea. Why don't you suck his fucking dick for a Christmas present? I know you want his fucking cock, the way you're always talking about him!" Another several minutes of silence on Mike's end before he finished with, "Well, don't fucking threaten me by saying you want to spend time with Terry Morris. I don't play those kinds of games, and frankly I don't want a girlfriend that does!" He savagely punched a button on his cell phone, ending the call.

We ate dinner in relative silence. Mike was stewing, but I figured he'd bring up the call if he wanted to talk about it. After we ate, we retired to the couch, and he pulled out the game console. He held up a basketball game. "Mind if we play this?" he asked.

Normally, I'm more of a Halo-type guy and steer away from sports games, but I'd do anything to help Mike's mood, so I nodded enthusiastically. While the game was powering up, he went over to his dad's liquor cabinet and found a bottle of Johnny Walker Black. Without a word, he poured us each a glass and then settled down next to me on the couch for some gaming action.

After he beat me soundly in several games, we put in a movie and watched Bruce Willis shoot up an office building. The whiskey was gone before the movie was over. Mike, not being much of a drinker despite being a popular jock, was obviously tipsy. I wasn't much better myself. When the end credits rolled Mike stood up on slightly unsteady legs. "I'm going to bed," he said.

"I am, too," I said. I didn't move, however. I was enjoying the sensation of being drunk.

Mike looked down at me, his head bobbing oddly from intoxication. "Then I will bid you goodnight," he said. After a pause he added, "Goodnight." He shuffled over to the stairs and had to use the rail to haul himself up. This made us both giggle uncontrollably.

I waited several minutes before following and going up to my room. I knew that in order to sleep, I'd first have to beat off while imagining Mike fucking me. I wanted to give him a chance to get to sleep before I started. I didn't want to hear jokes about squeaky bedsprings over breakfast.

In my room, I peeled off my sweats and, clad in only my boxers, crawled into bed. I thought of Mike in his tank top and shorts and was instantly stiff. My hand crept down to my crotch and slid under the waistband of my boxers. Before I got a good hold onto my dick, though, a noise out in the hall made me stop.

I figured Mike had gotten up to use the bathroom, so I was surprised when my bedroom door opened. There were no lights on in the hallway, but I could see his tall dark shape coming toward my bed. He was giggling softly.

I pulled my hand out of my shorts. “Mike?” I asked.

With a short laugh, he threw himself on the bed, landing right on top of me. The basketball shorts were still on but the tank top was gone. His erection, however, had returned. I know because he was thrusting his hips against me, pressing his hard cock against my leg. For a moment, I didn’t know what to do. Then I put my arms around him and smiled. He giggled some more.

“You’re fucking heavy, you know that?” I said quietly.

“Sorry,” he replied, shifting some of his weight off me. He kept his dick pressed against me, however.

I glanced briefly down at our crotches and then into his eyes. There was enough light coming in through the window that I could see he was as scared as I was. “Do you want me to take care of that?” I asked.

He nodded silently and turned onto his back. My hand was shaking as I pulled down his basketball shorts to reveal Big Mike in all his glory. I shifted my position, wondering if I could manage to swallow the huge monster. Mike ran his big, strong hands through my hair as I leaned in and took the head of his cock into my mouth.

It was heaven. It tasted of ... well, Mike. It was the dick of the tall, slightly dopey guy that I'd secretly (or maybe not so secretly) been in love with for ages, and it was perfect. I gagged a little once I'd gotten about halfway, but Mike chose that moment to let out a groan. "Oh, yeah," he said. "Suck that fucking dick."

I don't know how Jenny felt about sex talk, but it drove me crazy. I relaxed my throat and began to bob up and down on his shaft like a madman. I wanted Mike to remember this blowjob for the rest of his life.

He was undoubtedly enjoying it. I could feel his body tense as I licked and sucked on his pole. He squirmed. "Fuck, that's fantastic!" Suddenly his hands were pulling me off his cock, though. He positioned me so that I ended up lying next to him on the bed. There was an almost pleading look in his eyes. "Do you think you could ..."

He didn't finish the sentence for he quickly leaned in to kiss me hard on the lips. It was one of those kisses like you see in the movies and you think, 'No one really kisses like that!' but Mike did. It was as if he was trying to make us one person attached at the mouth. When he came up for air, he tried his request again. "I don't suppose you'd let me fuck you, would you?"

As an answer, I pulled him on top of me and kissed him. Our tongues entwined. I thought about pinching myself to make sure what was happening was real, but the feel of his weight on me was answer enough.

Off came my underwear and his basketball shorts. He must have come into the room holding a bottle of lube and a condom because the next thing I knew he had sheathed himself and was smearing a large glob of lube over the head. I barely dared to breathe. Then he lifted my legs and placed them gently on his shoulders.

Slowly his cock invaded my ass. I winced a few times as the monster entered, but each time Mike paused to allow my muscles to relax. Finally, he got the whole thing in and slowly began to fuck me.

"God, that feels so good," he moaned.

It did. My own cock was ready to burst, and I began to stroke it. "Fuck me harder," I said softly. "Give me that big dick."

A smile spread across Mike's face. "Yeah?"

"Yeah. Fuck me hard."

Mike increased his thrusts until he was slamming into me furiously. I thought the bed was going to collapse. We were both shouting out as I came, shooting all over my hand and stomach. This made Mike even more excited. He rammed into me hard, pounding and pounding and pounding. Then his face scrunched. "Shit! I'm coming! Fuck, yeah!"

He tensed, and then, I felt him shoot inside me. It was the most marvelous sensation I'd ever known.

When he'd rolled off me and tossed the dripping condom over the side of the bed, we suddenly got the giggles. After those subsided a little, he kissed me again. "Merry Christmas," he said.

"Christmas is days away yet."

He shrugged. "We're not done yet, either."

We weren't, either. After a short break, he face fucked me. We propped a few extra pillows under my head and he held on to the headboard. This time I didn't gag at all and swallowed that cock like a pro. He pulled out when he came, shooting a huge load over the side of my face and onto my pillow.

He sank back onto the bed, exhausted. I put my arm around him. He didn't object.

"You're kind of dumb, aren't you?" he asked.

I laughed. "What do you mean?"

"You probably think that this happened by accident or that it was the Jack Daniels. I planned this."

I snuggled against him. He brought his long left arm around me and held me tight. "What do you mean?" I asked.

He chuckled. "I knew that we'd get a huge snowstorm and be stranded up here. Hell, every weatherman said it was going to be bad. I've wanted to do this ever since you told me you were gay. I just didn't know ..." He struggled for the words. "I didn't know how to bring it up to you, I guess. I figured, though, if we spent a lot of time alone together that something would happen."

I grinned. "I'm not that dumb. I saw the box of condoms in your bag when we first got here. Part of me thought that maybe they were for me, but the rational part of my brain insisted there was another reason for them. I couldn't think of one, though."

He turned his head to look at me. He tried to be serious but broke out into laughter. "You've got cum in your hair. Let's go take a shower."

The next day, the guy with the snowplow called back to say he might be able to squeeze us in Christmas Eve. Mike told him not to hurry.

SANTA BEAR

By R. W. Clinger

"Hunt, put some clothes on. You're going to freeze your pecker off out there." The animal biologist is buck-ass naked again, ten feet outside our insulated NASA-made plastic tent called the Ice Cube.

"I need some fresh air," he calls over his right shoulder, taking in the morning's darkness and two degrees.

I'm intoxicated by his good looks. Peter Hunt stands at six-three, has an awesome body that with broad shoulders. He has a narrow waist, thick mop of blond hair, and lets out a yawn. Everything about him is sexy. He stretches his bulky arms over his head, caught in the sixty-seven days of darkness in the Arctic Circle, and asks, "Niles, are you looking at my adorable ass again?"

Always. I can't help it. He's straight and I'm not. Shame on PB Services for putting us together in the middle of nowhere for the last four months and the next eight. Plus, I study animals, a biologist like Hunt. Like the polar bears that we observe for days on end, activity that consists of eating, sleeping, play-time, and sexual habits, I study Hunt just as much. And shame on PB Services for letting Julia and Penny go home for Christmas, returning at the end of January, which leaves me alone with Hunt, his hunky bod, and my ready-to-be-played-with cock.

"Check this out, Dr. Niles," he says. He spins around and steps up to the Ice Cube.

I study him like Oslow, Icon, Britta, Newbe, and Georgette, our family of polar bears. Hunt is just as beautiful with his blond pelt of massive chest and striking blue eyes. A nine-inch flag stands between his pumped legs and he begins to jerk it up and down with his left paw. He jokes, “Is this what you want from Santa Bear this Christmas?”

It’s a game that never gets old. And yes, I do. For the last four months I have wanted Hunt all to myself: against my skin, in my mouth, up my ass – anywhere! I don’t share this with him, though. Hunt knows I’m gay. Not that it matters, since he has coupled with Penny, not my peter, and will most certainly be all over her when she returns from her leave. Instead, I say, “Get in here before you freeze to death.”

“Two days,” he says, thumping his extension of beef against his firm torso, “and you can have me as your Christmas present. Santa Bear promises you a good time.”

He’s kidding. His game continues, which I ignore. Hunt is known for his devilish and playful antics, similar to Oslow’s behavior with the other bears. A troublemaker. Always in it for the joke. He likes to use my weakness against me: his ripped torso and bear-body, the pole between his legs, thighs as strong as ice, and ...

“I’m making breakfast, Hunt. Get in here and eat, or starve to death. I don’t care.”

He gains entrance to the Ice Cube, locking us inside from the cold. Again, he pulls his boner away from his torso, releases it, and it thwaps against his muscular skin. He informs, “Forget the breakfast, I have other things on my plate.”

“Like what?” Damn, is he fine looking: multi-layers of muscles, perfect dong, great hair, smile, and eyes. He could be Mr. December in the Arctic Circle calendar.

Hunt is face to face with me. Our noses almost touch like an Eskimo kiss. He says, “I’m going to give you a pre-show of what to expect on Christmas morning.”

"What are you talking about?"

"This," he says, and rolls a palm up and down his thick shaft. "I'm going to jerk off for you. What do you think?"

What I think is quite simple and logical: he's teasing me again, playing games.

"'Tis the season to be naughty," I respond, ready for whatever he has to offer, even if he's teasing me. "First, I need one thing clarified."

He aims his dick at me like a harpoon. "Shoot."

"I thought you were straight. I'm under the impression that Penny and you are a couple."

Is he blushing? I think so. A devious smile forms on his face and he responds with: "Penny knows about my secret."

"What secret?"

"That I want to fuck you."

I'm still not convinced and say, "Prove it, Hunt. I have all the time in the world. Knock my socks off."

Hunt grins with a horny twinkle in his Artic-blue eyes, and says, "I like it when you beg. It's a total turn-on for me."

Our heated cots are side by side. Hunt lies down on them and grabs his ice icicle with both fists and says, "Get comfy and enjoy the show."

"This is so *Brokeback*," I say, and find a cooler to sit on.

"Whatever you want to call it," he responds, starts to work his meat up and down, up and down, up and down. Hips rise against the southern motion of his fists. Friction mixes with pleasure and causes the biologist to groan. Sweat builds on his massive chest and forehead.

Each hand-hump forces another groan. Hunt begins to breathe heavily, and his face turns into a combustible red hue. He moans, "In two days, Niles ... this is going to be in your ass."

I'm uncomfortable with his self-exploration, and intoxicated. His motion causes a vibration to form between my legs, and a stinging rod springs to life under cotton. I desire nothing less than similar hand-work on my own tool, but refrain myself, overjoyed with his performance.

A pre-bubble of spew leaks out of his pipe. It hangs at the tippy-top of his tool's mushroom cap. I half-expect Hunt to release one of his hands from his spike and use a fingertip to remove the sap, eating it down for breakfast. On the contrary, he lets the bubble turn into two, three, four bubbles, which he uses as lubricant.

Hunt spreads his legs a little wider, showing me his center: tight, hairy, poundable – exactly what I'm interested in.

Helplessly, I feel lost and bedazzled by his motion. The scene on the cot is almost too much for me to witness. Hunt's action is mind-blazing and dick-twitching for me. Without notice, a few of my own bubbles of pre-ooze leak into my pajama bottoms. I'm certainly eligible to blow a load, with or without resistance.

Following five minutes of palms-working-poker, Hunt exclaims, "I'm going to bust."

"Do it," I encourage. "Let the stuff fly. I want to watch you blow."

His hands continue to thrash up and down on the nine inches of meat. Hips thrust upwards. Murmuring ensues, which sounds like the night's wind. His tight pecs move with his palms. Nipples glow with fresh sweat and ...

White ooze shoots out of his tool in three beautiful arcs. One arc decorates his hairy pecs. The second flies against his chin and bottom lip. The last arc splashes his navel. During his ejaculation, Hunt moans in a state of bliss. Both hands still continue to work his beef, draining it. Hips subside from their steady movement. And eventually, his hands drop away from his tool.

Our eyes meet. He smiles. There's a very short pause and he informs, "Dr. Niles, it's not over yet."

Edgy, left with an ice pick between my legs, ready to combust, I nervously bite at my lower lip and inquire, "What now, Hunt?"

"Just watch," he teases, winking at me. He raises one hand to his chest and rubs fingers along spew-residue. Pleasuring the both of us, he moves three of the appendages up to his nostrils, takes a healthy sniff, and whispers, "This is my favorite part."

"You're not ..."

It's too late. He does. Hunt slips the fingers into his mouth and tongues the sap away, cleaning them.

"You did," I reply, feeling more spew-bubbles leak out of my untouched rod under its cotton.

Honestly, I want an invitation to clean the remaining goo off his abs and chin. When the invitation is not offered, I stand and readjust my swollen V-area with a balled palm, and ask, "Hunt, what do you recommend I do with this?"

Strings of white sap hang from his fingers. A dribble of the stuff takes residence on his lower lip. He stares at the protruding cotton between my legs and says, "In two days, Dr. Niles, that is what I would like to blow."

Dammit! Christmas can't come soon enough, and nor can I.

My notes for the day consist of: Icon and Oslo hunt for seals, Britta digs a den in a snow bank, Newbe plays in the snow, Phil eats more than his normal portion ... Hunt studies me more than the bears.

We get news from Anchorage via e-mail: one, a glacial storm from the northwest will be hitting the Ice Cube in a few hours; two, Penny broke her leg on a ski slope, which will further delay her return; three, Julia's enjoying her husband and says hello.

Once Hunt receives the news on Penny, he says, "Looks like you're officially my boyfriend."

"What about Penny?"

"She knows who I am. Penny is a good friend. Trust me, Niles, you have nothing to worry about."

"I don't get this," I respond, confused.

Hunt closes the gap between us. Our lips almost touch. He breathes me in and says, "Let's just say I'm ready to come out to PB Services, even if they're right-wingers."

"Say it. Tell me you're gay."

"I want you," he whispers. "Penny knows I want you."

"You're gay," I whisper, falling into his blue eyes.

His hands find my hips and his mouth connects with my own.

Once the kiss is complete, causing me to feel woozy and lost, I ask, "How long have you liked me?"

"Long enough."

"A month? Two months? What?"

He brushes one of my cheeks with a palm. "None of that matters."

"Who are you Peter Hunt?" I ask. "I want to know."

His response is simple and to the point: "I'll show you. Just give me time."

Hunt kisses me again, melting more of the Arctic with his hidden passion. Fingers find the denim-covered knob between my legs. The kiss ends and he asks, "Still hard, huh?"

"Since the day we met. You have a spell over me. What can I say?"

He unbuttons the denim, pulls down my zipper, kisses my neck, chest, a nipple, my tight stomach, and takes a whiff of my goods. He comes up for air and shares a dazzling blue-eyed stare with me, and says, "Can I taste it?"

"It's not Christmas Day yet."

"Close enough."

"It may burst in a second if you touch it. A man hasn't been down in that region for a very long time."

"Thanks for the warning. I'll risk it. Something tells me I'm sure I can handle it."

True to his words, Hunt handles it. He pulls the denim away from my skin, lowers the jeans to my ankles, and takes a greedy lick of my cock, from its south pole to its north pole, moaning the entire time. His right hand gently cups my balls, massaging their hairless skin. Hunt slurps and groans, hungry for my goods, but doesn't pop my beef into his mouth, which he knows cannot happen until Christmas Day. There is no blowjob or a shower of pent spew. He only licks my eight inches in one stroke, pleasuring the both of us, and now he pulls away in a gentlemanly manner.

"Nice work. Too bad you can't finish."

He stands and locks his mouth with my mouth: heated, intense, intoxicating, melting. When he pulls away from me, he says, “No can do, buddy. I don’t want to spoil your Christmas present.”

“Dammit,” I whisper. “Santa Bear sucks.”

He reaches for my jeans and pulls them back up onto my hips, and shares, “He’s pretty good at that, too. You’ll just have to wait and find out.”

My observations for the day read: Icon chases a seal. I want to chase Hunt around our lab. Britta rubs against Oslo. I want to rub against Hunt. Newbe licks Phil’s face. I want to lick Hunt’s face. Georgette sniffs Icon’s bottom. I want to sniff Hunt’s bottom. Icon plays with ...

Still hard. Always so hard. Iceberg hard. Earth’s crust hard. I can’t get Hunt out of my mind. Almost Christmas. I’m going to pop between my legs. No, I’m going to erupt. I can’t wait to feel Hunt’s skin against my own: lips connected, chest smoldering against chest, rod touching rod, his fingers pinching a nipples, his hot ooze bursting into my face, his cock in my ...

We sleep together to stay warm, but never make-out. He lets me spoon him during the cold night, and my boner is snug against his bottom. I want to wake him up and fuck him into a state of bliss, but we sleep, man against man, motionless, at peace – or so I believe.

The next morning is Christmas Eve, dark as night out, still. A pounder feels as if it’s going to spray a blizzard of cum against his body. I whisper into Hunt’s left ear, “You awake?”

“For the last hour. You’re a master of dry-humping in your sleep.”

“Tell me I didn’t.”

“You did. You also stroked me off, but I stopped you before I came.”

"You're lying."

"I'm not."

I sort of laugh behind him. "I'm sorry."

Hunt rolls over, and I get to look into his handsome face again. God, I could wake up to him every day of my life a happy man.

He kisses me with scruff on his chin and cheeks.

I can't help myself and reach into his flannel boxers and find exactly what I'm looking for.

"Hey, Mr. Scientist, it is not time for your present yet." He reaches down and pulls my hand away from his tool. "I know you want me. And you know I want you. Let's compromise."

"How so?"

"Like this," Hunt says, and pulls back the covers, yanking the flannel bottoms off my legs. Before I know what's happening, my legs are pushed into the cold air and his face is buried in my bottom. A seal-like tongue laps at my hole in a feisty manner.

"Nice compromise," I moan.

Hunt's tongue pushes into me, pulls out, and laps again and again. I hear him slurp, grunt and catch his breath. The inside of the Ice Cube spins above me. Pure satisfaction zooms throughout my system by his mouthy touch. My cock bounces against my torso, ready to shoot a wad. I beg Hunt to touch it, but he doesn't, resisting a meeting between his fingers and my swollen rod.

Continuous laps of his wet appendage rock my world. I huff and puff, completely unsettled by his mouth-action. In and out. North and south. Hunt provides a hearty tongue-tour with my ass; exactly what we both want, our compromise.

When I move one of my hands down to my eight inches of pick, Hunt pulls it away and pins it to the cot beneath me.

"Please," I beg, "just a few strokes. I can't take it anymore."

Hunt ignores me as he continues to tongue my hole – fast, smooth, diligently.

What transpires next is not expected. A rush of pre-sap leaks out of my boner and clings to my tight torso. Hunt sees what happens and sits up between my legs. He leans over my abs, sticks out his tongue, and licks the white stuff away, cleaning it off my skin. Once this is accomplished, he rises, and says, "Tomorrow you get the works. This was a just a tease."

"What's the works?"

"Whatever you want from Santa Bear, of course."

Tomorrow, I decide, is never going to come, but I might in the meantime from his taunting deeds.

Fourteen hours later, the Arctic storm hits, and the polar bears take cover in their snow bank dens. Our radio is out. The computer is turned off. A generator supplies the Ice Cube with electricity and heat. The wind outside is fierce, crying and howling.

I'm on the cots, reading a Jean Auel paperback, waiting the storm out.

Hunt is refining some bear notes at his desk before sending them to PB Services after the storm passes. He removes an attractive pair of reading glasses from his handsome face, places them down on his desk, looks over at me, and informs, "It's almost one in the morning."

"Christmas Day," I reply, looking over Auel.

Hunt provides a boyish grin, stands up, and removes his shirt, jeans, socks, and rushes to the cots. He instructs, "Move over. I'm coming in."

Hopefully in my ass, I think. The paperback is lost, and I snuggle under the bedding with him.

"You leaving your clothes on?" he asks.

"You leaving your boxers on?"

"Let's get naked ... I think we're both ready for your present."

Hunt laps at my bottom, stops, and sucks my eight inches of ice pick. He carries out this process for the next ten minutes or more, which causes my entire body to sting with man-elation. I groan and he slurps, a united balance of pleasurable sounds behind intense actions. I moan, and he buries his tongue deeper into my rump. I murmur something indecipherable, and he massages my balls with the softest and most playful movements.

Eventually, we end up on our sides and accomplish a sixty-nine position. Santa Bear plunges his rod into my mouth with consecutive blasts. I gag and munch on his meat while my own pole enters his mouth, and gently pulls free. Both of us work in a synchronized motion: to and fro, in and out of mouths, hands holding cock-stems, and gagging with harmless beauty.

Fingers are so close to our cores, tips caress tight openings. Melodies of closed-mouth moans fill the Ice Cube. Because lips are at work, oxygen is lost. Hands pet and pull balls. Torsos gain sweat, which mixes and clings to each other's skin.

Santa Bear, carrying out this primal action between naked men, sits up on the cots. He decides to spoon me from behind, and begins to kiss my right shoulder and part of my neck. In doing so, he whispers, "Niles, I'm going to rock your world from back here."

"I was hoping you would say that," I respond, ready for his extension of meat in my needy ass.

Hunt finds lube and plastic, which are nearby and happily applied to his tool. He snuggles up against my behind again, lifts my right leg and ...

The tip of his swollen shaft enters my center, which causes immediate pain to roll through my torso. Hunt coaches me, "Take another few inches, Niles. You know it's going to sting, but you want it."

As promised, another four inches of his dog pops into my man-hole. I let out a whimper, which is only drowned out by a masculine grunt from Hunt, enjoying his ride.

With his palm pressed over my right pec, and his arm locked again my chest, he informs, "All of it is sliding in, buddy. Hang on to whatever you can."

I reach around me and feel his hairy hip and thigh, clinging to his skin. I call out in a demanding manner, "Punch it into me, Hunt! ... Do it!"

This happens. His entire stick invades my hole while he hangs onto me, clinging to my skin. Hunt begins to thump into me, continuously, pragmatically, needingly, again and again.

His gift causes sweat to form on my chest and legs. I quiver by his constant humping. The boner inside me rocks to and fro, and his tempo builds to an unbelievable quickness. Hunt bolts his hitch into me, pulls out, and bolts it into me again, still hanging onto my chest with a squeezing paw.

"Bang it," I whisper, overwhelmed by the moment and his glacier shifting movement. "Don't stop."

"Naughty Niles," he chants, fully intoxicated with our connected touch, "here comes the blast."

Another bang batters my bottom. Another. And another. Pounding. Thumping. Rocking inside me. Still holding my leg up. Still clutching my chest. Heavy breathing. Intoxicating. Moaning. Blasting my ass. In and out. In and out. In ...

"I'm going to cream," he announces and drops my leg. Hunt pulls out of me and loses the condom. He spins me onto my back and sits on his knees between my open legs and sore ass. Santa Bear inquires, "Do you want to come together?"

He already has our rods in both palms, kissing their sensitive skins and working their upright bodies in a north and south motion. Hunt studies my smooth and sweaty chest, and shifts his handsome view up to the tight cords in my neck and flushed face. He says, "You're adorable. I should have hooked up with you sooner than this."

"Better late than never." I barely get the words out, and feel a vibrating sensation rattle my body. I gasp for air by his constant touch, tight inside his fists, semi-unconscious beneath him, ready to burst at any second.

"You going to blow?" Hunt asks, smiling above me.

"Any second."

His palms build up a steady crescendo with our cocks, and he says, "It's time, buddy. Let it snow."

Three upward juts of my hips mixed with Hunt's handy work causes my cream to twirl out of my yanker and splatter against his furry torso.

Santa Bear comes with me, huffing and puffing, whispering my name over. White shoot flies higher than mine, between us, and falls to my stern abs and sweaty pecs.

"Shit," I whisper, "your spew is stinging hot."

His hands let go of our rods and he huffs, "I like it hot." Hunt leans over me, drops his face to my come-covered chest, and licks up his goods, mumbling, "Santa Bear is hungry. I've been waiting for a snack like you for a long time."

I run fingers through his hair and reply, "It's almost as good as milk and cookies."

"No. It's better," he says.

Right again.

Sticky, sealed together on the cots, looking up at the Ice Cube's transparent ceiling, Hunt holds me in his arms and kisses my left temple. "Merry Christmas, Niles."

"It was the best gift."

"And, hardest."

"That, too."

Another kiss is added to my temple, with a light squeeze. Hunt whispers into my ear, "Santa Bear really likes you. This wasn't a one-time fling."

"I'll let PB Services know in my report," I joke.

"Let's keep it between us. What do you think?"

"What's in it for me?"

Hunt stares deep into my eyes, presses his solid body against my own, and whispers, "Me ... Santa Bear."

Before we start another session of man-inside-man action, I smile and reply, "That sounds worth it. I'm in."

Hunt doesn't object, falling into my skin again, growling like a bear.

STRIP DREIDEL
By Rob Rosen

The shade was up for the first time ever. Well, for as long as I had lived across from him, anyway. Typical New York apartment buildings. Windows facing each another, separated by maybe twenty, thirty feet. Neighbors who know all of your business. And vice-versa. Not this guy, though. Private dude. Shades always down. Though, like I said, not this time.

There it was, framed in brick, behind glass, dead center, all in silver. A menorah. The first candle lit, mirroring my own from across the alleyway, ten stories up. Guy was a Jew. Go figure. Then again, New York Jews are about as rare as gays at a pride parade – in San Francisco. Still, all this time living across from him and this was the first tidbit of information I'd come by. As I said, go figure.

I grabbed my binoculars and had me a look-see. Nice apartment, maybe a bit larger than my own. Well, the living room, at any rate. Leather sofa, modern lamps, stocked bookcase, Tom of Finland print. Wait, go back. Tom of Finland print? Guy was Jewish and gay. Happy Hanukah to me.

Yeah, yeah, Hanukah. Hence the menorah. Growing up, it was the holiday that replaced Christmas for us kids. As I recall, it has something to do with the re-dedication of the Temple in Jerusalem, some miracle with one-day's worth of oil lasting eight, and those heroic Maccabees, though I could never quite figure out who the fuck they were. Not that I'm all that religious, in case you couldn't tell, just hedging my bets with the big guy upstairs. God.

And keeping you-know-who happy and out of my hair. Mom.

Anyway, it seemed like a whole new world had suddenly opened up for me. Okay, a whole new window, I mean. Now I just had to see who lived behind the glass. Was he tall, dark, and handsome? Short, squat, and handsome? Fine, so long as he was handsome I'd be happy. Call me shallow, but it's easier to tread in that end of the pool.

Thankfully, I didn't have too long to wait to find out. Next morning, I woke up and headed to the living room to clean the wax from the menorah. I glanced up, and there he was, doing the exact same thing. Fucking fickle finger of fate, gotta love it. Mainly, because the dude was wearing nothing but a towel. Boing went my boxers. Handsome, as it turned out, was a gross understatement.

Guy was tall, easily six feet, dark, probably from all the fur that covered his big fucking pecs and washboard tummy, and, as I said, handsome. Way, way handsome. Chiseled scruffy jaw, a mop of curly black hair, and, when he looked up from the task at hand, eyes as blue as sapphires.

I waved and pointed at my own menorah, so he didn't think I was some peeping Dave, which is my name. Not a lot of Jewish guys named Tom. Anyway, he grinned, shooting me a wink and a nod, and pointed down to his menorah. That was that. An awkward ten seconds of nothing later, he waved again and was out of eye shot, his towel falling the split second before I lost sight of him, the most perfect ass this side of the Mississippi coming into view. Nix that, make it both sides. Stunning. And jerk-off provoking. Meaning, I slid out of my boxers pronto and let one rip, a gusher of spunk spewing into my outstretched palm.

Next morning, repeat performance. Buffed dude, towel. Only this time, I came prepared, and I, too, was in nothing but a towel. I lifted a handmade sign up after the wink and wave. "Happy Hanukah!" it read. He laughed and mouthed the same. I flipped my sign over. "Name's Dave," it read.

He held up a finger, indicating I should wait, and then he dashed out of sight, only to return with his own sign. "Marvin." Not that he looked like a Marvin, but it was a start. Then he surprised me by turning the sign over. "Nice towel."

I gulped, smiling a nervous smile as a flush of red splashed across both cheeks. I pointed to his, and mouthed, "yours, too."

He nodded his approval, looked around to the other windows in my building to make sure the coast was clear, and then dropped it with a shrug. "Oops," he mouthed.

Fuckin-A, Marvin was hung like a mule, and a large mule at that. Needless to say, my own towel did an oops-drop lickety-split. He gave me a thumbs-up and disappeared from sight yet again, only to return with a new sign. "Saturday morning? Spin the Dreidel?"

Really? Spin the dreidel? Was he speaking euphemistically? I hadn't played that Hanukah game since I was a little boy. I echoed his shrug with one of my own, adding a nod for good measure. "Sure," I mouthed.

He pointed to the street down below. "Nine."

I nodded back at him, my smile in full-force. Thank goodness it was already Friday. A mere twenty-four-hour wait. And with that, he disappeared. I got ready for work, severe lumpage in my slacks for the rest of the day.

Next morning, I showered, got dressed, and headed downstairs. He was waiting for me, his smile big and bright and beguiling, those eyes of his like pools on a hot summer's day, despite the fact that it was a blustery thirty degrees outside.

“Dave,” he said, his hand outstretched. “Nice to meet you, neighbor.”

“Marvin,” I replied, reaching out for a shake that lingered and sent a volt of adrenalin eddying through my belly. “Um, kind of cold for a game of sidewalk dreidel.”

“Bagels and coffee first. The dreidel’s upstairs.”

Wise move on his part. A pre-date date. Making sure I wasn’t some raving lunatic. I handed him a bag of *gelt*, gold-foil-wrapped chocolate coins. “Happy Hanukah,” I told him. His grin widened, revealing a set of glistening pearly whites. Guy must have had a stellar orthodontist when he was a kid.

“Yum,” he said, leaning in for a thank you kiss on the cheek.

“Ditto,” said I, returning the kiss in kind with a chaste if not eager one on the lips.

We walked down the street, heading to a local coffee shop. “I don’t usually pick up guys in windows, by the way,” he admitted.

“Considering Mister Lipshitz above me and Mister Miller below, I’d say you did pretty good for a first time.”

He laughed, his hand palming my lower back. I was pretty certain I was passing his test. And, considering how fast we scarfed down breakfast, I’d say I passed with flying colors. In other words, we were in his apartment not thirty minutes later. And yes, it was larger than mine, but just by a smidge. The city being what it is, it was bigger than a bread basket, but not by much.

I spotted the dreidel on the coffee table, first thing.

“So we really are playing spin the dreidel?” I asked.

He laughed, taking my coat. “Of course we are.” He reached around and pulled me in tight, those magnificent eyes of his now an inch away. “But with a twist.” His lips brushed mine, soft, tender, perfect, a million tingles riding up and down my spine in response.

"A twist, huh?" I asked, my hands cupping his ass, my boner poking his thigh.

"I don't play for pennies," he replied, cryptically, the kiss repeated, harder, more insistent, just as perfect, maybe even more so.

"Raisins? Candies?" I tried.

Again that laugh, the sound like pebbles tossed at the shoreline. "Clothes, Dave. Strip dreidel. High stakes."

I leaned in, mouth to neck, a quick suck and a slurp, a nibble on a tender earlobe. "I've seen you naked already, Marvin. So, count me in."

He pulled away, and we both sat on the floor, setting the dreidel down between us. I stared at the toy, a four-sided spinning top with letters of the Hebrew alphabet on it, a gambling game played only during the holidays. Though never quite like this, I imagined.

He spun the dreidel, the wooden toy whirling like a dervish. "The letters," he began. "*Nun* usually stands for nothing, *Gimel* for whole, *Hay* for half, *Shen* for put in." The dreidel fell on its side. He looked up, grinned, his eyes locking with mine, laser intense, my breath suddenly ragged. "Land on *Shen* and a piece of clothing gets put in the pot. *Nun*, and nothing happens. *Hay* gets a kiss."

"And *Gimel*?"

The smile grew devilish. "The first person to land on that gets fucked."

I coughed. "Not the way they taught it in Hebrew school."

He reached up and stroked my cheek. "Then you went to the wrong Hebrew school, Dave."

I spun first. "Apparently." It landed on *Hay*, yielding a kiss, lips pressed up tight, two tongues lashing out, snaking, coiling, swapping some heavy spit, eyes open, locked, not missing any of the action. "Your turn."

He spun. "*Shen.*" The shoes came off, brown, suede, expensive.

I spun. "*Nun.*"

His turn again. *Shen*, again. Socks, thick and white, slid down and off. His feet were large, hairy knuckles, high arches. I bent down to suck a toe, too, eliciting a ticklish squirm and a boyish giggle.

Again I spun. Still with a *Nun*.

Shen again for him. He stood. "Shirt or belt?" he asked, arms akimbo.

"Shirt," I managed. "Definitely shirt."

I stared up, eyes big. He started from the top and worked his way down, button after button, the matting of chest hair quickly visible, a cleft between muscled pecs, a furry six pack with a seemingly spare set of cans, two eraser-tipped nipples, sinewy forearms. Skin white, hair all a beautiful chestnut. The shirt joined the shoes and socks.

"Those things sensitive?" I asked, pointing up at his nips.

"Uh huh," he replied, with an eager nod. "You gonna suck on them, too?"

I smiled and motioned with my finger for him to bend down. He did as I asked, his hands on my shoulders, his chest in my face. I ran my hand through all that dense wiry hair, across solid muscle, my fingers coming to rest atop a nipple, which I tweaked and tugged on, causing a soft moan to escape from his cushiony lips, his eyelids fluttering in appreciation. I grabbed for the other one, working both between thumb and index finger, pulling him farther down, so I could suck and bite on them, tease them with my teeth.

"Fuck yeah," he sighed, rubbing his dick through his jeans. "Hurry up and spin."

He moved away, reluctantly, and sat back down. I winked at him and set the dreidel in motion. "Fuck, a *Nun* again. Sorry."

He shot me a wry smile. "You sure you're not cheating?"

"Nope, but I'll toss you a bone." I kicked off my sneakers.

He spun, the *Shen* landing on the topside, once more. The belt was unhooked and slid through the loops. "Your turn, and I better start seeing some flesh pretty soon."

"I'm trying," I replied, the top already spinning. "Hay, a kiss at least. Better than nothing."

"Hell yeah." He pounced, his body landing on mine, pinning me to the floor, his mouth smothering mine, kiss after kiss after kiss, wet and wonderful. My hands reached up and around, caressing his shoulders, his back, sliding inside his jeans, playing with the tuft of hair above his crack.

"Your turn," I said, when he let me up for air.

He sighed and rolled off, sitting with his legs crossed, Indian-style. The top went spinning, gliding across the hardwood floor, and landing, not surprisingly, all things considered, on the *Shen*. The sigh was echoed as he stood up, his deft fingers sliding down the zipper, popping open a button. "Damn, you're lucky," he said, mock-upset.

I stared up, my smile turning northward. "Amen to that," I retorted. "You're going commando."

He laughed, his thumbs inside his jeans, yanking them down an inch, two, his bush coming into view, the base of his prick quick to follow. "Makes the game go by a lot faster." He pushed the denim down, his dick bouncing out, semi-hard, the mushroom hid already slick. The jeans came off. He stood there, naked, his cock growing and growing, eight steely inches, arced to the side, balls the size of lemons. "Your turn," he said, though moving in instead of sitting down, until his dick was face-level with me.

"Gladly," I replied, my tongue darting out, licking the salty-sweet jizz of the tip before engulfing him whole, a happy gagging tear streaming down my cheek. He fucked my face while I tickled his nuts, playing with the fine hairs that ran rings around his hefty sac.

"Damn," he groaned, grabbing my head as he shoved his prick down my throat. Then, "Spin, Dave. And let's see some of those clothes come off."

Sadly, that old dreidel landed on *Nun* for me one more time. Then again, it had other plans for us because, oh happy day, he spun it into a *Gimel*. In other words, his ass was mine.

He stared at me, and I at him. "Well," I said. "I gotta get naked for that, a least."

"Finally," he added, lying down, spread out before me like a veritable buffet, his cock vertical.

I stripped for him as he stripped for me, slow and seductive, a flash of skin here, a flash of cock there, until I was naked, hard as granite, and standing over him. "Better?" I asked.

"Getting there," he replied, his legs instantly up and out, bent at the knee, his pink, crinkled, hair-rimmed hole winking at me all come-hither like.

Naturally, I came hither.

I crouched down, ass to face, a spank across each cheek, another, a deep whiff, the smell of musk and sweat invading my sinus cavity. I took a cursory lick, a suck, a slurp, my tongue sliding up his chute as his ass bucked into my face, his balls banging up against my nose. "Yeah, suck it," he moaned in one long gravelly exhale.

"I can do better than that," I replied, spitting on his ring and gliding in one, then two, slick fingers up and in and back.

He sucked in his breath. "Oh yeah, better. Much. What else you gonna shove up there?"

I rose my head above his horizon. He was looking down at me, stroking his thick prick, winking and grinning. I turned around and got on my back, my own billy club raging hard, pulsing in my hand. "Feel like taking a spin of your own?"

He laughed and jumped up, his mighty cock swaying as he ran from the room, his alabaster ass disappearing from sight for a brief moment before he returned, a bottle of lube in one hand, a rubber in the other. "I think I'm up for it," he quipped.

"That I can see," I said, beckoning him in with my dick.

He grabbed for it, sheathed it, and lubed it up before straddling me, his hole looming over it, his mammoth hard-on pointing down at me like a divining rod. "You gonna fuck me hard, Dave?"

"Oh yeah, Marvin. Fuck yeah."

He grinned, rubbing his ring around the head, and then pushed down, my dick disappearing inside, millimeter by millimeter. Marvin sighed, breathed in deeply, and then shoved his ass farther down toward me, engulfing my cock until balls were battering up against ass, sending every nerve-ending in body into overdrive.

I got up on my elbows, he bent down, our lips meeting in the middle, parting, his hands running through my hair, mine pulling mercilessly on his rigid nipples. He moaned, long and low, while I shoved my cock deep, deep inside of him. “Mmm,” he hummed, eyes wide open, staring into mine, lips gliding over lips, soft as down.

“Mmm,” I hummed back, breathing into his mouth, down his throat, bucking and fucking and pounding on his rump at the same time.

“You gonna fill that rubber up with your load, Dave? Gonna make me come with that big dick up my ass?”

For a Jew, he sure had a dirty mouth. That, of course, I liked. “Fuck yeah,” I told him, reaching down to jack at his thick cock. He leaned away, sitting up, grinding his ass into me as I stroked and stroked away, his pole growing fat in my hand.

He grabbed for his nipples, which he twisted and turned, his head now tilted back, his mouth open, a steady groan spewing out. “Gonna come,” he rasped, his dick immediately exploding, a stream of white-hot man-sap shooting out, drenching my chin, my chest, my stomach, as I rocketed my cock one final time up his ass, quickly matching him ounce for creamy ounce, both of us howling in ecstasy as we shot and shot and shot.

He collapsed on top of me, my dick popping out of his ass, his mouth again finding mine, both our bodies slick with sweat, sticky with his spunk. He laughed, suddenly.

“What?” I asked.

“Shoulda lifted that shade sooner,” he replied.

“Why didn’t you?” I asked, truly curious, as I always had been.

“That Mister Lipshitz above your apartment, guys got a powerful set of binoculars zoomed in at my building. Creepy.”

Mister Lipshitz, huh? Go figure. Still, it all worked out in the end. My end, that is. Which he fucked silly the next morning, just after we played spin the dreidel again. Same for the sixth and seventh and, at last, eighth days of Hanukah, that menorah of his burning big and bright and beautiful. As I said, Happy Hanukah to me. Whoever those Maccabees were, I sure owed them one. Big fucking time.

MIRACLE

By Stephen Osborne

Christmas Eve, alone. Worse, Christmas Eve alone in a hotel room. A hotel room in Des Moines, of all places! Zack knew exactly no one in Des Moines and didn't feel like going out and making anyone's acquaintance, even briefly. Why had he agreed to go to this conference in the first place? True, it put him in good stead with his boss, and he needed all the brownie points he could accumulate. He should have known, however, that the decision would end up kicking him in the ass.

A sudden and fierce snowstorm had all but shut down the city. Zack's flight had been canceled, and it didn't look as if he'd be able to get back to Pennsylvania until Tuesday, which meant missing not only Christmas with his family, but also not spending his usual day after Christmas with his friends hitting the clearance sales.

Des Moines sucked. His job sucked. Christmas, at least this year, sucked.

Zack poured a little more of the eggnog into the little plastic cup the hotel had provided and gazed mournfully out the window. The snow was still coming down, thick and wet. If he wasn't in such a sour mood, he might have thought it pretty. He sipped the eggnog. Store bought eggnog just didn't hold a candle to his mom's. She always made a batch from scratch every Christmas Eve. He and his brothers always spiked it and then got a little tipsy watching Christmas movies while their dad snoozed in his favorite chair. Zack looked at his watch. Yep, back home they'd be happily zonked right now, watching *Scrooged* or *A Charlie Brown Christmas.*

Through the falling flakes, Zack could pick out a particularly bright star. Was it the North Star? Zack didn't know stars. This one was blazing like hell, that's all he knew. Did one make a wish on the North Star? Zack didn't know that either. And what would he wish for, anyway?

"Something to make this Christmas not quite so crappy," he said aloud.

The star seemed to twinkle in response. Zack snorted and set the eggnog carton down. He sighed heavily and padded over to the bed. At least he didn't have to worry about his state of dress. No one cared if you roamed your hotel room wearing just your tighty-whities and your socks. At his parents' house, the dress was casual, but half-naked would be frowned upon. Zack picked up the television remote and pressed buttons. Maybe a good Christmas movie would help to cheer him up.

Channel surfing gave him few options. The best he could find was some old version of Dickens' *A Christmas Carol.* It was in black and white and looked very old. Zack didn't recognize any of the actors, but that was hardly surprising. They were probably all long dead before he had even been born. Still, it beat the Home Shopping Network. Zack sipped his eggnog and settled back onto the pillows he'd propped up against the headboard.

Zack's old boyfriend had loved black and white movies, but Zack usually gave them a miss. They just didn't look realistic. Plus, the guys in them were rarely hot. The costumed actors on the screen before him were no exception. The film seemed to be populated with ugly, bloated old English actors one wouldn't want to touch with a stick. Was there some kind of rule back then that cute guys couldn't be in films?

The movie changed scenes, and Zack sat up a little straighter. The actor playing Scrooge's nephew, Fred, was actually pretty hot. He looked a bit like Orlando Bloom but of course it couldn't be. Orlando Bloom was only a little older than Zack, certainly too young to be in this antique of a movie. Whoever it was, he had wonderfully wavy dark hair and the prettiest eyes Zack had ever seen. "You are fucking gorgeous," he said to the TV screen.

"Why, thank you."

Zack blinked. It had almost seemed as if the character, Fred, had replied to him. The actor had even turned to look directly at the camera, giving the impression that he was staring directly at Zack. "That's fucking weird," Zack muttered under his breath.

"I'm sorry," Fred said, "I couldn't catch that. You'll have to speak up."

The other characters in the scene, Scrooge and Bob Crachit, were carrying on with their lines as usual, but the actor playing Fred seemed to have forgotten the scene entirely and was just talking with someone off-camera. How did they leave this in the finished film? Was he watching out-takes from the movie? Although he'd never seen this particular version, Zack was familiar enough with the story to know that at this point Fred should have left Scrooge's counting house. Here he still was, seemingly looking at Zack. Zack looked at the nearly empty cup of eggnog and set it on the nightstand.

There hadn't been any alcohol in the drink, but maybe he'd gotten hold of a bad batch.

"It isn't the eggnog," Fred said.

Shocked, Zack tried to speak, but all that came out was a tiny, strangled moan.

"Look, this will go much easier if you let me out of here," the character of Fred said. Behind him, the movie still seemed to be going on as usual. What was going on?

Zack shook his head and looked up at the ceiling. "I swear," he said, "I'll never smoke pot again." Zack rarely did, but what other explanation could there be than some freak delayed reaction to some particularly potent weed? Zack tried to remember the last time he'd smoked. Maybe two weeks ago? It hadn't even seemed like good pot at the time.

The character on his TV screen seemed to point to a spot on the bed. "Look, if you'll just pick the remote back up and push the 'Enter' button, I can come and join you."

"It's the eggnog," Zack said. "It has to be the eggnog. It's spoiled, and I'm hallucinating and close to death and ..."

"I said it wasn't the eggnog." Fred sighed heavily. "It's a Christmas miracle. If you just accept it and have fun with it, this will all move a lot faster."

Zack moved slowly as he picked up the remote. This couldn't be happening. Characters in movies don't talk to you. They certainly don't tell you to push buttons on remotes. So why was he picking it up?

"And make sure you don't change the channel," Fred warned with a wicked smile. "Otherwise you might get Martha Stewart coming into your hotel room to bring you apple cobbler or something. And I'm not knocking apple cobbler. I just think it would be more fun my way."

"What's your way?" Zack asked. He'd finally lost it, he thought. He was talking to the television set.

Scrooge's nephew smirked. "Push 'Enter' and find out."

Zack, knowing that he'd probably gone insane and figuring he might as well go along with it, shrugged and pushed the button.

The image on the TV distorted briefly and then began to push itself forward – through the screen. First a pale hand emerged, followed by an arm and then a shoulder. The figure of Fred pulled itself out of the television headfirst, landing rather unceremoniously onto the carpeted floor with a thud.

Zack gasped as Fred stood and briefly dusted off his frock coat. The fictional character looked down at himself with a frown. "I'm still in black and white. I hadn't expected that. I hope that's alright with you."

"Um," Zack said, unsure of what to say, "sure."

The monochromatic figure smiled. "You don't believe in me, do you? You still think I'm some hallucination or an effect of bad eggnog. Blimey, I feel like Marley's ghost more than Fred. You know, 'Man of the worldly mind, do you believe in me or not?' It's not my line, but it's certainly appropriate. Look, you made a wish, it came true. Just deal with it."

"I wished for you?"

"Well, you were wanting to get laid for Christmas. Deep down, that's what you were thinking. Otherwise I wouldn't be here." The black and white man sat down on the edge of the bed and began to remove his boots.

Zack pressed himself back against the pillows. "What are you doing?"

Fred raised an eyebrow. "Stripping. Then the fun can begin."

"You mean you want to ..." Zack couldn't bring himself to finish the sentence.

"I thought we'd fuck, yeah." Fred let his boot drop to the floor.

Zack frowned. "They said fuck back in Dickens' day?"

Fred paused as he was removing his left stocking. "You get a Christmas miracle and you want to split hairs?" The living image stood with a smile and unfastened his trousers. He quickly pulled them and his underwear down to reveal a large, thick, monochromatic penis. “Merry Christmas,” he said.

Zack gulped. “Same to you,” he said. Tentatively he moved forward. The dick did look tempting. He reached out to touch it. It felt real enough. It even twitched as his hand made contact. He looked up at Fred, who had removed his frock coat and was tossing it aside. The look on the man’s face registered pleasure. Still, the dude was black and white. Freaky, Zack thought.

“That feels good,” Fred moaned.

That was all the encouragement Zack needed. He moved his face forward and took the man’s dick into his mouth. It seemed real. Real enough that Zack gagged a little as the man shoved more of the hard cock into his mouth.

Fred ceased the thrusting of his hips. “Sorry about that,” he said.

Zack took the cock out of his mouth long enough to say, “Don’t be.” He then quickly swallowed as much of the dick as he could. It tasted so good and felt so good sliding into his mouth, that Zack didn’t care that he was sucking off a fictional character (or was it an actor?) from a movie. He didn’t know if it was a ghost or a hallucination standing by his bed or what, but he decided he wasn’t going to worry about it. Zack finally got his throat to relax enough that he could swallow the huge cock in its entirety. He was rewarded by a long groan from Scrooge’s nephew.

Fred’s fingers were entwined in Zack’s hair. He had to use a little pressure to slow down Zack’s eager movements. “Hold on there, sport. You’re going to make me come if you keep that up, and we haven’t got to the fucking yet.”

Zack reluctantly released the penis and looked up into the man’s beautiful dark eyes. “I don’t have any condoms," he said, disappointment showing in his voice. "I didn't bring any."

Fred smiled. "I don't really exist, so they really aren't necessary. Are they?"

Thinking about that for a moment, Zack nodded. "I guess that's true."

"Then lie back on the bed and point those toes to the heavens, my boy, because I'm going to give you the drilling you deserve!"

As Zack threw himself back onto the pillows, he laughed. "You don't really sound like a Dickens character."

Fred climbed onto the bed and positioned himself between Zack's legs. Zack's underwear was off before he even was aware of the man's hands around his waist. "Well, I'm sort of part Dickens character, part actor from an old film, and part dream. Believe me, the actor who played me in that movie didn't have a cock this big. This," he said, pressing the head of his dick into Zack's crack, "is all because of your wish."

As the huge cock invaded his ass, Zack found himself thanking whoever was responsible for making his innermost dream come true. Okay, it would be better if the guy shoving his cock into him wasn't black and white, but it felt so good that Zack didn't really care. Fred's dick felt as if it was made for Zack's ass. When Fred began to pound into him, Zack had to turn his head and bite into one of his pillows to keep from giving out a yell that would wake up everybody in the hotel. Unable to hold off any longer, Zack began to stroke his own swollen cock. He licked his lips, enjoying the taste of the sweat that had formed over his upper lip.

Fred continued to slam the huge cock into Zack's ass. Zack thought for a moment that some color had come into the man's black and white hued face but he wasn't sure. He could tell, though, that the man was ready to shoot. Fred's face scrunched up in pleasure as his cock exploded.

Simultaneously, Zack shot his own load. He could feel Fred's cock pulse inside him as his own dick shot onto his abs. "Holy fuck!" Zack gasped as waves of pleasure rocked his body. A heavily panting Fred grinned as he collapsed on top of Zack.

They stayed there for a moment, sticky with sweat and cum but not wanting to move. Finally, Fred whispered into Zack's ear. "I've got to go. The movie's waiting for me."

"Do you have to?"

Fred turned his head. On the screen, Scrooge was conversing with the Ghost of Christmas Present. "Yeah, I'd better leave soon. I'm in the next scene."

Zack stroked the man's unnaturally white cheek. "Thanks for the best Christmas present ever."

Fred's eyes twinkled. "Anytime," he said as his image began to fade.

With a sigh Zack rose from the bed and got a towel from the bathroom. After wiping the cum from his stomach, he got himself another cup of eggnog and settled back to finish watching the movie. Was he wrong, or did the character of Fred turn to the camera there to wink at Zack? It didn't matter. Des Moines was great. The hotel was great. Christmas was great.

Best of all, Zack felt great.

SANTA'S RED FURRY BRIEFS

By Derrick Della Giorgia

"Holiday, sensitive, naughty guys wanted. Candidates can send CV and photos to santasredfurrybriefs@northpalace.com." Would I ever apply to a job position like that? Out of boredom or maybe curiosity, I did as soon as I ran across the ad on www.jobsnobodyknowsabout.com.

Five emails and a wire transfer later, I was on my first class flight to Copenhagen. Luckily, I belong to that carefree generation that never knew what it meant to sign a work contract and forget about it until retirement. My engineering degree had been hard to get and just as hard to sell, and at the age of twenty-six, I shamelessly and whole-heartedly accepted any kind of job that could pay my bills and offer me some kind of fun. To start with, I had never been to Denmark, and the extraordinary skills required anticipated a world that I probably wasn't going to explore in my everyday life in Rome. Well, if Santa won't come to Valentino, Valentino must come to Santa!

I had always been told that Scandinavians were different, much better behaved than Italians and blond, hot and tall; nevertheless, that surely didn't even begin to describe the entertainment that expected me in the gelid land. As soon as I stepped into the Scandinavian Airlines Airbus 319, three details wiped the early morning sleepiness off my still hesitant face: the Valkyrie assigned to first class was taller than I – which meant not less than six three -, wearing high black leather boots and a beige shawl with which she wrapped her upper body as if she was preparing herself for an imminent snow storm. After her guttural “God Morgen,” Sissel accompanied me to my seat and smiled to the other five people behind me, probably happy the flight was almost empty and she could hold on to her shawl without much trouble.

On the other side of the two thousand km carpet of snowy clouds, I was welcomed by “blond, hot and tall” Aksel, the chauffeur of my red limousine. From this point on, the information on my printed schedule became cryptic and limited. The only thing I knew was that I would have been driven to Santa’s palace where I could finally offer my service.

“You were the first one to be selected, Valentino,” Aksel shortly commented when I investigated about the palace, Santa and the party.

“Really?” I replied, approaching the front seats to hear his voice that most of the times was swallowed by the grinding noises of the black ice under the tires.

“Out of 11,239 applications!” His tone changed for the first time, showing emotions and interest. A smile bloomed on his face.

“What exactly is the party?” I attempted, even though it had been clearly explained to me that no detail would have been provided beyond what was in the emails until the night of the festivities.

“As you have probably been informed that I cannot disclose!” He went back to his almost military rigidity, never neglecting the road.

“Will you be there?” I thought that if I had to be naughty, I wouldn’t have minded his sexy presence. His monumental hands dominated the steering wheel, and his black suit stretched with every movement of his muscular arms. More than once, he caught me searching for his blue eyes in the driving mirror, after which he would formulate a question to justify that inadequate closeness.

"I will assist you through the whole process," he felt comfortable telling me, making me forget I was actually there for work and not for fun.

When Aksel dropped me in front of the main entrance, I realized with a sudden sense of suffocation that there was nothing but snow around me. Miles and miles of untouched white fluffy congealed water. The limo moved slowly away from me and the red of its body melted into pink and then disappeared. I hesitated by the time my thighs commenced to hurt from the cold, and I banged the doorknob as I had been instructed. Inside, time and space didn't matter anymore. I was left alone for what seemed five minutes because the Asian guy that opened the door ran away after his blond friend and the laughing coming from a far away room on the right. He was naked from head to toe except for a pair of cherry red furry briefs and the mistletoe tattoos that began on his chest, decorated his arms and from his crotch descended to his ankles. Shoeless, his feet made a fleshy noise on the dark wood floor and with every jump a puff of silver powder was released from his black hair into the air behind him. I was suffocating again. The temperature was insanely high, and the first thing that crossed my mind, coming from the uniform white outside, was to take off my clothes. I peeled off my jacket and searched for the source of that strong cinnamon fragrance. Everywhere I turned I felt as if my head was stuck into a bucket of warm cookie dough. The music was a holiday carol I wasn't familiar with.

"Welcome!" A mighty voice preceded a man I couldn't see yet, up on the immense spiral stairway in front of me. Red and white, a mastodontic candy cane that climbed to the higher floors.

"Hello," I directed toward the ceilings, feeling on my cheeks the redness that inflamed my white skin and my dark eyes. Then, I couldn't believe what or who was in front of me.

"Hello Valentino! Welcome again!" Santa came down the stairs, only he didn't look like the Santa that used to come down my chimney when I was a kid. A shirtless, heart-stopping, groin-convulsing, thought-annulling man jogged down the steps in his red silk Christmas boxers, making the candy cane necklaces around his neck teasing every groove of his muscular torso. A Santa furry hat, dangling on the right side of his face, covered his silver grey hair. "It's a pleasure to meet you. I am Santa." He seized my right hand with both his and shook my entire body before I could say anything. His golden skin was slightly oiled and smelled like hot sugar. I had to force myself to avoid licking him – unstoppingly.

"Nice! To meet you, I mean ..." My head started to float, and I wondered if I had been drugged by Aksel in the limo or by Sissel on the plane. I was in Denmark, at Santa's palace, weeks before Christmas. And Santa was stupendously hot.

"Don't worry! Aksel will be here in a few and explain everything to you. Just come with me, and I'll show you your room, would you?" Santa rubbed the back of his palm against my left cheek and ruffled the back of my hair, still wet from the snow flakes that had landed on me outside. As he did that, I felt a whirl of emotions invading my body, but I could only concentrate on his cinnamon imbued caress.

# # # # #

"... and approximately ten days before leaving for the holidays, Santa organizes a week of festivities with the guys he has picked from all over the world. The flux of energy keeps him young and in touch with the new generations." Aksel finished his introductory lesson on Santa's secrets while painting the mistletoe leaves on my neck and all the way down my back as I had chosen. All the selected guys had to exclusively wear the tight furry red briefs and have their bodies decorated with mistletoe tattoos to carry on the Christmassy atmosphere. Personal bedrooms were furnished with a round red make-up table, on which rested a weaponry of vanilla, peppermint, cinnamon and an infinity of other fragrances, glitter, sparkling powders, oils, shiny little stars and every sort of decoration you could use on your body. After that treatment, you were not a guest anymore but part of the holiday yourself, undistinguishable from the rest of the palace.

"Can you tell me, now, what exactly happens during the parties?" I inquired when he was bent over me, a few inches from my lips, painting the last mistletoe on my forehead. His breath was minty fresh, and the blue of his eyes reminded me of the gelid whiteness outside the steamy palace.

"Well, it depends how much Santa likes you. Sometimes he just enjoys admiring your naked body and your decorations, he watches you running around and playing with the other guys. Sometimes, he picks a few and plays with them, and if he really really likes you, he takes you to his rooms. But that only happened once in so many years. No one is allowed to enter his rooms." Aksel stopped talking but went on savoring how special it is to be the fortunate one.

"Where are my furry briefs?" I stood up and slipped out of my underwear without waiting for Aksel to turn around or leave the room. Blame it on the stories, the perfumes or the music, but I was craving to be touched after having his warm palms grazing my skin for so long. I sat on his knees and said again: "Where are they?"

"Oh no!" He landed his almost trembling hands on my naked hips and invited me to stand up. "Please, Valentino. You have to get ready for Santa. Your first party will start in less than an hour." I was Santa's property, and he would have never violated that law.

At eight thirty sharp, I was taken to the salon where all the other furry briefs were, and I was introduced to everybody. There were over forty-nine naked guys, laughing and teasing each other while sipping eggnog and sucking on colored candy I had never seen before.

"Tonight, I am gonna resist! I will enter Santa's rooms, you'll see." A blondie two furry briefs away from me was telling his concerned friend.

"If only ... Aksel told me the last guy that managed to be with Santa remained here. Do you think it was him? I haven't seen anybody else in here ..."

"Oh, let it go! Your briefs are puffing out already!" A hyperactive redhead made fun of the two and then turned to me. "You are the new onc, aren't you?"

"I got here three hours ago. My name is Valentino." I shook his hand and grabbed a purple cup of eggnog.

"Guys, guys ... it's time. Santa is coming down!" As silence fell into the room, the music swelled in the air, all around the ten ceiling-scraping Christmas trees scattered among the garnished tables and white couches. A few furry briefs spread some more silver or gold on their chests, and then we all gathered in front of the dark wood doors that apparently concealed Santa.

"Good evening furry briefs! Let the party begin!" Santa announced, bowing before us. His hat was gone and his silver hair sharpened his honey eye stare. He uttered a few more words that I completely missed, too enthralled by his harmonious voice and gestures, collapsed into the couch in the center of the room and gulped down a quarter of his glass of eggnog, fixing his red silk boxers with his free hand. Immediately, at least five guys launched themselves on him and started whispering irresistibly funny things into his ears because they kept laughing and rolling over each other.

"Please, please!" Each and every one kept begging as they rubbed their warm booties on Santa's lap and kissed his neck or licked his nipples.

"You lose ... don't you see?" With a provoking smirk, Santa wiggled out of their asphyxiating embrace and kept changing couches, until he found a shelter behind the fat tree crammed with clock ornaments, toning down the desire on everybody's face. He was supernaturally sexy. Something inhuman but irresistible lingered around his body, and the drops of eggnog, the signs of the fight on his chest, made my stomach twist with yearning.

"It is impossible. How can you not get hard?" The guy beside me mumbled and sat on the green and gold embroidered tablecloth behind us.

"What do you mean?" I asked confused.

"Well, you know, if you can rub your briefs on him without getting a hard-on, he will take you to his rooms. That's the rule." He exhaled in despair and stuffed his beautiful mouth with gingerbread cookies. The lights dimmed even more, and a gold shiny fog started descending from the ceiling covering us with more colors and sweetness. The eggnog reached all my nerve endings, and I started laughing, too, locking my eyes on Santa and monitoring all his movements. I was eager to conquer him. My whole body emanated a bursting energy with every breath, a wave that swayed back and forth in unison with all the other furry briefs. And Santa absorbed it all and looked younger and sexier with every smile. He seemed especially stimulated when the furry briefs fooled around with each other. After failing in the unattainable deed of awakening the fascinating host's sexual appetite, three of them diverted their attention to a holiday orgy behind the couch. The carol gave them the pace and the imminence of an orgasm drew many a jealous look. From the opposite side of the happening, I could only spot the end of it, announced by the hyperactive redhead that I had met earlier, picking some of the red fur stuck on his lips.

By the time the most uninhibited furry briefs captured Santa's lips into a long sensual kiss, the party drew to a close, and one by one, surrendering to the impossibility of the task, the Christmas guys walked the candy cane spiral stairs up to their rooms.

"And you are hard," Santa commented as his hand still lay down on the adventurous furry briefs' crotch. He kissed him again, licking the last sweet drops off the red lips and spanked him away with a smile. "Time to go to bed."

"Not yet, Santa!" I approached him from behind, the second he reached the first step. "I hadn't had my try yet!" I pushed my whole body against his smooth firm torso and finally kissed those lips as I anchored myself to his hair.

"Valentino! I thought you were the shy one!" He was pleasantly surprised, and he slipped his longing hand down my briefs, feeling my butt from every angle.

"I have been good all night. Now I want my present!" I rubbed my red fur against his crotch trapped in my embrace and watched his eyes illuminating with excitement. His red silk warmed up under my fingers and among the tensed muscles of his legs I felt his hard-on. "You lose ..."

"You win." He kissed me and lifted me off the ground, carrying me up the sixty-nine steps to his rooms. When he opened the door, I couldn't believe my eyes. My heart weakened. I don't think a human being can imagine all that.

The ancient maps, the wood art, the miniature toys, the sparkling gemstones, the intricate glass ornaments amassed in his room were breathtaking. A soft orange light inundated every object and perfectly glued them all together, delicately falling on the white feathers covering the entire floor. What struck me the most were all the things I had never seen before in my life and whose use I couldn't even start to imagine. Wherever I turned my head, I discovered more of that man's secrets and all that excitement turned into sex for an outlet valve.

Santa sweetly abandoned me on the Pompeian red mattress by a huge dark blue puffy pillow and locked the doors of his kingdom. The candy cane necklaces were gone, his hands looked free and hungry, and the only thing that separated me from his hard-on was a thin silk veil. I adjusted my hips and invited him between my thighs, sweetened by all the eggnog that was accidentally spilled during the festivities; he smiled, spread his legs and crossed his arms over the golden tight chest two feet away from the right corner of the bed.

"I knew you'd make it." Those words were delivered to my ear followed by an open mouth kiss that migrated to my neck. Aksel, who had entered the room unnoticed, grabbed my wrists and blocked them above my head. Then he slid down on me, taking his mouth to my nipples and passing his Norse chest only millimeters away from my nostrils that desperately sought the aroma of his flesh.

When more hands landed on my body, I saw Santa scanning my ankles and exchanging quick love looks with Aksel. Aksel in fact was the one chosen. The only other one, Santa's closest furry briefs. Like each and every one of us, he had entered Santa's palace wondering how such a marvelous place could exist and had joined the parties, but he had never left since.

The red limousine chauffer's shoulders took away the thick orange light when he stood on his knees facing me from above and his finally naked body reinvigorated my already unquenchable erection. Unlike mine, his furry briefs were golden and protected a praiseworthy tool. Santa inserted his arm in between his smooth thighs and teasingly caressed his bulge, uncovering the tiny mistletoe tattoo on his groin. "One more test and you, too, will have golden briefs." They both looked at me and smiled in their own different way, the supernatural silver haired ageless Santa and the glacial stare Dane without his uniform and composure.

"I wanna earn them!" Grabbing the fur and the silk in front of me and the steady sticks underneath, I pulled them both closer to my body, and I alternately made them sigh wetting their pleasure canes until I traced the origin of those sounds and stole a three way kiss that ignited their most feral desire. They nailed me to the mattress and had me strip off my briefs, exposing my hard-on and everything else they were looking for. Suddenly, I found myself facing down, with their lips following the mistletoe line on my back all the way to the last vertebra, where they met for another kiss.

For an instant, the sighing multiplied in the distance, and I realized that everybody knew I was in Santa's rooms; the nervous steps, the scratches and the breathing of my forty-nine mates in the palace randomly rustling behind the sepia tall doors. But my moaning erased everything else in the room when their tongues furtively and voraciously explored my most secluded surfaces.

The tension accumulated in my flesh during those long hours of temptation, subsided, and the physical happiness initiated its journey from my crotch to the farthest extremities of my limbs. A sweet burning reclaimed my hand where the action was occurring and, with the help of my fingers, I shamelessly fed both men my precum. Then, Santa lifted my hips, making me feel lighter than the feathers I kept admiring in ecstasy from my position, and Aksel slid underneath me. The chauffer clutched my turgid balls and dipped them in his heated Nordic mouth, giving Santa free access into my body. The moment Papà Noel found his way up my special gate, I finally felt the flames parting and my thirst was completely alleviated. His impetuous fury pervaded my insides and catapulted me into a pleasure ride that lasted forever, culminating with everybody's satisfaction on my panting stomach.

SCREWOOGED

By Logan Zachary

Mark was dead. A car accident ended his life and our relationship. I staggered to the house as the snow fell, almost slipping on the slush covered stairs. The alcohol, I was sure, had no effect on my unsteady climb.

The doorknocker swam in and out of focus, as the key tried to find the slot. The damn cold chilled me to the bone, making my hands shake, preventing the unlocking process.

A Christmas Eve's gust swirled snow and cold around me. Inside the warm house, the phone rang as fumbling fingers finally found the lock, but the tumblers refused to turn.

"Eddie, I was hoping to catch you at home, but ..." A pause. "We'll see if Santa is good to you tonight. I hope that we can get together tomorrow. Santa may have dropped something off for you at my house. Besides, I'd really like ... you know. Anyway, Merry Christmas."

The locked clicked, and the door swung open.

"Why didn't you call my cell ..." and I noticed it still plugged into the wall, charging.

I took off my coat and threw it on the chair next to the phone. The heavy snowflakes quickly melted in the house. A damp chill hung in the air as I made my way to the living room. I flipped through the piles of DVDs and slipped in Mark's audition disc. He tried out for the Guthrie's *A Christmas Carol* and landed the part, but on the way home to tell me, a drunk driver crossed the middle line.

I slipped the DVD in and settled on the couch. Reaching over to the coffee table, I clicked the remote for the fireplace, and a warm glow filled the room.

The DVD clicked and thumped. It was an old player and refused to work half the time. The drawer slid open, and the disc shined in the fire's light.

I pushed play again and the drawer pulled back in, and the DVD tasted the disc, deciding if it would play or spit it out again.

I closed my eyes and rested my head against the back of the overstuffed couch and drifted off to sleep.

"Eddie, you have the chance to change your life," boomed out of the television, and I startled awake. Rubbing my eyes, I tried to focus my eyes on the screen.

"I will send three ghosts ..."

"What the ..."

"The first will come on the stroke of one."

I shook my head.

The audition tape?

My dry contacts floated into place as Mark's face looked at me.

But the movie looked more live than recorded, and why wasn't Mark's face painted with the make-up?

This was Mark.

"This is the only way ..."

The screen fogged over, obscuring Mark. It turned a bright blue with the DVD player's logo in the background. "This disc is not able to be played," flashed on and off. The little drawer stood open with the shiny disc glowing.

"What the hell?"

The Ghost of Christmas Past

The clock struck one. I jolted awake. Maybe it was time to go to bed. I picked up the television's remote. The channels started to change. A black and white game show from the fifties started. The happy music tinkled a tune from an innocent time. "Edward Stewart, this is your past."

I leaned forward. Someone from the fifties had my name. I had to see this.

A baby picture filled the screen. My baby picture.

"It was June 13, 1979, over thirty years ago." Pictures from baths to birthdays, Christmas to Halloween, grade school to high school raced by. Friends, family, pets, picnics, camping.

Shane skinny dipping. Roger showering after gym class. Jeff slipping out of his jockstrap. Ken's hairy butt mooning. Strip poker at a birthday party. Camping at the lake. The lifeguard in the red Speedo.

My body started to tingle. My heart beat faster, and my loins started to swell.

A *Playboy* magazine. *Hustler. Playgirl. Playguy. Torso.* Images of naked men, hairy, smooth, tan, black, white.

My hand touched my chest, feeling my heart beating. I caressed my pecs, traced the muscles, the ridge, the nipples rose underneath, tender and sensitive. I unbuttoned my shirt and worked down my belly. The blond hair that covered my chest thinned slightly over my abs and trailed down under my waistband.

Favorite porn stars and scenes of videos played across the screen. My arousal grew in my underwear. All the beer at tonight's bar didn't slow my erection.

My first kiss. My first boyfriend. His skinny body and long awkward limbs as he slowly removed his shirt.

His pale skin and small nipples. His knobby knees sticking out from baggy boxer trunks.

How sweet and innocent he was, how nervous and unsure. We fumbled around, touching, exploring, tasting, and holding.

My hands slipped into my pants and adjusted myself. Wetness greeted my fingers. I smoothed it along my shaft and continued to watch my life.

The trip to Mexico on spring break. A semester abroad in France. A ski trip in the Upper Peninsula of Michigan. A hot tub at a cabin in the Black Hills.

I pushed my pants down to my ankles and caressed my hard-on through the cotton briefs. Cupping my balls and squeezing them, stroking down the shaft.

I kicked off my shoes and slipped off my shirt. My legs wiggled out of my pants, and I settled back clad only in my shorts.

My sexual history played out on the screen, the good, the bad, and the furry. Then Mark appeared. Football player body, hairy legs, chest and butt. A white wife beater stretched across his broad chest, a thick pelt of fur poured over the neckline. A red jock framing a tight furry ass.

My hand worked my arousal inside my briefs, pre-cum oozed across my hand, and I worked it down my length. Inhaling deeply, his scent returned. Orange from the one he peeled each morning, a hint of wood smoke from the neighbor's backyard, cinnamon from the Big Red he chewed, and a manly sweat mixed with soap and water.

My hand worked harder, faster, as he posed in different positions. His long hairy legs, his bright, white smile, his low hanging testicles. The scar across his knee from hockey practice, the one on his finger from helping his mom peel potatoes.

My skin remembered his caress. Slow and firm, tender with desire, how his finger tips would explore every crease and crevice, made me moan with pleasure and beg for more.

I pushed down my briefs and felt the short nap of the upholstery tickle my ass. I could still feel his touch, his thickness as it entered me, filled me up. I could feel his body on mine, how his tight bubble butt felt when I rode it, the thick hair tickling my legs, my balls.

Pressure rose with pleasure, my toes curled as my balls pulled up alongside my shaft. My breaths came in short violent bursts.

Mark smiled at me on the screen.

My orgasm hit, shooting a load across my belly. I closed my eyes and savored the feeling of my hand stroking my flesh as I drifted off to sleep.

The Ghost of Christmas Present

The clock struck two. I lifted my head from the back of the couch. The fire burned and a thick towel lay on the floor within the circle of heat. A hand towel and a bottle of massage oil rested on the hearth.

"You're awake," James said as he entered the room. He carried two glasses of wine and joined me on the couch. He wore a white towel around his waist and nothing else. His tan skin glistened with oil. The scent of pine and eucalyptus hung in the air.

Candles illuminated the room. Their flickering soft light danced around the room.

I took a long sip of the wine. "It looks like you have a plan."

James' eyes glowed with desire. "I wanted to do something nice for you." He clicked his glass against mine. "Cheers."

I took another sip of the wine, and James stood.

He held out his hand for me, and I joined him. He guided me to the towel and helped me lie down. "Face down," he said.

He picked up the bottle of oil and poured a palmful. He rubbed his hands together to warm them and the oil. His hands touched my shoulders and caressed over and back to my spine. One by one, his hands followed my spine down to my butt. His hands rode the ridge of my bubble bottom before heading back to my neck and down again.

Tension flowed out of my body. My arms and legs became heavy and settled on the floor. I took a deep breath and exhaled slowly.

His hands fanned out to my sides and worked over my love handles and along my ribs. His touch was light, almost a tickle as he stroked under my arms.

I resisted the urge to pull my arms close and prevent his access, but I took another deep breath and let the wine warm my insides as his hands worked my outside. He adjusted his towel higher on his legs, so he could straddle my waist. His hairy legs hugged my hips as his butt sat in my lower back as a saddle.

I wanted to say 'ride me cowboy' but I felt he wanted a calm massage, so I didn't.

James adjusted his butt on me, and a soft furry sac rubbed up and down my low back as he made long strokes over my back.

I breathed in deeply, the eucalyptus cleared out my sinuses and was able to breathe even deeper. The Christmas tree added pine as the fire's wood snapped and crackled. Sparks flew across the hearth and quickly extinguished.

James slipped off my back and worked over my right arm. His muscular hands worked my hand and arm. One hand slipped under my chest and brushed my nipple. It rose under his touch.

I could feel my erection swell to full length. I raised my pelvis off the floor and allowed it to flip up against my belly.

He worked both arms and hands. The sensation made my hard-on grow and ooze pre-cum. A small pool spread on the towel and soaked in.

"You're legs are next," he said. He started at my feet, explored between each toe and pulling one by one to make them snap and relax. His thumbs dug into the ball of my foot and stroked into the arch. He hit every reflex point in my foot, sending positive energy through my body. His hands moved to my other foot and sent more waves of pleasure. His fingers combed my hairy calves, played behind my knees, and worked up to my butt. His finger tips traced along the lower crest of my gluts, brushed the crease, and slid down my legs.

He repeated the path, but this time, his fingers were more adventurous, exploring deeper. The sensitive opening puckered when brushed. He spread my butt cheeks and inhaled at the sight.

He added more oil to his hands and started to massage my ass. He kneaded and oiled me up. My tight muscles unclenched and relaxed as he worked me over.

James took off the towel and straddled my upper legs. His erection brushed against the curve of my butt and bounced off it. A thick wet spot dotted my skin with each tap. His hand applied oil to his shaft and then massaged my lower back. His fingers worked up my spine as his penis slipped between my cheeks. His length burrowed along my crease as he worked higher on my back.

As his hands worked lower, his cock pulled out and worked down my crack. His thick penis's head rested at my tight opening. As he rubbed up my back, the tip sought entrance and then slid up. Back and forth his hips rocked, as his cock plowed the cleft. Each time the mushroom tip tried to drill deep inside.

My balls pulled up underneath me as he massaged me. I fell into a trance until he whispered in my ear, "Roll over."

He helped me onto my back. My erection flipped up and slapped my belly.

James poured more oil into his hand and spread it up my leg. His long firm strokes worked the blood up and down my leg. His fingertips tickled the hair on my balls as he reached up and quickly pulled them down to his ankles. Once in a while his finger would linger on a ball and gently circle the fleshy orb.

Pre-cum oozed out and filled my belly button. A long strand pulled from my torso to my penis' tip.

James thumbs rode higher and higher on my belly, working along my balls toward the root of my shaft. His hands teased my flesh and stimulated each nerve.

My body tingled, and my cock pleaded to be touched, rubbed, caressed. I pressed my hips to his magic touch willing him to work the hardest muscle in my body.

James shifted his body to sit on my waist. He picked up the bottle and gently sprinkled oil droplets over my chest. The oil glistened in the firelight and slowly ran down the coarse strands to my skin. Warm rain drops covered me.

James smiled as he looked down. He bent forward and kissed me. His lips stayed on mine for a while. He finally sat up, and his hands settled down on my chest and rested there, riding the in and exhalations of my lungs. His fingers fanned out and worked the oil through the hair and across my skin.

I shifted my hips under his muscular ass.

“Not so fast. Relax. Let me do all the work.” His hands worked on my pecs as his fingers circled my nipples. He pinched them, and they rose into sharp points under his touch.

I rocked my hips again and felt my hard-on slip between his cheeks.

James rose, reached back, and lubed his butt. He found my dick and oiled it from tip to balls. He sat on me and wiggled back and forth as his hands worked over my chest. He traced my muscles and worked my flesh with his butt muscles.

I reached up and caressed his body. I ran one hand over his hairy thigh. His skin was warm from the fire, and sweat beaded off from the hard work. His wet body mixed with the oil and slipped easily along my body. Man sweat, wood smoke, and pine swirled in my nostrils, and I breathed deeply. My body relaxed even more from the touch.

James massaged my ears and sent shivers through my frame. He started on my ear lobes and worked up the cartilage ridge.

He bent forward again and kissed me, long, hard, and full of desire. He reached behind him and spread his cheeks. He guided my hard cock to his opening and pressed back on me. The oil made everything slip easily, and soon he was riding along my shaft.

My tip poked his hole and sought entry.

James pushed his body down and straddled my pelvis. The oil and sweat made me start to slip inside. He threw his head back and moaned. He bounced up and down on me. My swollen head pressed in and filled him. He moaned in pain as I pushed in deeper.

I grabbed his thick cock and rubbed it up and down. I felt my cock move in deeper. The fat ridge passed the tight opening, and James rocked his hips as he rode my dick down to my balls.

He squeezed his butt cheeks together and milked my penis. He rose up and my shaft pulled almost out, before he clamped down on me and sat back down.

Shivers ran down my spine. My toes curled, as my hand clamped down on him.

James repeated the thrust and the withdrawal, increasing the speed as he continued. My thrusts matched his, faster and faster. My hand worked his erection at the same rate. Deeper, faster, harder.

James' massage worked all my nerves to the edge, and my cock wouldn't take long with his tight ass. The heat from the fire, along with the pleasure, flushed my body. A sheen of sweat broke over my body, which added to the lubrication of the oil and helped quicken our pace.

Our rhythm and our breathing became one. We moved like a well oiled machine, piston into cylinder, faster, slicker, harder, and deeper. My back arched as I drove in deeper, and then there was no turning back.

I felt my balls explode and shoot a white hot load into James. As my wave hit his prostate gland, my hand squeezed down on his shaft and liquid fire burst out. As I emptied myself into him, his cock shot his load over my fingers and across my hairy chest.

Neither one of us moved, the sensory overload too intense to survive any more stimulation. Slowly, James rose, freeing me from his body. He lay on me, his weight felt wonderful. His mouth found mine, our tongues tasted each others, and we fell asleep in each others' arms.

The Ghost of Christmas Future

The clock struck three. I rolled over on the couch, and the doorbell rang. James was gone, he was nowhere in sight. I wrapped my shirt around my waist and stumbled to the door. I prayed that this would be the last visitation of the night.

I opened the door.

"James, what are you doing out there?"

He stepped into my house and pushed the door closed. "Let's get you inside where it's warm. I hate to make you sick." He guided me to the living room, and we sat on the couch.

"I couldn't wait to give you this." James knelt down at my bare feet. He pulled a small box from his parka and handed it to me.

Opening the lid, a silver ring shone in the velvet interior. "I don't understand."

James took the ring out of the box and slipped in onto my finger. "Sometimes your present can turn into your future."

At that moment, the DVD player's drawer pulled in, clicked, and Mark's face appeared on the television. "God bless us, everyone." He winked and blew me a kiss.

FATHER CHRISTMAS GOES DOWN UNDER

By Wayne Mansfield

It was forty-two degrees Celsius. There were people everywhere; hot, sweaty people wearing frowns and leading grizzling children around by their hands. Outside, the car park was filled to overflowing. Some people had even parked on the footpath. The traffic warden was getting writer's cramp with all the tickets he was issuing. It was Christmas Eve, and as I threw the last of my shopping into the back of my car, I sighed and slammed the boot shut. I was glad to be getting away from the chaos.

Once I had got home and unpacked the car, I set about wrapping the presents I'd purchased for various people. There was a bottle of Chanel Number 5 for my mother, a book on football and some lottery tickets for my father, various toys for various nieces and nephews, and a bottle of wine for the old dear across the road. When I had finished, I arranged the whole lot under the silver Christmas tree in my living room and stood back to admire the little Christmas scene I'd created.

Just for old time's sake, I hung a red felt stocking at the foot of my bed, and although I knew it wasn't going to be filled, it reminded me of my childhood when Mum would sneak in and fill it with lollies, comics, games and puzzle books. I missed those days when Christmas was exciting; when I promised myself I would stay up to catch Father Christmas in the middle of delivering his bounty but always seemed to fall asleep before he came. And in the morning we would wake up, my two brothers and I, and we would run into the lounge room to look at all the presents.

But those days were long gone. I was twenty-eight years old now, and my appetite for anything to do with Christmas was waning more and more with each passing year.

I spent Christmas Eve watching a horror DVD and then went to bed at about eleven. As I lay there waiting for sleep to whisk me off to Dreamland, my mind wandered to the hot looking guy who had served me at the lottery kiosk. I felt myself growing hard beneath the bed sheet. I started jerking off, imagining us together in the toilets by his kiosk, me sitting on his cock, kissing him while he fucked a load into my tight, hairy hole, but I was too tired to keep the fantasy up, and I ended up drifting off to sleep, semi-erect and a little frustrated.

A while later, I was awakened up by a noise. At first, I just lay in bed, eyes still closed but ears pricked. Had I dreamt it? No. There it was again. My eyes sprang open and my heart started racing. Adrenalin flooded my body. I slid off the mattress and without even bothering to pull on a pair of shorts I stalked out to the living room. I saw him straight away, the dark figure of a man by my Christmas tree. My hand felt along the wall for the light switch and with one flick of a finger the room was filled with bright light.

"What are you doing?" I demanded, balling my hands into fists.

The man, dressed in red clothing trimmed in white fur, turned around. His snowy white moustache and beard hid a surprisingly youthful face.

"Ahh great," I said dryly, "I'm being robbed by Father Christmas!"

The man put his hands in the air.

"I'm not robbing you," he replied. "I'm delivering some presents."

"And I suppose the reindeer are on my roof as we speak."

"Oh God no," he laughed. "I haven't used reindeer for years. I've got a truck now. Much more efficient. It's parked out in front of your place now if you want to take a look."

I sidled over to the window, keeping my eyes on the stranger in red. I pulled the curtain open and peered out into the lamp-lit street, and sure enough there was a huge truck stopped there and something that looked like an elf sitting in the passenger seat with his little legs dangling out the open door. He was smoking a cigarette and staring back at me through the window. My wide eyes blinked, but nothing had changed.

I turned back to Father Christmas, my mouth gaping.

"Th-that's impossible," I managed to babble. "There is no such thing as ..."

"Father Christmas? Elves? The Tooth Fairy, perhaps? Well, there is," he explained. "And that Tooth Fairy is a real bitch! You guys get such a bum deal from her. The profit she makes on those teeth. Sheesh!"

I couldn't believe what I was hearing.

"Aren't you a little young to be Father Christmas?"

"Regeneration," he replied. "I regenerate every fifty years. I've actually just undergone my latest one. You wouldn't believe how good I look under all this. Most of it is padding. You know, keeping up appearances and all that."

"At this stage, I don't know what I believe," I said.

"Well check it out."

He began to undress, first taking his hat and boots off and then his coat. Underneath was a large belly-shaped cushion, which he untied and dropped to the carpet, revealing a rock hard six-pack, which was lightly haired and a set of pecs that brought the blood rushing into my cock. As he hooked his thumbs into the top of his pants he glanced up at me and flashed me a killer smile. My cock twitched and started growing. I could feel my cheeks burning. I placed my hands discreetly over it in a vain attempt to hide it.

He pulled his pants and underwear down in one fluid movement, stepped out of them and stood there, hands on hips for me to admire. I had to admit his body was mighty fit. Better than mine! While I was lean, athletic and lightly tanned, he was stockier, more defined and had a small trail of blond hair going from his navel to the thick bush above his massive cock.

For the second time that night, my jaw hit the carpet.

“What do you think?” he asked with a knowing smile. “Pretty good for a two thousand-year-old dude, hey?”

My hands rearranged themselves over my hard on. “Er, yeah, it is.” I agreed.

“I can see that you’re impressed,” said Father Christmas as he walked across the room to me. “I can see that you are really impressed!”

He took my cock in his hand and gripped it firmly. I closed my eyes. It felt good to have someone else’s hand on my cock for a change. I think I even shuddered slightly at his touch. Then I felt his lips on mine. I opened my eyes and stared into his crystal blue eyes. His lips were full and firm on mine, his tongue explored my mouth. I wrapped my left arm around his shoulders and pulled him closer to me.

"Are you okay?" he asked me, his voice barely a whisper.

"Yes," I managed to reply.

I felt his hand leave my cock. As our kisses became more heated, he wrapped both arms around me and held me to him, our dripping cocks pressed together. I cupped my hands over the twin orbs of his buttocks, kneading them and pulling them apart. My finger found his anus, and I started to rub it gently.

"Lick it," I heard him whisper.

He turned around and bent over, pulling his muscular ass cheeks apart and exposing his lightly haired fuck hole to me. I leant in. I could smell the earthy aroma already and my cock twitched as my tongue came into contact with the puckered flesh around his hole.

"Get right in there," said Father Christmas, and he began to grind his asshole into my face.

I gripped his hips with my hands and used them to steady myself as I pushed my tongue deep inside his ass. When the tip of my tongue came into contact with the smooth tissue inside, I heard Father Christmas groan.

"That's it, boy. Get right inside my fuck hole. Lick it out good."

I didn't have to be told. I was eating him out as if it was my last supper. I munched his furry chute with gusto, rubbing my face over it in between licking the puckered flesh surrounding the entrance and probing the space beyond the sphincter muscle. My tongue darted in and out, and then I started kissing his ass lips, sucking on them while my tongue ran riot over the tight folds of flesh.

Then, without warning, he spun around and shoved his cock into my open mouth.

"Get stuck into that, mate."

I wrapped my lips around the swollen cock head, sucking on it and probing the piss slit with my tongue. I savored the slightly salty taste I found there for a second or two and then slowly took the entire nine-inch monster down my throat. I slid my lips firmly up and down, and I could feel every vein on his thick shaft. I nearly gagged a couple of times, but I controlled myself, breathing through my nose as I slid my mouth towards the tip of the cock and holding my breath as his thick shaft filled the back of my throat again.

I felt his hands gently grip my head, guiding me slowly back and forth along his cock. Each thrust of his hips against my face was accompanied by a grunt. He was obviously enjoying himself. I could feel his heavy balls slapping on the skin beneath my chin and still smell the musty odor of his asshole on the tip of my nose. I breathed that man perfume in and concentrated on keeping my throat open to accommodate his pulsing prick. I soon became aware that his balls were beginning to tighten, but I didn't want him to blow his load down my throat. I wanted to feel that thick piece of meat sliding into my asshole.

"Okay boy. That's enough," he said, as if he had read my mind.

He pulled his cock out of my mouth, and the next thing I knew I was being lifted up by my arms. My feet had barely touched the carpet when I was thrown over his shoulder and carried down the semi-lit hallway to my bedroom. I dangled over his right shoulder, limp, like something just killed in a hunt. I could feel the muscles in his back moving beneath me. His strength was intoxicating; his scent still strong in my nostrils.

He walked into my bedroom and threw me onto the mattress. I landed with a bounce, but almost immediately, Father Christmas had me by my ankles and was dragging me to the edge of the bed. Once he had positioned me where he wanted me, he pushed my legs apart and rubbed my tight hairy hole with his finger.

"That feels tight, boy. Maybe you won't be able to take my cock."

I assured him that I would try. "There's some lube in the side drawer over there."

Father Christmas leaned over, pulled the drawer open and took out the small bottle of lube. He flipped the lid open and poured a generous amount onto his erect cock. He threw the bottle back into the drawer and began to smear the clear gel over all nine inches of his hard meat.

"I'm going to fuck you like you have never been fucked before," he said, fingering some of the lube into my eager hole. "You'll believe in Father Christmas after I have finished with you."

I gasped when I felt the head of his cock press against my tight pucker. I heard him laugh.

"I haven't started yet, boy," he said.

But I didn't have long to wait. I soon felt my asshole being stretched taut as he pushed his engorged cock head past my ass muscles. I gritted my teeth.

"How does that feel?" he asked.

"Good," I lied.

When he was all the way in, he waited for a few seconds, so my ass could get used to his thick pole. I lay on my back, impaled on his cock, and focused on the way my anal muscles began to relax around the invading organ. He leaned down and kissed me tenderly on the lips, his hips beginning to thrust while my mind was occupied with his full lips sucking on mine, his tongue sliding over and around mine and his warm breath mingling with mine. I moaned as his thrusts became more vigorous, the sound muffled by a kiss. Yet it wasn't long before I was pulling him deeper into me. My ass was full of cock, filled to capacity, but I wanted more of it. I wanted him to fuck me harder, deeper.

He grabbed my ankles and pulled my legs wider apart. Suddenly the sensation of his cock sliding in and out was intensified. I moaned again and began to twist my nipples between my fingers. My first instinct was to grab my cock, but I knew the minute I touched it, I would explode. But I wanted to wait, wait for him to blow a load of white Christmas up inside me. Instead, my cock just slapped against my stomach in time with his thrusts.

Suddenly I was aware of someone else in the bedroom. My eyes had become accustomed to the darkness, and I saw two dark figures climbing onto the bed. I looked up at Father Christmas and then back at the two figures. The whole situation was surreal.

"You don't mind if they join in, do you?" asked Father Christmas. "They gct so little pleasure."

The two elves were naked. I could see their tiny stalks sticking straight out against the dim light from the hallway. They stood on either side of me, neither of them any taller than a garden gnome. Already they were breathing heavily. Immediately, they knelt down and began sucking my nipples, licking them and slurping at them. With nothing to do with my hands, I wrapped one around my cock and the other one roamed over my belly, gently caressing it.

Father Christmas was pounding me now, and the two little elves were finding it difficult to stay attached to my nipples. But I'm glad they did. I could feel their little tongues flicking back and forth over each erect nub, sending little bolts of electricity coursing across my chest and down to my groin.

Father Christmas was really ramming me now. Drops of sweat fell from his body and splashed against my toned body. His panting was getting deeper and faster.

"I'm getting ready to blow, boy. I'm going to flood your guts.

I was glad to hear him say that because I could feel an orgasm building in my own loins. My nipples had always been little powerhouses, and between them being sucked and the massive cock massaging my prostate, I was helpless.

"Here I go, boy. I'm coming. I'm fucking coming!"

I felt him blow a great load up inside me. The warm splashes of his cum spewing into me set my own cock off. I felt it pulse and then a great jet of cream flew over my head. Jet after jet shot out covering my chest and stomach. My whole body shuddered as my balls were emptied.

The two elves had stopped pleasuring me and were instead jerking their little cocks so that soon I felt two more streams of cum splashing across my naked body. For such little creatures they sure produced a lot of spunk. I could feel rivers of the stuff rolling off my torso and onto the mattress beneath me.

Father Christmas pulled his cock out of my soggy fuck tunnel. I felt the tickle of a trickle of cum running down between my buttocks and immediately clenched them shut to keep the rest inside me. The elves didn't waste any time in mopping up the three loads of cum that had basted me like a Christmas turkey. They were on me immediately, sucking up all the cum they could, running their tongues up my sides to collect every last drop and flicking my nipples with the tips of their tongues at every chance they got.

"They sure love their cum," said Father Christmas. "They don't get much chance to play, what with making all those toys. But you have given them a real treat tonight."

He leaned over them and tousled my hair. I started laughing. The elves tongues were tickling me, and my asshole was still throbbing from the pounding Father Christmas had given it. For a moment, I felt as if I could float right off that bed and out the window. I couldn't remember a better fuck.

"You did a good job tonight, boy. I really needed to drop that load. Been hanging onto it for a year you know."

I sat up on my knees. "It felt like it," I replied with a smile that he probably couldn't see in the dark. "My ass is going to be pulsing for a few more hours yet after the work out you gave it."

"Glad you enjoyed it," he said as he turned and left my room; the two elves scampering after him. "Now you two get back to the truck," I heard him say to the elves. "You know you shouldn't leave it unattended. There are a lot of kids depending on us tonight."

I grabbed a towel from the cupboard in my room and wiped up the drying cum while hurrying out to the living room.

"You know, if you wanted to you could come back again," I said, but as I arrived in the room I saw it was empty. I dashed across to the window just in time to see the lights of the truck being switched on and hear the roar of the engine starting up. And then the strangest thing happened. The whole truck sped down the street before lifting off the road and shooting up into the sky. If I hadn't seen it for myself, I would never have believed it. It streaked across the night sky like a comet before disappearing behind a bank of cloud.

I turned, shaking my head, and under the tree was a present that I couldn't remember wrapping myself. I walked over to it and picked it up. I undid the bow and tore the paper off. Inside was a long box, and inside the box was a nine-inch dildo. The card attached said: "So you're prepared for next time. – F.C."

JINGLE BALLS

By Rob Rosen

Santa was beside himself. Two days until Christmas, and three of his elves were out with the flu. He could lend a hand in the workshop, but even then, the toys would never get finished in time.

"What can we do?" he asked his wife, who was also busy, sorting out the good and the bad girls and boys on her Mac.

She scrunched up her nose and strummed her chubby fingers on her equally chubby chin. Staring at her computer screen, her eyes suddenly lit up. Quickly, she Googled a search term and came up with a solution. "Elf temp," she soon replied, pointing at the monitor. "Right here on the North Pole Craigslist."

Santa scratched his wooly white head. "I thought only we made lists up here, good wife. Who is this Craig fellow?"

She laughed at her behind-the-times husband. "Never you mind, Santa. I'll just email this temp and see if he's available."

Santa shrugged and let her have at it. She typed lightening fast and waited for a response. Seconds later, they heard the lilting "you've got mail." She smiled big and bright as she read the reply. "He's free," she shouted, her voice filled with glee. "And if we all pitch in, the toys will get finished just in the nick of time."

Santa's grin stretched from east to west, the jowls beneath his chin jiggling like Christmas pudding. "It's a miracle, wife," he proclaimed, with a relieved sigh. "An honest to goodness miracle."

The miracle arrived the next morning and only twenty minutes late.

"Jingle's the name," he proclaimed, with a bow, "and toy makings my game. From China to Uzbekistan, and all the sweat shops in between. I can make a Yo-Yo with just one Yo and a Slinky that hops down stairs two at a time."

"Oh, no," laughed Santa, as the little elf bounded in, his head nodding up and down as he did so. "No cutting corners here, Jingle. Our Yos come in pairs."

The elf winked and grabbed his crotch. "Yeah, Santa, I got your pair right here, and they're itching to get to work, if you know what I mean." The wink repeated itself.

Again Santa laughed, not sure what to make of this strange little elf. Still, beggars couldn't be choosers, and he happily showed Jingle around and then planted him at his station. "Here you go, Jingle. The work is hard but enjoyable enough, especially when you see the smiles on the happy children's faces." And with that, he was gone.

Jingle glanced around, cute little elves on all sides, all toiling away, their sinewy arms and sweat-covered brows glistening in the ambient factory light. "Man," he groaned, "something's hard alright, and it ain't the work."

"What's that you said?" asked the elf next to him as he hammered and nailed and screwed a toy train together.

Jingle turned and looked at the adorable elf by his side, his sleeves rolled up as he labored away, rippling little muscles moving to and fro as the train took shape. "I said," Jingle replied, sidling over, "I can hardly wait to get to work."

The other elf looked up, his twinkling blue eyes locking on to Jingle's, his candy-cane-crisp breath mingling with Jingle's slightly gin-soaked one. Nervously, he said to him, "Um, name's Tweeker."

Jingle grabbed the elf's hand and gave a firm, if not lingering, shake. With a leer, he said, "Oh, I'd like to tweak you."

"Excuse me?" said the other elf, apprehensively.

Jingle coughed. "Oh, I said, pleased to meet you. Name's Jingle. Jingle Balls."

Tweeker, his hand growing sweaty in Jingle's, swiftly went back to work, pulling his slender fingers away. "You start on the tracks, Jingle, while I finish this train," he told him, a quiver to his reedy voice.

Jingle laughed and smacked him on his butt. "Well, Tweeker, the caboose is looking mighty fine, already."

Tweeker jumped in place. "But I'm just starting on the engine car."

Jingle winked at his coworker and retorted, "Exactly, Tweeker, exactly." And then he began the business at hand; though his hand ached to return to his neighboring elf's end.

Which gave him an idea.

He toiled long and steady, the tracks churning out lightening fast, the trains boxed and gift wrapped in no time flat. In fact, Jingle was soon ahead of schedule and even managed to whittle out a gift of a different sort.

Tweeker looked over, and asked, "What do you have there, Jingle? Is that a train whistle?"

Jingle held the long, spherical object up for the other elf to see. "Nah, it's for a good little ho, ho, ho in Minneapolis."

Tweeker played with his blond chin hairs, which coiled down to a tapered point as he twisted them between his dexterous fingers. “What’s it do, though?”

“Do?” Jingle asked, shifting over once again, locking laser-sharp eyes with the curious elf. “It’s a smile maker.” He paused, inching in even closer. “Don’t tell me you’ve never seen a smile maker before, Tweeker.”

The elf blushed, a crimson red flush spreading from one pointed ear to the other. “Of course I’ve seen a smile maker,” he replied. “I’ve just, well, I’ve never, um, played with one before, is all. How’s it work?”

Jingle looked at the clock on the toy factory wall. “Our break is in ten minutes. Wanna play with it then?”

Tweeker smiled, a brilliant white array that lit up the room like a moonlit night. “Oh, yes, I love to play,” he replied, wholeheartedly.

“Oh, I bet you do,” Jingle fairly moaned, and counted down the seconds until their break, churning out the toys at a jarring pace.

Soon thereafter, the clock began to chime, and all the elves stretched their tired little arms up high, or at least as I high as they could go, and filed out for some hot cocoa and cookies. All, that is, save for Tweeker and Jingle.

“Where can we play with the smile maker?” Tweeker eagerly asked.

“Where’s your room?” Jingle asked in return.

“My room? Can’t we play with it outside?” came the hesitant response.

“Oh no,” Jingle told him. “Good boys and girls play in bed. With the smile maker, I mean.”

“I see,” was all Tweeker could think to say and led them both down a long corridor to his small room, closing the door behind them as he hopped onto the undersized bed. "Now what?" he asked, his eyes wide and the nervous grin returning to his adorable face.

"Now?" Jingle said, his breath instantly growing shallow. "Now we hide the smile maker."

"Oh," said Tweeker. "You hide it and I find it?"

"Sort of," said Jingle, jumping on the bed with his playmate and taking out the toy from his back pocket. "Only, trust me, you'll know just where it's hidden."

The elf shrugged. "I don't get it."

"Yeah, you will," Tweeker rasped, setting the wooden object down, and then changing the subject with, "I like your little blond beard." He paused, then added, "Does the carpet match the drapes?" Jingle pointed from Tweeker's face down to his crotch.

"My carpet?" Tweeker practically whispered. "Well, um, yes, I suppose it does. Why, doesn't yours?"

Jingle grinned. "Actually, I don't have a carpet. I clip it off. Elfscaping, I call it. Want to see?"

The little elf gulped and nodded. "Sure. I mean, I've never seen an, um, elfscaped carpet before." In fact, he wasn't even sure what one was.

Tweeker stared in rapt wonder as Jingle got on his knees and unbuttoned his leather shorts. He slid them down a few inches, revealing nothing but brown stubble. "See," he said. "No carpet." Then he pointed back down to Tweeker's suddenly burgeoning crotch. "Now it's your turn."

Tweeker slowly did the same, his shorts bunching up as a thick, blond bush came into view. He laughed. "Yep, they match the, um, drapes, alright." He paused, his hands still on the waistband. "They even match the, um, the rear doormat," he informed, again a red blush blossoming on his already rosy cheeks.

"Do they now?" Jingle asked, leaning back on the bed. "That I'd like to see." A gross understatement if ever there was one.

Tweeker grinned, sheepishly, and pushed down on his shorts, his prick bouncing out as he flopped on his back and kicked the leather material off. He held his teeny feet in his tiny hands and bowed his short legs out, revealing a pink, crinkled hole, lined, as promised, with a matching blond whirl of fuzz. "See," he said, swirling his finger around the slot, "everything matches." He chuckled and chortled and winked at the gazing Jingle.

The kneeling elf groaned the faintest of groans. "My oh my, everything most certainly does," he whispered, admiringly. "And now, would you like to see where we hide the smile maker?"

Still ticking his hole, Tweeker replied, "Yes, please."

Jingle giggled with a wicked if not completely captivating grin. He quickly shucked off his leather vest and wriggled out of his tight shorts, leaving him in nothing more than his green and red striped knee-socks. Tweeker stared upwards, and noted, "Now I see where you got your apt name from."

The turgid elf swayed his low hanging balls, and sang, "Jingle all the way." Then he leaned in and took an appraising sniff of Tweeker's chute. "Smells of cinnamon and spice and everything really nice," he practically purred, taking a lick and slurp and suck on the blond hair-rimmed ring.

The sprawled out elf moaned and bucked his ass into the lapping mouth. "Oh hole-y night," he gasped.

Jingle laughed and grabbed for the larger than average, by elf standards at any rate, cock, downing it in one fell swoop, while sliding a spit-slick finger to the farthest reaches of Tweeker's tiny tush. "Ready to see why I call it a smile maker?" he asked, in between hungry sucks and gulps.

Tweeker looked between his outstretched legs at the eyes starting intently at him. "Are the five rings golden?" he replied.

Jingle took that as a yes, and reached over for the wooden phallus. Back on his knees, he stared down at the randy elf, now stroking his Yule log while he waited to see where the smile maker would get hidden, and then happily surprised where it did.

Lubing up the virgin territory with more thick spit, Jingle pressed the end of the toy up against Tweeker's tight hole. Then, with one easy glide, he slid it down the chimney with care. The prone elf sucked in his breath, his eyes fluttering as a million tingles, enough to light up an entire evergreen forest, coursed through his shortened limbs. And then, as the oaken shaft butted up against a granite-hard prostate, he smiled, big and full and wide and blissful. Just as was promised.

"Ah," he moaned. "Now I see where it gets its apt name."

Jingle laughed, knowingly, and bent down to suck on the shiny, plumb-sized knob that sat perched high above the thick shaft, while the smile maker slid in and out, in and out. And then he suddenly stopped pushing and prodding and sucking and slurping, and looked up at the enraptured elf. "Would you like something to make you smile even brighter, Tweeker?" he asked.

"Is that even possible?" giggled the elf, now stroking his fat prick.

"Only one way to tell," replied Jingle, popping the wooden rod out, and then reaching over for his shorts, from which he removed two more items. He jumped off the bed and stared back down, holding the objects in his hand.

"What are those?" asked Tweeker.

"I'll tell you, but first remove your vest and socks, and then lower your legs."

The elf did as he was told, soon lying naked on the bed. Jingle crouched down and ran the palm of his hand across smooth skin, sending goosebumps rising in its wake. His slender fingers ran up silken hills and down sleek valleys, coming to rest for a time on two pink nipples, tiny raisins that he plucked like a harp, causing the elf below to sing in turn. "A more beautiful elf I've never seen," moaned Jingle, taking in the sight like a starving man would a Christmas goose.

"Then gaze in the mirror," responded Tweeker.

Jingle grinned. "Good one," he said, and hopped back on the bed, swinging Tweeker's legs up and placing his cute, little feet atop his shoulders. The first item he held in his hand he slid down the length of his steely prick. "For safety's sake," he informed.

"And the second object?" Tweeker asked.

Jingle grinned and bent down, placing it over the elf's head. "Mistletoe," he told him, stealing a soft, lush kiss on Tweeker's full, pouty lips, their mouths meshing together as the top's cock pressed up snug against the bottom's tight hole, before it rammed in and up and back.

Jingle groaned as he entered, and then pulled his face away to stare down into two crystal-clear pools of blue. "Better?" he asked, noticing the smile grow impossibly broad.

"Oh, much," Tweeker replied, again stroking his cock as he leaned up for another wonderful kiss.

They sighed in unison, rocking their sweat-soaked bodies in pitch perfect harmony, their tiny torsos flush together, their mouths locked as one. And then they heard the jarring bell, their break apparently over.

Tweeker's eyes popped opened. "Hurry," he said in alarm. "We have to get back. Santa doesn't like us to go missing."

And so hurry Jingle did, letting loose like a rocket, pummeling Tweeker's ass with his rigid prick, pounding away at the farthest recesses. Pump, pump, pump, he went. And then, his head tilted back as he finally shot, filling up the rubber with ounce after creamy ounce of molten hot cum, enough to melt the very North Pole itself. And speaking of poles, Tweeker's exploded a split second later, dousing their miniature bodies in a pungent glorious mess, before Jingle collapsed on top of him, giggling in a mix of both pleasure and exhaustion.

"Merry fucking Christmas," he whispered into Tweeker's ear.

"I must've been a good elf this year," came the response, "because I just got the best present ever."

They hugged for the two seconds they had left, and then rushed to wash off, get dressed, and return to their work stations, the faint lingering aroma of cum wafting over them, causing two well-deserved smiles to suddenly appear.

The toys were made in record time, with Santa overseeing in obvious delight, stunned at the progress they'd made. And when Christmas Eve rolled around, enough presents for all the good boys and girls were loaded onto the sleigh and jolly old Saint Nicholas was off like a light.

Tweeker returned to his tiny room and his teeny cot, and stared glumly at the mistletoe that had been left behind.

And then there came a knocking on his door.

"Come in," he said.

The door creaked open. "I already did," came the giddy reply. "Inside of you, that is."

Tweeker lit up like a Christmas tree. "You're still here," he practically shouted. "But the season is over. And so, I thought, was your temp assignment."

Jingle skipped to his side and landed on the bed. "Santa liked my work. Fastest elf he'd ever seen. So, no more sweat shops for me, little one." He grabbed the mistletoe and held it above Tweeker's head. "Lucky me," he said, with a deep, perfect, wonderful kiss, before adding, "Oh, and Merry Christmas." He handed him the gift he had hidden behind his back.

Tweeker grabbed for it and joyfully ripped it open. "A new smile maker," he proclaimed, his shorts already tenting at the sight of it. "And a longer, thicker one at that."

"Double headed," Jingle informed, already shucking off his leather outfit. "To help ring in the New Year right."

"And what a good year it will be," Tweeker moaned, sliding out of his shorts, his prick already rock hard.

The smile maker seemed to have its desired effect, causing two grins to beam like the moon that Santa was flying past at that very moment.

ABOUT THE AUTHORS

CHRISTOPHER PIERCE is the author of the novels *Rogue: Slave* and *Rogue: Hunted.* His short erotic fiction has been published most recently in *Ride Me Cowboy, Surfer Boys* and *Don't Ask, Don't Tie Me Up.* He is the editor of the STARbooks anthologies *Men On The Edge, Taken by Force* and *SexTime: Erotic Stories of Time Travel.*

CLIFF MORTEN is German, a teacher of art and a licensed guide for free climbing. Aiden Kell is American, working as an Insurance Analyst in North Dakota.

DAVID C. MULLER currently lives in Tel Aviv but works at a prominent position somewhere in the Jewish Industry in Jerusalem. His writing has come out in a few places: a story entitled "The Beekeeper" appeared in *Love in a Lock-Up* in 2007, published by STARbooks Press and in 2008, a story called "Miza'zeyah" came out in Tel Aviv Short Stories, published by AngLit Press. "My First Jesus" appeared in the erotic anthology *Cruising for Bad Boys,* edited by Mickey Erlach and "Gan Ha'atzmaut" appeared in *Nerdvana,* edited by Fred Towers and also published by STARbooks Press.

DAVID HOLLY's stories have appeared in *Best Gay Romance, Best Gay Love Stories, Boy Crazy, Ultimate Gay Erotica, Surfer Boys,* and *Cruising for Bad Boys.* "The Yule Goat" is his second story published by STARbooks Press. Readers will find a complete bibliography at www.gaywriter.org.

DERRICK DELLA GIORGIA was born in Italy and currently lives between Manhattan and Rome. His short stories have been published in several anthologies: "Courtesy of the Hotel" in *Island Boys* (Alyson Books), "Couch with a View" in *Cruising for Bad Boys* (STARbooks press), "A Secret Worth Keeping" in *Pretty Boys and*

Roughnecks (STARbooks press), "Pyramids in Rome" in *Best Gay Love Stories 2010* (Alyson Books), "Antimatter Matt" in *Unmasked II: More Erotic Tales of Gay Superheroes* (STARbooks Press). Visit him at www.derrickdellagiorgia.com.

Published in dozens of gay erotic anthologies, **JAY STARRE** pumps out fiction from his home in Vancouver, Canada. He has written regularly for such hot magazines as *Torso*, *Mandate* and *Men*. His work can be found in titles like *Love in a Lock-Up, Don't Ask, Don't Tie Me Up, Unmasked: Erotic Tales of Gay Superheroes*, and *Ride Me Cowboy*. His steamy gay novel *Erotic Tales of the Knights Templar* came out in late 2007. Look forward to his upcoming erotic book *Lusty Adventures of the Knossos Prince* in spring 2009.

LOGAN ZACHARY lives in Minneapolis, MN, where he is an avid reader, writer, and book collector. His stories can be found in *Hard Hats, Taken by Force, Boys Caught in the Act, Ride Me Cowboy, Service with a Smile, Surfer Boys, Ultimate Gay Erotica 2009, Time Travel Sex*, and *Best Gay Erotica 2009*. He can be reached at LoganZachary2002@yahoo.com.

With almost a quarter-century experience in the publishing industry, **MILTON STERN** has written several short stories for the Eric Summers anthologies, including, *Unmasked: Erotic Tales of Gay Superheroes, Don't Ask, Don't Tie Me Up, Ride Me Cowboy, Service with a Smile, Unwrapped – Erotic Holiday Tales*, and the upcoming *Teammates*. He is also the author of several books, including *Harriet Lane, America's First Lady, On Tuesdays, They Played Mah Jongg* and *Michael's Secrets*. Residing in Rockville, Maryland, with his toy parti-poodle, Serena Rose Elizabeth Montgomery, Stern is also an active volunteer in his community, where he serves as a neighborhood representative for the Leukemia and Lymphoma Society, car club liaison to the Washington Animal Rescue League, and the president of the Straight

Eights, a gay antique car club. He is presently researching his next book about a boxer in New York in the 1880s. You can read more about Milton Stern and his work at www.miltonstern.com.

PEPPER ESPINOZA works full time as an author and part-time as a college instructor. She has published with Amber Quill Press, Liquid Silver Books, and Samhain Publishing. You can find more information about her work at www.pepperverse.net.

R. W. CLINGER is the author of numerous gay erotic fiction including "Just a Boy" and "He Likes It Rough." His novels include *The Pool Boy* and *Soft on the Eyes*. His short fiction has appeared in the magazines *Men* and *Freshmen*.

ROB ROSEN, author of *Sparkle: The Queerest Book You'll Ever Love* and *Divas Las Vegas*, has had short stories published in more than sixty anthologies, most notably in the STARbooks Press collections: *Ride Me Cowboy*, *Service with a Smile*, *Unmasked II: More Erotic Tales of Gay Superheroes*, *Cruising for Bad Boys*, *SexTime*, *Pretty Boys and Roughnecks*, *Teammates*, and *Boys Getting Ahead*. His erotic fiction can frequently be found in the pages of *Men* and *Freshmen* magazines. Please visit him at his website, www.therobrosen.com, or email him at robrosen@therobrosen.com.

RYAN FIELD has been contributing to STARbooks Press for a while. He has a story in the upcoming *Unmasked II: More Erotic Tales of Gay Superheroes*. "Home for the Holidays" was originally published by ravenousromance.com in an e-book. To find out more about STARbooks Press and other works by Ryan, check out www.ryan-field.blogspot.com.

STEPHEN OSBORNE has had stories published in numerous anthologies, including *Boys Caught in the Act*, *Ride Me Cowboy*, *Unmasked*, *Unmasked II*, *Frat Sex 2*, *Best Gay Love Stories 2010*, and many others. He is also the author of a book of ghost stories and legends called *South Bend Ghosts and Other Northern Indiana Haunts*. He lives in Indianapolis with Jadzia the One-Eyed Wonder Dog.

TROY STORM has had a lot of hot stories published in a lot of hot magazines under a lot of hot names, most of which have cooled off by now. But, he is also in a lot of hot anthologies, which are still hot, the latest being STARbooks' *Ride Me Cowboy*, also edited by the hot Eric Summers. In this current collection of very cool holiday tales, Troy is doubly hot – and wishes his readers Happy Hot Hot Holidays!

WAYNE MANSFIELD hails from Perth, Western Australia. He has had stories published in *Boys Will Be Boys*, *Ride Me Cowboy*, *Boys Caught in the Act* and *Pretty Boys and Roughnecks*. Additionally, his story "An Afternoon in the Life of…." was chosen for inclusion in this year's Sydney Gay and Lesbian Mardi Gras online anthology *I Am a Camera*. Find out more at: www.myspace.com/darknessgathers.